Lock Down Publications and Ca$h
Presents

A

GANGSTA'S

KARMA 5

The Route of All Evil

WRITTEN BY

FLAME

First Edition 2025

Printed in the United States of America

Lock Down Publications
P.O. Box 944
Stockbridge, GA 30281
www.lockdownpublications.com

Like our page on Facebook: Lock Down Publications
www.facebook.com/lockdownpublications.ldp

Stay Connected with Us!

Text **LOCKDOWN** to 22828 to stay up-to-date with new releases, sneak peaks, contests and more…

Like our page on Facebook:
Lock Down Publications

Join Lock Down Publications/The New Era Reading Group

Visit our website:
www.lockdownpublications.com

Follow us on Instagram:
Lock Down Publications

Email Us: We want to hear from you!

PROLOGUE

May 15, 2011
Satellite phone rings
He knew exactly who it was. Nobody else could reach him on that device.

"Da," he answered in his native tongue.

"I have the when and where. Do you have the you know what?"

He understood from the beginning of all this that the satellite phone was critical to the operation. But he was still having a hard time understanding why they couldn't speak freely on them. They were supposed to be secure and encrypted after all, so why did he have to mind what he said.

"Da, I have everything."

"Good. And your pawns, are they situated?"

"They *vill* be soon."

"Soon! Why not now? Why are you procrastinating? Should I be concerned? Because you absolutely must not mismanage the pickup."

In a display of his displeasure, his forehead furrowed. *He still insists on talking down to me and blaming me for that one missing container. But how does he not see that I'm in control and he's my pawn? And instead of accusing me for that container that vanished three years ago, he should blame this so-called secure channel of communication he set up for us. I strongly sense someone has been listening in on our calls for a while now.*

"Nyet. You shouldn't be concerned."

4

"Okay. Now what about the takers?"

Had the time finally come for him to confess to his associate how he was really getting rid of the stuff?

He had wanted to spill the beans about the side partnership he'd set up. But he didn't want to share the extra proceeds. He needed the additional cash flow to pay for exclusive pursuit.

"The demand exceeds the supply," he retorted.

"Great. If you meet your requirements, we're headed for glory. Now stop procrastinating and get to work."

"Just call me vith the time and place." He disconnected the call.

In a bit, he'd begin the not-so-difficult task of mobilizing his expendable assets.

***

Happening at the same time…

"The call ended, *jefe.*"

"It's okay. I heard just enough. *Bien hecho,* Vicente. You are a priceless gem. Contact me immediately the next time they communicate with each other. *Me entiendes?* I need to know the day and location of that pickup."

"Si, jefe."

With nothing else to address, he hung up with his IT guy. *In due time I'll have one less player to compete with. And rather than throw my dog this bone and let her reap the benefits, I'll take care of this one myself. I'm going to shovel that poison down his own people's throat with joy for thinking I'm foolish enough to swallow his red herring. He'll learn, when it's too late, that no amount of money impresses me.*

He smiled villainously.

Chapter 1

May 16, 2011/ 9:22am/ West Palm Beach, FL
Palm Beach County Jail

"At last, you're out, baby. How does it feel to be free again?"

JuneBug hoped it wasn't going to take long to acclimate himself to being home again. First, he'd have to mentally erase the conditions he'd been living under for the last eight months.

He was more than a bit paranoid. The butterflies he experienced in his stomach leading up to his release wasn't the same feeling he felt now. This feeling was more intense. Instead of "butterflies," it was more like winged razor blades fluttering in his gut. Nevertheless, he sighed in relief as his ride-or-die pulled away from the jail complex on Gun Club Road. Despite the unpleasantness in his gut, there was a flash of joy to put this stint behind him.

A little less than four hours later, they arrived at their destination.

"Baby, we're home. Better yet, you're home for good." She killed the engine, then turned in her seat toward Bug. "And your rowdy-ass, spoiled rotten sons, I let them stay home today. I know they've been up since early this morning, drivin' my mom crazy, because they're excited to see you."

JuneBug nodded subtly as he surveyed the serene scenery. He hadn't said much since he got in the car – for good reason.

He was a changed man. The old animated JuneBug was gone forever.

He stared through the windshield at his most prized investment: a three bedroom, three bath townhouse in Orlando's MetroWest community. He became oblivious to everything else. *Man, it's a miracle I lived to see this place again,* he said to himself while reflecting on all the shit he went through since September of last year.

"What's wrong, Dayvan? You haven't said more than a few words at a time the whole trip. You're actin' like you're not happy to be home or somethin'."

Bug looked at his baby mama, whom he informally upgraded to wifey status yesterday. Her actions through his recent ordeals were grounds for the status upgrade. Although he'd told her months ago she'd forever be his lady love. Prior to his last arrest she had routinely demonstrated her worthiness. But it was her endless support and steadfastness while he was away that made it clear she was worth walking down the aisle with.

"Shella, don't get it twisted. I'm happy as fuck ta be outta that hellhole an' wit'chu an' my boyz. I'm just … I just gotta ton of shit on my mind now that I'm fresh out. My agenda—"

"What? Your agenda?" Shella snarled. "Dayvan, the *only* thing you should have on your to-do list right now is how many different ways you goin' ta fuck me once we get in this house. It's been six long months since I had some dick. I'm hella horny and need to be dicked down. So, as soon as you're finished huggin' and playin' with the boys, my mom is goin' home, and my sister is comin' to take the boys and her kids to GAMESTOP and Wet 'n Wild water park for being good in school this year. Until they return tonight, we're fuckin' like rabbits."

"That's wassup, boo, becuz I'm in desperate need of some gush-gush." He smiled, flashing his mouth full of lackluster gold teeth. "But I can't help that my mind is runnin' at a hunnid miles per hour. I have –"

"I know good and damn well, Dayvan, you're not thinkin' about hustlin'. That absolutely better not be on your mind. I didn't hold you down this long and put up with all the shit that I have for you to go right back to jail because you want to get back in the game. I'm puttin' my foot down now. The game is over! You hear me? Or you can go be with a sour pussy, chicken head hoe and abuse her because I'm not goin' to be your duck bitch anymore. If you thought I was a bug-a-boo then, you wait and see."

"Be easy, Shella baby. I ain't gonna thug ya like that no mo'. The well-bein' of you and the boyz is always on top of my mind. It's just hard fo' me to keep from thinking 'bout ways ta get my chips up." He got quiet briefly. Then, he decided to stretch the truth. "I ain't thinkin' 'bout husslin'... at least not on da illegal tip. I'm thinkin' 'bout how long it's gonna take ta get my CDL an' start haulin' product up an' down the highway legit."

Shella's manicured eyebrows drew up. She smelled something was fishy. By now she was hip to Bug's deceptiveness. "CDL? Haulin' product on the highway legally. If you ask me, what you're talkin' about sounds *illegal.* You can't piss on me and say it's rainin'. I know you too well, Dayvan."

"Naw, boo. On some real shit, I'm talkin' 'bout getting my commercial driver's license so I can drive eighteen wheelers. A few of my dawgs been drivin' semis fo' years, so I know it's good, legit money. But I learned durin' my time in there that I can make up to a hunnid Gz a year drivin' big rigs. Of course, that don't stack up wit what I was rackin' in da streets. Gettin' my CDL an' drivin' trucks, tho', is way betta than otha nine-to-fives that's out'chere fo' felons."

Shella fell for it once more. "That's... that's good, baby. However, it sounds... bittersweet."

"How so?"

Shella slowly took in air and let it out even slower. "Now that you're out I was hopin'... I want you home every day, plain and simple. I know we never lived under the same roof, but I don't want to be left alone no more in your house."

"Our house," Bug quickly corrected her.

Without skipping a beat, she resumed, "I don't want to be raising our sons alone in *this* house once you get off home confinement. You drivin' trucks means you'll be on the road for days at a time. I know that sounds like I'm bein' insecure... Well, I am insecure, all thanks to you. So, once again, it can be M.O.B. but not with this bitch."

"I hear all that, baby girl. I don't plan on bein' a ova-da-road trucker out da gate. I myself wanna be in da house er'day, even after I complete these few months on house arrest. But shit is diff'rent now since my..." He refrained from speaking about his ailment. "Look. If criss-crossin' the USA in a truck fattens my pockets, you gotta undastand I'm doin' that fo' us. You helped me out tremendously, handlin' all of my finances an' takin' care of *our* house an' kids while I was on ice. I owe you big time. It's on me now ta take back da steerin' wheel an' cater ta you."

"Ugghhh... See, you don't get it, Dayvan. You're failin' to realize... Never mind. Forget it."

"Speak ya mind, boo. What don't I get?"

After a moment's pause, she said, "Listen closely... I didn't do what I did for you for practical reasons. I did it all because I downright love you. I sacrificed a lot for you, and I'm willing to do more if it keeps you out of trouble. I've been committed to this relationship since the beginning, Dayvan. I knew you were no good back then, so I shouldn't have gotten involved with you. There was just somethin' about you, though. When we finally hooked up it was no joke to me. It was all a game to you, however, Mr. Playa. When you got me pregnant and I gave birth to Deuce, I was hopin' you'd take our relationship seriously. But you didn't. I endured a one-sided relationship, doin' all the lovin' and givin' and prayin' you'd change. Then, Trey came and you still chose to run the streets, stickin' your dick in every mutt

9

bitch you came across because you were too scared to be exclusive with me. And still I chose to stand at your side. You finally opened your eyes to see that I'm the real deal when I stepped up when you went down hard." She shook her head disappointedly.

"The only compensation I need from you is to reciprocate the love I've always had for you. As far as I'm concerned, our relationship can thrive with you workin' at Burger King. I'll get a job, too, and take the rest of my college courses online and we'll struggle together. I'm good as long as we love each other unconditionally… and you're in bed with me every night at a reasonable time. How you treated me back then, it'll be none of that. I'm drawin' the line here."

Me, workin' at BK and livin' check to check is out of the question, Bug thought while looking at the stylish, mortgage free townhouse that was in the name of his mother, who was a CPA. *I'm down to six hundred stacks, according to my old girl, so it's a must I recoup my losses and top off my safe before I fall back …or worse.*

Before his most recent hardship could encumber his mind again, he leaned over and kissed Shella's MAC-covered glossy plump lips. The taste of cherry stirred him. His tongue intertwined with hers before he knew it. His hands fondled her full D-cups.

Drawing on all her willpower, Shella pushed herself away. She was breathless, as well as thrown open and wet. "My mama inside with the boys and my sister, Stanika, should be here any second," she managed to say while stroking the stiffness in his rumpled Givenchy jeans. "We don't need them seein' us fuckin' in the driveway. Besides, how I want it, this small space won't let you hit my spot. So, let's go in the house and do this properly. Plus, I got a surprise for you." She gave him a quick kiss.

Just as they got out of the car, a dark-tinted vehicle pulled in the driveway.

"Is tha'cha sista?" He asked.

"No."

"Who that then?"

"Umm, I have no clue, baby."

Bug's insides spasmed and his heart pit-a-patted all at once. Other than his momma and Shella, he hadn't told anyone his exact release date, so he wasn't expecting any visitors. And since Shella only mentioned her sister swinging by, he got on his toes and ready to take flight. *This better not be her doing because I told her I didn't want a surprise party.*

A well-dressed black male exited the sedan. In his hand was a black tote bag. Gayly, he approached Bug and Shella.

"Mr. Stubbford?" the middle-aged man asked.

"That's me," Bug spoke up as Shella joined his side and hooked her arm on his.

"I'm Mr. Vickers. I'll be your probation officer for the next year and a half. I'm simply dropping by to evaluate your place of residence. If this home passes my inspection, which it should from the looks of it, I'll be affixing an electronic monitoring device to your ankle and setting up the boundary around this place that you mustn't go beyond. The whole process should only take an hour." Mr. Vickers gestured towards the house. "Shall we?"

Damn. Instead of doing this weeks ago like he was supposed to, he decides to show up when a nigga 'bout to set foot in the house, Bug griped inwardly as Shella led the way. *There's no chance now for me to stop by mom duke's crib real quick after I beat Shella's back out.*

"Dad," Deuce, Bug's thirteen-year-old son, yelled once he saw his father. He charged ahead joyfully and hugged him,

Right on Deuce's heels was eleven-year-old Trey. "You're finally home, dad. I missed you."

Bug winced in pain from being clutched so tightly by his boys. Yet, he ignored the extreme discomfort in his abdomen and firmly squeezed Dayvan junior and Dayvan III.

"Okay, I'm gone. I'll call you once I make it home," Ms. Athena, Shella's mom, said, appearing suddenly. And just as quick as she appeared, she was in her car and gone.

Ms. Athena hated JuneBug, and she made sure he knew it every chance she got.

There was no mistaking the animosity between Bug and Shella's mom. But he didn't give a fuck.

Shella… she just stayed out of it. She'd been gave up trying to be a peacemaker.

"I missed y'all, too," Bug assured his young men. Misty-eyed, he kissed their foreheads. He subsequently looked sideways at Mr. Vickers and said indirectly, "An' I promise, y'all will neva miss me like that again becuz I'm home ta stay fo'eva."

Chapter 2

September 1, 2011/ 6:21pm/ Orlando, FL
Restless.

Notwithstanding being confined to his home nearly twenty-four hours a day the past three and a half months, his mind was always on go. He'd become an insomniac due to incessantly sorting plans out in his head. He understood that the best way to hit on a plan was to devise lots of plans, because so many things were achievable if he didn't think they were unachievable.

In the rare moments he wasn't mapping things out and getting at key individuals, he was scratching a need that was incapable of being completely satisfied.

Presently, it was one of those moments.

Shella bit her inner cheek and clawed her long French-manicured nails up and down Bug's spine as he buried his bone deeper and deeper in her garden of Eden. With his five-eight, one-hundred-twenty-pound lanky frame smushed against her five-five, one-hundred-fifty-pound curvaceous body in the missionary position, he rummaged her depths. The ecstasy radiating from their flesh left them drenched in passionate sweat. His proficient dick-work soon caused her pussy to speak the language of wetness.

"Oh my God… That's it, baby… You know the spot… Yes… Knock the bottom out, why don't you? Don't stop. You better not stop," Shella talked shit sexily while opening her legs wider and grinding her hips underneath him. She was nearing eruption. She sucked hard on the side of his neck and whimpered erotically.

Her customary moaning, along with the twisting and grinding of her abdomen and pelvis, incited Bug. He picked up the pace as she began to bite at his neck, fervently pumping in and out. It seemed like her divine box was a hapless victim and his well-above-average cock was the Ghostface killer from the SCREAM films. He returned the favor and forcefully sucked on the spot where her shoulder and the base of her neck merged, which was one of her erogenous zones.

She left new teeth indentations all over his neck. And he covered her neck and shoulder with fresh hickeys.

"Yes. I'm about to cum," she announced.

Upon her announcement, Bug put an end to his savage impaling. He pushed himself off her while keeping his bulky shaft stowed away between the creamy walls of her love tube. In a high plank pose, he proceeded to grind against her. He moved his hips in a circular motion, simultaneously stimulating her clit and stirring up her slick insides.

"Oooohhh, you know I love it when you do that shit. That shit feels sooooo good," she breathed lustily. "Harder… Do it harder. And faster."

Bug happily complied with her command.

"Mmmmhmmm… Oh, yes… Yea. Yea. Yea… I feel it!"

Abruptly, Shella shimmied, cueing him that she was a wink away from gushing. He repositioned himself. In no time, he fastened his mouth to her pearl like a remora fish clung to a shark. He nursed on her clit madly while tweaking her "surprise," which was her newly pierced VCH right above her clit.

Ssphish ssphish ssphish

The back-to-back jets of warm nectar shot into his mouth so fast that he almost choked trying to drink it all. He thought he'd be used to the amount of flavorful fluid that squirted out of her since, amazingly, it was close to the same output every time she came. When the last drop of her juice went down his throat, just barely bypassing his windpipe, he lifted his head from between her thick thighs, looked into her dreamy cinnamon-hued slanted eyes, licked his lips theatrically, and said, "Ahhh... That was mmm mmm mmm so tasty." He kissed his fingertips like a chef admiring his handiwork. "That pineapple diet you on got me wantin' ta call them fruit people at Dole an' gettin' you a lifetime supply. It got this pussy tastin'—" he dipped his head down, gave her a quick lick and came back up "—sugary."

"Damn, Dayvan, your tongue... It will make me... I'll kill a bitch!" Shella beamed. "Well, baby, let's see if the same diet kicked in yet for you and got your sauce tastin' fruity." With a X-rated expression, she gestured for him to "come here" with her index finger.

Bug smooched her silk like labia once more before kissing his way up her cocoa butter-scented, peanut butter-toned smooth flesh. Once he arrived at her sweet mouth, he spent several seconds kissing it before straddling her chest. In the middle of her pillowy breasts, he placed his Grade A meat. He pushed her large round tits together until the set up resembled a jumbo hot dog. He then began sliding his pole within her titties, inserting his inflated crown into her welcoming jaws every time he thrusted forward. Her saliva soon lubricated the passage between her breasts, which allowed him to titty fuck her with gusto.

"Squeeze 'em together fo' me, boo," he instructed. "I'm 'bout ta bust."

With joy, Shella did as she was told.

Bug tweaked her stiff Skittle-sized nipples as he drove his dick in and out of her slippery mammaries. The euphoric smile on his mug eventually contorted. His lips contracted next. Lastly, he grunted.

"You ready?" he rhetorically asked, slobbering a bit while removing his pulsating member from between her titties. He moved around until his bulbous head was pressed to her juicy, puckered lips. He started jacking his spit-coated dick. "Here it cums."

"Boy, shut up and let that shit fly." She opened wide, anxiously standing by for his flow, while massaging his big balls.

His eyes rolled upwards.

Skeet skeet skeet skeet

At irregular intervals, he squirted his seed. Unlike her gushing like a malfunctioning water fountain no matter how many times they fucked during the day or week, his discharge volume was short of diddly-squat. At the rate they'd been going at it the last few months, it would take him at least two full days of no fucking to release a full load.

A good bit of his semen found its intended target. The rest spackled some of her lips, cheeks and chin.

"Yes, baby, them pineapples are definitely workin' for you, too. It wasn't much to enjoy, but it tastes better than the last batch," Shella confirmed immediately after ingesting his sperm. She then used her fingers and lips to clear away what was left on her face. "Waste not, want not." She smiled. "I'm fiendin' for more already."

Bug finally dismounted Shella. He laid down next to her. He positioned a pillow behind his head and stared at the ceiling. Instantly, he reverted to his routine of late.

"I want to get married," she said very fast. She'd waited the longest to say that. She felt that now was a good time to say what had been on her mind.

Shella's unexpected words interrupted Bug from building on and fool proofing the vision he was just a few weeks from actualizing. As a matter of fact, her statement left him blank for the first time in a long time.

She cozied up against him. She laid her head on his shoulder and threw a leg over his groin. She subsequently traced the still extra sensitive six-inch long ragged scar on his belly lightly with a fingertip. In his ear, she whispered, "Do you love me, Dayvan?"

"Yeah," he replied flatly.

"Do you love your sons?"

"C'mon now. Get real. Why would you ask me sumthin' stupid like that?"

"Just askin'. I meant nothin' by it. I'm sorry, bae." She sighed, then asked, "Are you *in* love with me?"

"Yeah," was his response.

However, it wasn't said with conviction.

Deep down inside, though, Bug loved the shit out of Shella.

Doubt or not, yes was all Shella needed to hear.

"Well, wife me if you're in love with me, Dayvan. Let's take this relationship to the next level and officially form a household. There's no bond greater than family. That's somethin' I really want with you because I love you with all my heart and soul. I want to spend the rest of my life with you.

"And if you ask me, this twenty-four-seven time we've been up under each other lately proves that I'm worth wifing. I do all the cookin', nearly all the cleanin', and I primarily take care of the boys' needs and hobbies outside of the house. I'm a certified dime piece, and my pussy surpasses premium. Am I lyin'?"

"Naw, you ain't lyin'," he said truthfully before adding, "You also gotta good head on ya shoulder an' y'know where you wanna be in life. So, all in all, you got da works an' what it takes ta be da missus."

"When we tyin' the knot then?" she jumped to a conclusion. She lifted her left hand in the air in front of them. "This finger needs a chunk of ice. And the venue needs to be spacious because my dream has always been to have a huge wedding."

Before Bug could play out all of what was happening in his head, his phone rang. *Perfect timing,* he said to himself as he grabbed the phone from the nightstand. *This better not be that Vickers nigga talkin' 'bout he comin' over here*

17

because I just went in for a piss test yesterday. He looked at the screen and recognized the caller. *Thank God.*

"Wassup, blood?"

"I'm outside, homes."

"I'm comin' ta unlock da door now," Bug said before ending the call.

"Who was that?" sought Shella.

"Blue."

Bug scrambled out of the mahogany California king four-poster bed. He hurriedly dressed in a wife beater and Dickies and left the bedroom. He opened the front door. He clasped Blue's hand and gave him a brief hug before showing him in.

They settled in the family room, Bug's temporary sanctuary these days.

"It's been a few weeks since we last spoke, so what'chu been up to, homes?" asked Blue, getting comfy. "It look like you gettin' ya weight back up, too, I see."

"Yeah, I'm slowly puttin' on some pounds," Bug confirmed. "Otha than that, it's been nuttin' but plannin', mo' plannin', an' doin' that some mo'. I can't afford nuttin' fuckin' up what I have in mind becuz I ain't tryna end up goin' up da road. I neva been to da big house, an' I'ma do my best ta keep it that way."

Blue smoothed the deep waves in his hair with his hand. "Bro, as y'know, I been in da panhandle twice wit those racist crackas an' it ain't da beat. I most definitely ain't tryna go back a third time. So I'm glad ta hear you usin' extra precaution wit'cha plannin'.

"But, altho' you told me ta sit tight while you draw up a flawless play, my curiosity in wha'chu plannin' without my input is only makin' my nerves worse every day that passes. You're 'bout ta get off house arrest soon an' I'm still in da dark. You gotta run sumthin' by me now ta gimme at least a glimpse of what'chu got in store, homes. I don't have ta give ya feedback. Just bring into da light, even if it's a lil', an' that'll help calm my nerves."

Bug wasn't trying to be secretive about his scheme. He merely wanted to make sure his ducks were in a row, and stayed in line, until it was go time. He wanted to present Blue with a flawless plan just before they embarked on their pursuit of ill-gotten gains.

"Well, befo' I break anythang down ta ya," Bug said, "I need ta know sumthin' first."

"What's that?"

"Have you cracked open an' studied that CDL book I got fo' ya?"

The bummed-out look on Blue's face answered the question. Still, he explained, "I haven't, homes. Da reason why is becuz I been bizzy takin' care of a lotta old shit so I can be in order an' focused when we hit da road. That's also why we ain't spoke da last few weeks."

Let down, Bug shook his head. "Gettin' ya CDL is mandatory fo' my vision ta work, blood. I can do this without ya, but I'm tryna bring ya along fo' da ride this time."

"Yeah, it was fucked up how ya left me hangin' last time, homes. I swear shit wouldn't have went down like it did if I'd went ta Palm Beach wit'chu an' Chad. Becuz like it's always been between us, we all we got. We gotta have each othas backs fully."

"Ya right, which is why I need you ta be fully on board now or this ship gonna sink befo' we get out da docks." He paused to let his words sink in. "I know I had nuttin' but time ta study da last few months while you did what'chu had to do. But it's 'bout that time, so you gotta get on da ball, blood. Becuz if all goes right, we gonna get Master P bread when No Limit Records was at its peak."

Blue burst out laughing for no known reason.

"What? I said sumthin' funny, blood?" Bug asked with a stumped look.

"That. That's funny, homes."

Still puzzled, Bug said, "What'chu talkin' 'bout?"

"Where you get that *blood* shit from? You hooked up wit a gang while doin' ya lil' time down da way an' didn't tell me?"

"Hell naw! I ain't bangin' shit but my hammer when I have ta nail a nigga." He grinned, displaying his highly polished sixteen gold teeth. "But ta clear da air, I say blood now ta da few I consider family that ain't actually my blood. You ain't my real brotha, but'chu my blood. You fam. Got me, *homes?*" He said *homes* like he was a gangbanging Mexican.

"Homes...Bro, that...Ya explanation ain't make... Whateva, *blood.* I got'chu. As long as you ain't goin' hard fo' nuttin' but da color green." He chuckled some more.

Of both Bahamian and Jamaican descent, JuneBug, born in Orlando on April 6, 1979, was raised on the wicked west side of the city. On West Parramore Avenue, near the Beirut projects, was the first place he remembered living. It was him, his single mother, Tessemera, and older brother, Andric. His absentee father was a Jamaican Don Juan who was well-known all over O-Town. And because of his deadbeat father's philandering ways, he had at least a dozen other siblings. Some, he knew that lived nearby; more he didn't since they lived far away.

The merciless struggle that Bug endured and the extreme violence that he witnessed as a young whippersnapper robbed him of having a normal childhood. Additionally, his mother's bouts with depression from grappling with mounting bills and Andric's inconsistent household contributions due to his frequent, yet brief, jail bids forced him to come of age fast. By 1989, he was both a part-time student and thief. He started off swiping food from local markets because there was never much to eat in the house. Over time, he graduated from taking groceries to burglarizing residences and stealing vehicles.

It had been during the drop of a "chip" at the local chop shop when he ran into a familiar face he didn't realize was also into grand theft auto.

Blue was that familiar face.

Bug and Blue, both fifteen years old at the time, would ultimately team up to lurk and pull off elaborate heists up and down and across Orange County. Bug tried to get another homeboy, Chad, from around his way to join them so they could perpetrate even more complicated capers. But Chad's dopeboy father kept vigilant watch over him. Blue and he therefore proceeded to ransack so many homes that they could've opened a hybrid furniture and jewelry store. And they drove off with so many cars that they could've set up a full car lot.

Their two-man venture went on flawlessly for years until Blue's deepening cash fever got him jammed up on an impromptu solo mission in 1996. Blue's rash act put him away for six years in the FDOC. During those one thousand, four-hundred-twenty-four days up the road, Bug was the one that primarily kept Blue's books loaded. And because Bug had Blue's back like a sweater during a dire time, their friendship strengthened to where it was unbreakable. Bug became not only Blue's alter ego; Bug indeed became the brother Blue always wanted his real brothers to be.

"Anywayz, you gotta get up on da truckin' game, Blue, in order fo' us ta succeed. Show me you serious 'bout this shit like I am by learnin' this shit so we can breeze through da six weeks of truckin' school an' get our CDLs. I'ma have a lot ridin' on this an' it'll be smooth sailin' if you're on top of ya shit. Ya hear me, blood?"

"Ai'ight. You just see to it that this plan keeps us off da law's radar becuz da one ya cooked up while in Palm Beach County jail sounded crazy."

"Which plan ya talkin' 'bout, blood?"

"Da one ta take ova Palm Beach. That wasn't well thought out."

Bug chuckled. "Ya right. It wasn't. I was in my feelings then. I wanted to bite off mo' than I could chew. But don't trip. I got our best interest at heart now. You just get on what

I asked ya ta do ASAP an' lemme continue ta perfect this shit. All I'm missin' really is one big piece. Once that's in place, I'll bring you all da way ta speed. Bet?"

Blue nodded.

Beep beep beep

"Damn, I can't wait ta get this shit offa my leg," griped Bug before maneuvering to plug in his ankle monitor. Once plugged up he sat back and said, "Befo' we get goin', finish up er'thang you need ta handle, especially all ya family matters. It's all hands on deck when we start. We liable ta be on da road fo' weeks, maybe months, at a time."

"Months?" squawked Blue, wide-eyed.

"Yeah, blood, possibly months."

"Sheesh... Ummm... Okay... What—what did Shella say 'bout that? She cool wit that?"

"She got no choice but ta be cool wit it becuz I'ma marry her soon an' give her all da say-so ova da particulars of da weddin'. That there should play it down when I tell her."

"Bug, you ain't tell her 'bout ya plan?" Blue laughed. "You crazy if you think Shella gon' fall fo' that. You musta neva heard of 'Happy Wife, Happy Life.' She gonna be happy ta be ya wife, fa'sho. But she ain't gonna be happy 'bout you bein' gone on da road fo' months, homes. Real talk. I think you're a dead man once you tell her, honestly."

Silence.

"An' what about that bitch-ass P.O. of yours?" Blue asked next. "You talked ta him yet 'bout drivin' tractor trailers?"

That aggravating, Uncle Tom-ass nigga is the only major hurdle that I have yet to figure out how to clear without stumbling or busting my ass, Bug thought as he looked down at the irritating, charging monitoring device. *The way he has consistently been on my ass like white on rice these past few months, I can feel he's going to be a fucking headache until I finish my papers.*

Chapter 3

November 2, 2011/ 9:07pm/ Miami, FL

It was a drafty, brisk forenoon. The ocean's salinity being carried on the wind was zestier than Zest soap. The taste of the air was one of the luxuries of being in such proximity to the sea.

The pleasant elements created a utopian ambiance this morning. To tourists, the South Florida autumn weather was surreal. But to the locals it was just another typical nice fall day.

JuneBug finally arrived in Little Havana after an uneasy four-hour drive. In haste, he whipped into the parking lot of his destination. He parked crookedly, hopped out of his whip, and damn near sprinted up to the Cuban restaurant.

"Good morning."

Bug stopped dead in his tracks. He was a few steps past the man sitting at the shaded table outside the vintage eatery. He backpedaled and took a seat across from the man he only recognized by his speech.

"You Adrian?" Bug asked.

"Yes, Mr. Stubbford, I am he."

Adrian's response somewhat knocked him for a loop since he'd never made his last name known to Adrian during their two brief conversations. Bug began to size up the Latino that dressed stylishly, paralleling Tony Montana. He estimated that the dapper *hombre* was in his mid-to-late thirties and had lived in the lap of luxury for some time.

23

Besides his outfit, that appeared to be handmade from the finest materials, and his subtle but expensive jewelry, he concluded that Adrian's other possessions included the finest foreign cars and a fantastic mansion on or near the beach, which was likely visited by some of the most eye-catching women to be had in the area.

All I'm aiming to get out of this mission is a good portion of this migo's noticeable wealth and I'm gravy, Bug gathered as he silently admired Adrian's charismatic bearing. *But first, I must convince him to bet on me or it's back to the drawing board I go—humiliated.*

Unconcerned at the moment with how Adrian knew his last name, Bug got straight to it. "I don't have much time to kill. But, first off, I appreciate you fo' answerin' when I called. I know it was prolly strange an' unclear ta you 'bout what I was callin' fo' since ya dunno—"

"Do you want some breakfast?" Adrian abruptly cut in, his voice tinged with an accent. "Eggs and bacon? Or would you prefer a sweet roll and melon? Or perhaps you'd just like some tea or coffee, Cuban style?" He took a sip of his expresso.

Suppressing his agitation, Bug replied, "I'm straight. Like I said, I don't have da time. I'm kinda in a rush. I gotta—"

"I didn't want to address anything substantial over the telephone because you never know who is listening," Adrian commandeered the conversation again. "Now, tell me, how did you come by my number?"

Bug wasn't with being cut off, nor was he up for small talk. But since he was seeking to be put on by a heavyweight narco-trafficker, he knew he had to interact and be grateful for this opportunity, regardless of Adrian proving to be a habitual button-pusher.

"Like I said in our first convo, I'ma friend of both Bizzy an' Chad."

"Byron provided you with my number?"

"Byron? Who's that?"

"Byron is Bizzy."

"Oh… Ummm… Actually, he didn't give it to me. I got it from Chad, Bizzy's cousin. Chad, who'd been my dawg since we were knee high, passed it ta me ta use—"

"What are we doing here this morning?"

Bug had to laugh to keep from cussing the pompous asshole out.

Before Bug could say anything, though, Adrian continued. "Obviously, you're privy to who I am, so you must know I'm the one here who doesn't have time to waste. And just to clue you in, I'm wise to who you are and what your intention is. Now I want you to run down everything, from how you became involved with Byron to how you ended up at this table. Be truthful, because I'll know when you're lying."

Bug sighed defeatedly.

A lot had happened between the time frame Adrian specified. Some of what took place was sweet. But the long and short of it had been a shit show.

Beginning from the top, Bug concisely talked about how Chad and he grew up together in O-Town yet lived remarkably different lives. Next, he talked about how a privileged Chad left the city to attend Bethune-Cookman College in Daytona Beach when they were eighteen. He filled Adrian in about how he gave up the life of thieving and finagled his way up under Chad's father's wing and got introduced to the dope game. He described how he completed menial jobs to learn the ropes as Bubba's apprentice, such as buying large volumes of cut and pills and guaranteeing that all the packaged work was airtight and the correct weight. Once he got those tasks, and more, down pat, he was allowed to sell ounces of soft to select clientele. But he wasn't permitted, for any reason, to hustle on the block or out of a dope house. Eventually, his obedience, devotion and ability to operate clandestinely led to him nabbing his first block of white within a year.

From there, he spoke about the nine years he hustled at will until his grind came to a screeching halt the day Bubba, the man who considered him a son and the only person that provided him with powder, got locked up in June 2007. With a decent amount of cash stashed, he recounted how he put his felonious career on the back burner and proceeded to enjoy the creature comforts of life. His downtime didn't last long because Chad reached out to him in October 2008 and pulled him back into the game.

Bug continued the recountal by describing the day Chad requested he relocate to Nashville in January 2009. He discovered that Chad had paid for the house he moved into and supplied him with one hundred thirty keys, of which he was directed to sell a half brick or better every transaction. Then, in March 2009, he divulged that Chad called him and ordered him to return to O-Town without giving him a reason why. Once more, happy to admit, Bug kicked his feet up and had a blast living life.

Exactly a year later, in March 2010, he went into detail how Chad again drew him back into the life of hustling. Nonetheless, the short period he'd spent selling coke and pills with both Chad and Bizzy, whom he'd just been introduced to, had been plagued with bad breaks. He then opened up about the released video of Bizzy's father being killed, which resulted in Bizzy mainly focusing on finding out who murdered his pops, and how that ultimately led to Chad being killed and him getting shot and locked up afterwards.

Once Bug finished playing back how he became tied in with Bizzy and Chad, Adrian said, "There are two things I'd like to dig into further. First, I'd like to know more about the night you were shot."

"Uhh… What mo' do ya wanna know?"

"I want to know, in full detail, all that led up to that night." Adrian repositioned himself in his chair, awaiting Bug's story.

Bug peeked at his G-Shock. He noticed that he'd spent the last fifteen minutes telling Adrian all that he had already. He hoped they'd be talking business by now, but he decided to put up with what he deemed was unimportant. *As long as this extra babbling gets him to roll with me, I'll play along,* he thought as he finally chilled out and leaned back in his seat.

"Like I said, once Bizzy's pops' murder was put on that *Thugz & Gangstaz* DVD fo' da whole world ta see, Bizzy flipped da fuck out. He not only sent four deranged killas out in da streets ta track down who done it, he offered a Meal Ticket fo' any info that would lead to who off'd his pops, Kilo. Bizzy was already unda a lotta pressure at that time ova diff'rent shit. He was stressed out ova da war he was engaged in wit da lames callin' themselves Triple S, da two feds he learned that was watchin' him, an' da grand openin' of his first pain clinic in Mobile, Alabama.

"Bizzy eventually left town fo' Mobile ta open da clinic. He returned ta West Palm ASAP, tho', when I found out da bitch I was fuckin' knew sumthin' 'bout Kilo's death. Instead of capturin' an' toturin' da bitch ta get info outta her, Bizzy chose ta off her ta send a message ta da muthafucka who actually merked Kilo. Bizzy, Chad an' me had er'thang set up perfectly ta slump da hoe…or so we thought. That night, sumbody rode through da park we were gonna smack that bitch an' they got ta shreddin' shit wit a chopper. Chad was killed, I was shot, an' Bizzy… I dunno what happened ta that coward-ass nigga. I ain't heard from or seen him since. He disappeared. An' that's that."

"Okay. On to the next." Adrian shifted in his seat. "Tell me now what happened after you were locked up."

"What is there ta tell?" Bug's patience was wearing thin. He was close to saying fuck it and hauling ass and falling back on Plan B, which he didn't have yet. All his eggs were in this one basket. "I got shot, spent ova a month in da hospital first, then got booked fo' a quarter pound of krypt them boyz found in my 'Vette. I didn't get charged wit nuttin' that happened wit Chad."

"Why is that?"

"Why is what?"

"Why didn't you get charged with Chad's murder since you were the only one found on the scene with him?"

Bug shrugged. "I dunno."

"Was it because you ratted on Byron? That is what's being said in the streets of Palm Beach County at least."

Bug's blood had been simmering before now.

It started to instantly boil with that last statement, though.

This wasn't the first time Bug had heard the ridiculous allegation. He initially caught wind of the damning rumor his first day in Gun Club's general population. If it weren't for his discovery package, aka his paperwork, documenting that the police seized his phone and obtained a warrant to go through his phone records, he, as an out-of-towner, would've been assaulted. The local news had distorted his story. But they never once reported he was a rat.

Bug's best guess of who was responsible for starting the lie that was making the rounds in the streets and on social media was Bizzy. He prayed he bumped into the slimeball soon... real soon. He had to get some straightening.

Through clenched teeth, Bug uttered, "I ain't no fuckin' snitch. I'ma solid, thorough nigga. All da way ta da gristle. I knew to lawyer up da second five-oh paid me a visit in da hospital. I got proof in black an' white sayin' I ain't gotta fat mouth. So, fuck what da streets of Palm Beach say 'bout me, becuz my niggaz in da *O* know I don't name names. I neva rocked like that."

A dashing smile formed on Adrian's face. "My friend, your credibility is indeed solid. I know this because I always have eyes and ears everywhere. In fact, I knew beforehand everything you just told me. I did my homework on you after the first call. I know your history. I simply had you echo everything to check you out face-to-face."

Bug was tongue-tied. *Why this spic make me waste time telling him shit he already knew?* he asked himself as his blood turned to lava. *I clearly told him out the gate I was pressed for time, so he got another thing coming if he thinks I'm a simp or something.*

"Why do you look *extremely* mad, my friend?" Adrian asked as a gust of air blew open the unbuttoned segment of his dress shirt, putting his delicate and curly chest hair on view.

"Look, mutha—" Bug caught himself. "I. Am. Not. Your. Friend."

Throatily, Adrian guffawed. "Look, there's a reason I agreed to meet with you... my friend-in-the-making. Otherwise, you'd be home seeking out other means to get rich quickly and not here worrying about your probation officer discovering your whereabouts. So, lighten up and let's feel each other out during this informal introductory meeting. We don't have to discuss much now, but we can spend a little time chewing the fat. Because if Demetrius, the most successful businessman I'd ever dealt with, welcomed you into his fold and entrusted you with a hundred plus keys in another state on consignment, I can at least hear you out. I'm sure you have a top-notch plan that'll line both of our pockets with *mucho dinero.* And now I should inform you that what happens hereafter depends on what you're selling me, so smile."

Bug didn't smile.

But he no longer had a sourpuss look on his mug.

In an attempt to decrease the tension, Adrian said, "Did you know that Demetrius and his notorious RockBottom Family were the leaders of all the syndicates in the states?"

"Naw."

"Well, to give you a full scope of who you were in cahoots with, Demetrius, aka, Kilo, was the mastermind behind an enterprise that moved *metric* tons of cocaine in a matter of a few months. In fact, what you were given to sell in Nashville was a very small portion of the forty-three million dollars' worth of coke Demetrius purchased to peddle in numerous states east of the Mississippi River.

Did this nigga really just say forty-three MILLION dollars? Bug wondered in awe.

"I can see from the look on your face that you weren't aware of Demetrius' magnitude in the drug game. He was truly a titan." Adrian sipped his espresso again. "So, make your pitch, Mr. JuneBug. Prove to me you're a titan to be."

Once upon a time, not long ago, becoming a legendary figure in the game like his mentor, Bubba, was Bug's dream. Long gone was that vision now. He had his wake-up call the night before he was released. It was then that he gave up on his aspiration to be a big shot outside of his stomping grounds. All he wanted after he was set free was to reserve enough illegal money to maintain a lifestyle he didn't have to bend over backwards for once he checked out of the game.

Bug hoped his limited, yet outrageously deliberated plan would still win Adrian over.

"In a nutshell, I wanna get my CDL an' transport work fo' you."

After hearing the brief proposal, Adrian enjoyed some more of his beverage. He put his mug down and lightly rubbed his bare chin. Then, "You just want to transport drugs for me. That's it?"

The way Adrian put it made Bug feel...small. To him, his brainchild was fit for accomplishing his goal. But Adrian's reaction made it seem like he was asking to be a peon instead of an enterprising sub-contractor with an ambitious checklist to reach the top.

"It don't have ta be just dope. I'll... Well, me an' my trusted homie, Blue, will move whateva," Bug said, trying to boost his petition.

Despite employing plenty of transporters, Adrian always had use for more. D.O.T. and interdiction officers on stretches of major interstates were consistently pulling over and jailing his truckers. Americans may spend approximately ten billion dollars a year on illegal drugs, but the United States devoted close to fifty billion a year fighting the war against them. Nevertheless, as long as the insatiable demand for drugs was present, he, as well as other cartels, would supply the dopers by way of boat, plane, train, or semi.

"Will I have to provide the trucks?" asked Adrian.

"Naw. I'ma use my own bread ta buy two fairly new trucks."

"Good. So, once you register those trucks and become an owner-operator, are you going to work exclusively for me? Or will you look for work elsewhere through a broker to blend in?"

"If you ain't got nuttin' fo' me ta move, I'll haul loads legally fo' othas until ya call."

"What about your probation? Are you going to wait until you finish that before you begin?"

"I had to twist my P.O. arm ta get a lil' room ta move. I been goin' ta truck drivin' school da last couple weeks now wit my dawg. We gettin' this shit poppin' as soon as those CDLs touch our palms."

"Your ongoing healing from your colon cancer surgery won't slow you down, will it? You don't want to be out of state in a rural area and in need of help if a complication arises."

Damn, this motherfucker has done extensive research on me like I'm a history test, Bug concluded as his stomach spasmed. *I might need to think twice before going forward with this out-of-pocket spic.*

The near fatal shooting was both a gift and a curse to Bug. During one of his complex operations to patch up his guts, surgeons discovered polyps in his colon. After biopsies confirmed the polyps were cancerous, doctors successfully removed the genetically destructive growths, which were the cause of his father's death at the young age of forty-five. He was told by the specialists treating him post-op that the malignancies were detected in their early stages.

He was cancer-free.

And so, being shot was a blessing in disguise.

"I'm straight."

"Okay, my friend. Now, before I leave to plunge into my overloaded day, I'll fill you in briefly on the percentage you'll earn." He took a second to put on the elegant Panama hat that was on the table in preparation of his departure. "The aftermath from Osama Bin Laden being killed six months ago has ran up the prices of dope, so you're in luck. You'll get a cut of the total cost of the shipment, and your percentage for transporting depends on the distance. It's five percent in state and ten percent coast-to-coast. Anything in between is within those percentages. *Comprende?*"

Bug nodded.

"Good." Adrian stood up. "I'll contact you soon and we'll go over the ins and outs before I assign a load to you. Your first load will be a small one, and the delivery will be in state, just to see how you and your amigo handle it. The loads and distance will increase over time. So, in the meantime, stay on top of your health, my friend." He took a few steps then stopped suddenly. "Nice transportation," he added, acknowledging Bug's limited edition convertible Camaro, before confidently striding away.

Bug arose and cleared the scene, cautiously optimistic about the days to come.

Chapter 4

November 26, 2011/ 2:46pm/ Wellington, FL
Tinkle tinkle tinkle
Quietness.
Plink plink plink plink plink
"Enuff already wit that damn bell! I heard you. I'm on da way. An' it betta be a emergency."

"Oh, hell no! Don't address da queen like that. You wouldn't talk to me that way if I was healthy."

Phone in hand, Devon stormed into the twenty-five hundred square foot master bedroom. She halted just inside of the doorway and stared unamusingly at her mate seated upright against the maple headboard. "Miss me wit that Her Majesty shit right now. I'm on an important call wit RahRah. So, what is it ya *need*, Marie?"

Despite the seriousness in Devon's tone, Miracle pouted like a heartbroken toddler. Feigning feelings of hurt, she softly said, "I need some ice water. I'm dehydrated and hot." She extended the half-full glass of water in her hand toward her significant other. "Pleeeease."

"Honestly, Marie, this charade, you played it da fuck out. I didn't have a problem waitin' on you hand an' foot, day an' night, when you were physically unable ta do fo' yaself." She walked to the side of the bed and plucked the glass from her hand. "You been out da hospital about six months now. Ya physical therapist said two months ago you're capable enuff ta do low strain activities. Gettin' ya ass up out this bed an'

goin' downstairs an' gettin' water fo' yaself is low strain."
She turned around and trudged away. "This da last time I'm
doin' petty stuff fo' ya. An' FYI, I'm not respondin' ta that
bell no mo', so ya might as well throw that shit away."

"Thank you, Dee baby, my hero," crooned Miracle
gleefully.

"Whateva," Devon blurted out just before exiting. She
then said into the phone, "Rah, you still there?"

Six plus years, Devon and Miracle had been together. And
with any relationship, their union wasn't all rainbows and
unicorns. On occasion, they had to rise above adversity. Yet
none of it had really threatened to end their love story.
Except for the most recent ordeal they faced.

Because Devon righted an overdue wrong, which was the
slaying of the man that killed her mother and sexually
assaulted her, it set off a destructive chain reaction. Devon
steered clear of the resulting mayhem she set in motion,
while keeping her willing accomplice, Miracle, in the dark
about the truth of the matter.

However, Miracle soon discovered, by chance, something
vital that Devon had failed to disclose. Miracle flipped her
wig when she learned that Devon's machinations had
backfired and endangered not only their lives but the life of
Miracle's son, Kamani, as well. This put her in a predicament
where she felt there was no choice but to abandon Devon,
which she did posthaste. While separated and before she
could completely cast aside her feelings for Devon, she
received an unexpected call claiming that Devon was in
danger. Concerned about Devon's safety, she dropped what
she was doing and rushed to Devon's supposed location.
Upon arrival at the reported scene, she had been ambushed.
She survived being shot four times. After undergoing several
successful surgeries, and being in a persistent coma for three
months, she suddenly awoke while Devon and RahRah were
by her side. At first, she was unable to clearly speak at
length. Through mumblings and hand gestures, she was able

to implicate the person that likely organized the surprise attack on her.

Brimming with vengeance, both Devon and RahRah, siblings by way of Devon being fostered by RahRah's late grandmother, Miss Candace, had been doggedly hunting their prey ever since Miracle's non-verbal divulgence.

Prior to being beckoned by the servant's bell, Devon was on the phone receiving the latest news from RahRah about their target.

"My bad, bro," Devon resumed. "Miracle been on some real bullshit lately."

RahRah chuckled. "How my sis-n-law, tho'? Is she still laid up in bed?"

"Only becuz she wanna be in that damn bed, hoggin' it like it's all hers. Ain't nuttin' wrong wit that heifer. Da doctor said she way ahead of her treatment. Otha than da thirty, forty pounds she lost and some occasional pain, she almost one-hunnert percent." Devon sighed at the thought of how the five-eight, formerly one-hundred-seventy-five-pound Caribbean Amazon had shriveled up. The sorrowful feeling was fleeting, though. She became mad and got back on point. "So, you were sayin' that you found out sumthin' befo' Miracle bug me. What'chu got?"

"Does the bitch we lookin' fo' have family or know anybody that lives in Orlando?"

"Orlando? Hmmm…I don't think so. Why ya asked?"

"Well, we put feelers out there in da county an' swept it high an' low befo'comin' ta da agreement that she had ta have bolted from Palm Beach. So, I asked that bcuz a while back I decided on my own ta put a generous ticket on that hoe head. About fifteen minutes ago I gotta hot, credible tip that she might'a run off ta Orlando."

Who in the hell could she know up there? Devon wondered as she poured the lukewarm water in the sink and moved to get a bottled water and ice from the fridge.

Then something occurred to Devon. Their target had occasionally worked some weekends in various strip clubs in O-Town with Miracle. That led her to believe that her ex-employee-slash-side-bitch could've met someone during that time and was currently hiding in fear at the home of a tender-dick client.

"You might be on ta sumthin', bro," Devon admitted. She explained to RahRah what had dawned on her. "So, are you thinkin' what I'm thinkin'?" she concluded, heading back upstairs.

"A road trip ta Disney World?"

"Yup. Pack a big suitcase, too, bro. We might have ta camp out fo' a hot minute up there."

"As long as we back here by Christmas, I'm down. I didn't get da chance ta spend much time wit my jits this Thanksgiving. I told 'em I'ma make it up to 'em fo' Christmas."

"I got'chu."

"What'chu gon' do 'bout Miracle an' Kamani? You leavin' 'em behind?"

"Damn, I'm movin' so fast that I ain't think about them. Fuck!" Devon stopped halfway up the stairs and groaned in frustration. "Well…Since this is spur of da moment, I…I dunno. I can't lie ta Miracle no mo' cuz she been involved in this since day one. So…I'll figga it out befo' we hit da road tomorrow."

"Tomorrow?"

"Hell yeah, tomorrow. You wanna be back home fo' Christmas, right? I wanna get up there fast an' find out if that bitch there or not."

"I feel ya. I'll be packed up an' ready ta go when ya scoop me up."

"Oh, you think you so slick, nigga. Why I gotta drive?"

"Becuz my DL suspended, that's why."

"That ain't neva stopped you from driv—"

Ding ding ding ding

"Dee, where you at? My mouth is bone-dry and I'm about to overheat!"

I think not, she and Kamani aren't going with me, Devon finalized before continuing up the stairs. *I'll have Mystic and Peachez look after them and pay The Clean-Up Crew to protect them while Rah and I are out of town.*

"Kamani!"

"Yes, mommy!" Kamani yelled back from his room down the hall.

"Go see what's takin' ya mammie so long gettin' my water."

Devon shook her head wearily.

***

November 26, 2011/ 5:09pm/ Orlando, FL

Holy matrimony.

The nuptials weren't taking place in a glamorous tropical resort; however, the downtown banquet hall was spacious enough to pull off the Cleopatra, Queen of the Nile, theme Shella had imagined. The grandiose interior was bedecked wall-to-wall, floor-to-ceiling in gold and ivory. The balloons, streamers and other Egyptian-inspired decorations were said colors, as well as the tulips, lilies and irises.

With a veiled headdress adorned with jewels and a long train, Shella's bridal gown was designed by Dolce and Gabbana. And it was white as fresh fallen snow. Bug's black and gold tuxedo, accessorized with bowtie and cummerbund, was from the Hugo Boss collection. The maid of honor, bridesmaids and flower girls were dressed in white and gold gowns, and they had temporary henna designs on their hands, including Shella. The best man, groomsmen and ring bearer sported black and gold tuxes, and they wore gold crowns, with Bug's royal headdress eclipsing the others.

Surrounded by two hundred of their close family and friends, they exchanged vows. After Bug lifted Shella's veil and kissed his gorgeous bride, she cast the bouquet, and he tossed the garter. Next, the newlyweds sat and listened to several members of the wedding party toast and pay tribute to them. Following all of the heartfelt compliments and well wishes, Bug and Shella cut into the extravagant, seven-tiered wedding cake. They simultaneously fed each other some cake before smashing a handful of it into the other's face. Finally, to Jagged Edge's *Let's Get Married,* the twosome danced.

Once their first dance ended, and everybody took to the dancefloor, they were approached by the clearly inebriated best man.

"I gotta hand it ta ya, bro, this weddin' is one fo' da history books." He gave Bug some dap. "But I still think it's fucked up that her mom an' pops ain't have nuttin' ta say when it was time ta toast y'all. I know they hate ya guts, but damn...Look at'chu now, tho', Mista PFL. Ya ass on lock—"

"You need ta pipe down wit that PFL shit, drunk nigga," Bug attempted to say just loud enough so only the best man could hear. As inconspicuously as he could, Bug cut his eyes towards his wife, dancing an arm's length away.

"It's too late. I heard what Blue said about my mom and dad... Mister Playa For Life." She glared at her husband. "I'm glad he brought that up because you'll be gettin' that tacky leg tattoo covered up first thing tomorrow."

Bug and Blue laughed.

"Ha ha hell, negro," she said with a stoic expression.

"Say less, boo. I'll cover it up tomorrow wit sumthin' that symbolizes my love fo' ya." He grabbed Shella's hand and brought it to his lips. He then turned to Blue. "Er'thang grizzy wit'chu, blood? You came up on us mighty fast like sumthin' was on ya mind."

"Yeah, bro, I got sumthin' on my mind I need ta holla at'chu 'bout."

"Can it wait? I'm 'bout ta get ready ta dance wit my mom dukes."

With glazed eyes, Blue peeped at Shella. "Uhhh..."

"Whateva it is you have to say, Blue, you're going to say it now. This here—" she thrust the platinum five carat princess-cut diamond ring into Blue's face "—means there are no more secrets between me and Dayvan. So, what's on your mind, *blood?*"

Blue shrugged before blurting out, "I'm ready ta get zooted. Ain't you? Let's go outside an' burn this purp real quick. It's ya weddin' day. Enjoy it ta da fullest. Tomorrow you can get back on ya no smokin' bullshit."

Bug looked at Shella for the go-ahead to take a momentary leave of absence.

"*You* can think nothin' of it, but you know your ass is still on probation and that Mr. Vickers still closely keeps after you. So, if you violate and go to jail behind a failed urinalysis, you'll be unmarried." With that said, Shella walked away because she knew she'd never be able to tell Bug what to do. Regardless of what was at stake, he was going to do what he wanted, especially when presented with an ultimatum.

After Bug danced with his mother, he and Blue found a secluded area outside and sparked up.

"Bro, you an' Shella made fo' each otha like...Skippy crunchy peanut butter an' Smucker's strawberry jelly," professed Blue. "I don't get how her peeps don't like you."

Bug had just puffed the potent tree when he replied, lungs full of smoke, "Thank ya, blood." A dense cloud billowed out of his mouth before he started to cough. "Goddamn, this shit hittin'." He coughed on purpose to clear the itchiness from his throat. "Anywayz, altho' Shella treat me mo' like a jailbird than her man at times, she a great woman. She stood firm in da paint through all da bullshit an' troubles without givin' up on a nigga, so she has every right ta go off on me an' monitor my actions when necessary. She makes me think 'bout what I'ma do befo' I do it by givin' it ta me blood raw, know what I'm sayin'? Her being blunt keeps me in check an' on my toes. I appreciate that da most 'bout her cuz it furtha shows me she truly fucks wit me an' she not just wit me fo' my money. That's why I went on an' married her without her parent's blessing. Fuck them. Its officially death do us part now, know what I'm sayin'?" He hit the jay lightly the second time to not hack up his now delicate lungs.

Bug's trick didn't work. He began coughing uncontrollably.

Blue felt compelled to pat Bug's back like an infant. "Pass that shit befo' ya drop it, pink-lung-ass nigga."

Bug gladly passed it as he tried his best not to drool on himself.

"You geeked as shit, ain't ya?" Blue asked, taking the blunt while patting Bug's back still.

"Hell ta fuck yeah!" Bug responded froggily. "I know... Uhem... I'ma be bug as fuck... Uhhem... in a minute." Once he got himself together, he said, "Now what's really on ya mind? I know you ain't pull me outta there just ta smoke wit'chu."

Before replying, Blue pulled hard on the weed, held in the smoke for several ticks, and blew out a wisp. He showed no indication he had to cough. "Well, since we got our CDLs, an' you scratched da weddin' off ya to-do list, I wanted ta know when we gettin' ta work. I'm ready ta get this paper."

"I told ya... At least I think I told ya. I can't remba whetha I did or not, blood, cuz I'm higher than a bitch right now." Bug shrugged. "Anywayz, da plug hit me up a few days after we got our licenses an' said he has work fo' us. I put the job on hold, tho', until I got this weddin' out da way. I gotta number ta hit him up when I'm ready. I'm ready ta go now, so I'ma hit his line first thing tomorrow. It's on an' poppin' from there."

"It's 'bout time. I got er'thang in order like ya told me ta do. I'm psyched up ta get this show on da road. I'm ready ta stack up mo' bread than da French."

"Da French?"

"Yeah, homes. You done heard of French bread?"

"Ohhhh. I follow ya, blood. Stupid nigga."

They burst out laughing.

Blue hit the jay again, ashed it with a tap, and presented it to Bug.

Bug hesitated to take the blunt.

"Homes, stop hittin' it so hard. Take ya time. You gotta crawl befo' ya walk," Blue said, impersonating Smokey from the movie *Friday.*

Smiling, Bug grabbed the blunt and hit it with poise. The urge to cough struck him, but he resisted. He let out the smoke, then said, "We 'bout ta get *mucho pesos,* blood. But don't ya get greedy on me, know what I'm sayin'? I need ya ta stick ta da script an' don't get trapped up by a slimeball nigga or ratchet-ass hoe."

"Neva again, bro. I'ma be all da way on point. My hunger fo' cheese will neva get da best of me again. If... That's a big IF... If I do get jammed up by them folks again, I'ma hold court in da street. I ain't puttin' on anotha pair of cuffs again. An' a petty nigga or foot-draggin' mutt bitch won't get da chance ta cross me up an' knock me off my square."

"I hope you stand on that, blood, becuz we'll be neck deep in this shit in no time. Once we kick this off, we'll have a lot ridin' on this, know what I'm sayin'? An' rememba, da goal is ta make eight figgas quietly an' get out fo' good an' live comfortably, know what I'm sayin'? We can invest our money into a legit business, like expandin' this trucking business, know what I'm sayin'?"

"Yeah, *I know what'chu sayin',* zooted-ass boy. Now, hit da joint an' pass it. You lettin' it smoke itself." Blue laughed. He watched as his chinky-eyed homeboy puffed on the blunt twice before giving it back to him. "Back ta what'chu were sayin' now...It shouldn't take long ta rack up that much cabbage. Since you said we getting a percentage of what da plug sells his bricks fo', an' da cheapest brick in da street is movin' at twenty-four bandz right now, then we'll get twelve hunnid fo' each key we move in-state. It's double that fo' coast-to-coast haulin'. So, at da least, we gotta truck about seventeen thousand of them thangs in-state ta split twenty mill."

Damn, I never broke it down like that, Bug thought as the effects from the THC caused him to become immersed in thought. *How Blue had just laid it out, I need to make arrangements with Adrian to get all coast-to-coast shipments as soon as possible so we can reach our mark by transporting fewer keys.*

Then, out of nowhere, someone crept up on them.

"JuneBug."

Hearing his name broke his train of thought.

Simultaneously, Bug and Blue saw the silhouette of a busty five-two, one-hundred-forty-pound, dark chocolate-complected woman strutting in their direction. From a distance, neither of them could make out who the woman was. But they both easily sighted the baby she carried in her arms.

I'm glad it isn't my fucking monster-in-law, Bug said to himself.

Then it clicked to Bug who the woman was once she got to within a few feet of them.

Upon recognizing the person now standing in front of him with a frightened expression on their face, Bug's bloodshot eyes just about popped out of his skull. He did a double take just in case the purple haze had him hallucinating. His high was instantly blown when he was a hundred percent sure she was real.

"What da fuck you doin' here?" Bug inquired, raising his voice.

"JuneBug, I—I ain't come here to cause any problems. I'm only here becuz I need ya help."

"Hold up, homes. You know this chick?" Blue asked, looking back and forth between his partner and the unknown female.

Bug tuned Blue out. "You need ta get da fuck on sumwhere, bitch, befo' I snap an' fuck you up!"

Though the sun's light had not quite faded into darkness, her misty eyes glistened like the stars due to come out soon. "Bug, please, I really need ya help." The waterworks commenced.

"You gon' fuckin' need help bein' carried away if ya don't get da fuck outta here NOW!" Bug said with great anger as he stepped toward her.

Blue jumped in front of Bug and held him back. "Bro, slow ya roll! You trippin'. You don't wanna cause a scene on what's 'posed ta be da happiest day of ya life. Plus, you don't want Shella comin' out here an' seein' you fightin' wit… wit whoeva this bitch is."

"Who you callin' a bitch, nigga?" The tears ceased. "You dunno me to be callin' me a bitch. Besides, I ain't no bitch. I'm his baby mama!"

The statement left both Bug and Blue frozen in place, silent.

"Yup, ya heard right. This ain't no game. This here is yo' five-month-old daughter, Daylonna."

Bug turned his attention to the quiescent baby in her arms that was swaddled in a blanket. As soon as he locked eyes on the cute, curly-haired infant, there was no doubt in his mind the little one was his. The baby girl was the splitting image of both Deuce and Trey when they were newborns, except she was dark-skinned.

"You weedheads not done smokin' yet?" Shella said, walking up on them abruptly. "Y'all need to hurry up. My mom and dad want to talk to—" She ceased talking when she took notice of the woman with the baby that had not attended the wedding ceremony. Consequently, she eyeballed the female suspiciously and said, "Dayvan, who is she?"

Bug's stomach cartwheeled, causing him to double over in pain.

Chapter 5

November 27, 2011/ 3:19am/ Orlando, FL

Between a rock and a hard place.

That's where he currently found himself.

Just when he believed he had sorted everything out, lined up and ready to go, *that* had to happen. He couldn't let this unexpected crisis sabotage his impending mission. The quagmire he was in could be turned around, he firmly believed.

Fuck, why did our plot to cancel that bitch get derailed? He silently puzzled over the question as he was being excoriated early this morning. *I hope I can get Shella to see this embarrassing bombshell as an uncontrollable circumstance.*

After he took advantage of an opening to squeeze in and defend himself, he prayed his story, omissions notwithstanding, was accepted and didn't inflame her further. He wanted to end the dispute peacefully, and for good.

"I don't care, Dayvan, if you were fuckin' that hoe before you chose to make me your one and only! You should've kept it strictly business between y'all. If you would've only sold her pills and not stuck your lil' dick in her raw, you wouldn't be in this shit," Shella yelled, nearly in a psychotic rage. "But since you didn't keep it to strictly business, your fuck-up let her obliterate our household in less than three hours... THREE... of us exchanging vows. There is no fuckin' exclusively *us* now because she and your—" she struggled to say the words "—your daughter are permanently a part of our lives. It's no longer wherever you go I alone will follow. It's wherever you go I, along with them, will follow. Ugghhh! You and your hoe-ish ways have ruined my happily ever after."

Bug sighed. He decided to completely level with her and hold nothing back.

"Bae, calm down an' lemme lay it all out fo' ya."

Shella got up in his face. "Lay it all out for me? Oh, so you lied to me, Dayvan? Really? You swore you wouldn't lie to me no more."

Bug wanted to step back from Shella for his safety but thought otherwise. "Please, recognize that we weren't committed when all this fluke shit happened."

"You said that already, Dayvan. Tell me something I haven't heard because that isn't helping your case."

"I was truthful 'bout all that I told ya," Bug resumed. "Howeva, I had ta fake like I was really crazy 'bout da bitch when I first met her becuz my dawg Chad an' his cousin Bizzy, da two niggas I was gettin' money wit befo' I got shot, they needed me."

"They needed you! For what?" She crossed her arms over her chest and awaited his response.

"They needed me ta buddy up ta her once they suspected she had sumthin' ta do wit Bizzy's pops' murder. Since I was fuckin' already...yes, bareback...they felt I could easily extract info from her. After a few days of us kickin' it, I caught her off-guard wit da questions I was told to ask her. An' her reaction incriminated herself. I reported back that she was sour. After that, they wanted me ta lure her into a trap. I agreed ta help 'em. Unfortunately, that bitch ain't die that night." The flashback of that life-altering night caused his face to contort. "So, all this wasn't 'posed ta happen becuz she 'posed ta be dead."

Shella cringed. What she'd just heard showed her a whole new side of her husband. It was hard for her to visualize her soulmate conspiring with others to commit a homicide. She'd always known that Bug was a thug. But she didn't know he was heartless enough to play with a woman's emotions, primarily through sex, before setting them up to be murdered.

Who is this man I thought I knew well? She asked herself. *Who did I marry?*

Phone rings

Shella acted quickly answering her phone. "Hello…Yes, this is she. And you're KiKi, right?"

Bug's brows raised at once. "Stop bullshittin', Shella. That ain't that bitch on da phone."

Shella lowered the phone from her ear and said with a full-blown attitude, "Yes, it sure the fuck is her on this phone. You don't see me smilin' and laughin', do you?" She left the bedroom and resumed talking. "Hello? You still there?"

A now maddened Bug was on her heels. "What're ya doin' talkin' ta that bitch?"

"Hold on one more second. Don't. Hang. Up." She stopped and turned to face Bug. "What I'm doin' is getting the information I need because yesterday I was so mad that I couldn't think straight. But I was clearheaded enough to swap numbers with her off to the side before we went our separate ways."

"Bae, you can't trust that bum bitch. She knows I tried to kill her ass! She might be tryna set *me* up this time, so hang up da muthafuckin' phone."

With everything Bug had just confessed, she realized that there was a strong possibility he was right. She was close to ending the call.

Then again…

"Okay, no more interruptions. Anyways, we need to meet up to discuss a few things…Somewhere in public, yes, of course…I can't promise that because I don't know you… Yes, he'll be comin'… I'll text you where we're goin' to meet… Okay." She hung up.

"I'ma tell ya straight up right now; I ain't goin' ta meet up NOWHERE wit that bitch. An' neitha are you. Real nigga shit."

"The hell if I ain't! Real BITCH shit!" she snapped, freeing the hood bitch in her. "Look, negro, this is your fuckin' mess, not mines. There's no way I can let this shit slide. So, I'm goin' to help you clean this up as much as possible because I feel obligated to in order to move forward with our lives. This girl has your baby – and you better not even try to deny that innocent child that looks exactly like your ugly, big-lipped ass – so we must figure out where to go from here, ASAP."

"Bae, I appreciate you willin'—"

"Dayvan, I'm ready to walk. What I say in this matter is final. You should be countin' your blessings instead of objectin' to what I say. You're lucky I'm so self-controlled, because if I wasn't, I wouldn't have let you in this house last night. A hysterical woman would've packed up all your shit and left it on the lawn after being blindsided *on their wedding day* like I was. I should've kicked your ass to the curb. But my crazy ass didn't because, sad to say, I still love your stupid ass. All of my girlfriends and my parents say I'm not all there for stickin' by you, even though I told them that you were foolin' around and got her pregnant before we made it official. But I told them hatin', envious bitches and my parents that come hell or high water we're together forever. BUT, if you think for one second that you'll play wit my emotions again once we clear this shit up... Ha ha, you got another thing coming ifmore hoes come out of the woodworks talkin' about they're your baby mama. You think she has it out for you now, play with me *one more time* and you're goin' to see what I have in store for your ass. Now, I'm goin' to ask you this only once: Is there anything else you need to let me in on? I'm givin' you this opportunity to speak up now."

"I don't have any… anymo' secrets. But I can't say flat-out anotha bitch won't surface outta da blue on some bullshit. I can say, tho', if a bitch pop up wit a baby younger than this one here, that bitch straight up lyin'. You da only one I been wit since I got out. That's on Tessemera."

Swearing on his mother wasn't necessary because his body language and cadence let her know he wasn't being deceptive. "

"Good. Now I'm goin' to bed for a few hours before we link up with your baby mama."

"Don't call her that."

"Don't call her what? Your baby mama?"

"Yeah. You said it like…like I'm buddy-buddy wit that bitch."

Shella rolled her eyes. Ignoring his comment, she added, "And another thing I want you to know before we go to see her, I'm takin' my gun with us in case I have to give her the business for tryin' somethin' stupid."

Bug was heavily bothered, yet slightly turned on, with the idea of her bringing along her licensed Glock 27. As a convicted felon on probation, he wasn't authorized to be in possession of a firearm.

Bug kept a gun handy anyway. Mr. Vickers and his probation be damned. And he'd be carrying that reserved pistol to the meeting since he reluctantly gave in to Shella's pressure to go.

When Shella walked off toward the master bedroom, Bug followed.

"Umm, where do you think you're goin'?" she asked once she noticed Bug on her ass, literally.

"Ta bed wit my beautiful wife so we can consummate our marriage."

"Ha! Nope, correction to be made. You're goin' back to the beautiful couch. Consummate the marriage with your hand." She walked into the bedroom alone and locked the door behind her.

They both spent the next six hours tossing and turning in respite before arising in the midst of the late morning sun. They practically avoided each other as they prepared to leave the house. Once the boys were in order, Shella zipped her Range Rover Evoque to her sister's house to drop them off. They zoomed to their destination next. As planned, they were ahead of schedule when they arrived at the designated pavilion in downtown's Lake Eola Park. They scoped out the landscape from the cover of their vehicle for a couple of minutes before they strolled up to the open-air structure. They stood under the canopy and chitchatted awkwardly as they attentively anticipated KiKi's arrival.

Quite a few cars trundled by while they waited. The moment of truth soon came when they observed a Nissan Altima brake and pull into a parking space near their vehicle. On pins and needles, they watched KiKi hop out of the driver seat.

KiKi was inappropriately dressed for the occasion. She was killing the form-fitting Ann Hardy dress and Jimmy Choo heels. And her magenta-colored short bob hairdo complemented her babydoll face.

KiKi wasn't alone, either.

Bug eagle-eyed the male that had muscles for days exit the car.

Oddly, no baby was with them as they came at Bug and Shella.

Bug's uneasiness increased with every step they took towards them. Admittedly, the presence of the tall bodybuilder put him on alert. As a precaution, he lifted the hem of his shirt, doing his best not to be noticed, and gripped the handle of the gun Shella wasn't aware that he had brought along.

Subsequently, he glanced over at Shella. To his amazement she already had her Glock brandished by her side, and it was twitching in her hand. He wanted to take the small gun away from her because the angry look on her face suggested she was close to upping and busting them both at any second. *They better be coming in peace because wifey looks ready to bag these motherfuckers,* Bug thought as his heartbeat sped up. *But on the sly, it'll be thrilling to see my baby off that bitch.*

"Hi, y'all," KiKi said, her tone marginally conveying aversion and diffidence.

Together, Bug and Shella nodded at her and her... man? Friend? Bodyguard?

"Well... ummm... I hope y'all don't mind my guy friend joinin' us. Please don't see him as a threat. I didn't bring him along to start no bullshit. I just didn't want to come alone. I strictly came to address issues an' resolve misconceptions so Bug can help me."

"Why can't buddy help ya?" Bug blurted out with a unit on his face.

KiKi impulsively looked up at her six-foot-three friend. "Cam isn't in da streets, Bug. He's a personal trainer I met a while ago at... He's just my friend. Let's leave it at that. Anywayz, I went through a lot trackin' you down to see if you'd be willin' to help da mother of ya child."

"Alright, let's cut to the chase because I've had it up to here with this bullshit already," Shella spouted out. "Before we even think about helpin' you with whatever it is you need help with, I need to hear y'all history together."

"Whose history?" KiKi asked.

"We don't gotta history," Bug threw it out there.

"You, be quiet and let her speak," Shella warned Bug. "I heard your side of things. It's time for me to hear hers. Let's see if y'all stories align."

Bug and Shella had defied seemingly insurmountable odds in the past. But he prayed that the mess laid before them wouldn't lead to a casualty, or three, after KiKi's account.

KiKi quickly peered at Bug. Despite Bug looking extremely displeased, she recognized he was copping pleas via his eyes. If not for her seeking his help, she would have fabricated a story that would do more than shatter his wife's self-esteem. It would also erode her faith in her husband's integrity and trustworthiness. Instead, since she needed to play nice to manipulate them, she said, "Can we sit down?"

"And could y'all cool it with the guns?" Cam the he-man added in a voice that sounded like his vocal cords also pumped iron. "No hard feelings."

On that note, Bug and Shella relaxed.

They all took a seat on a nearby picnic table under a tree. Paired up, they sat across from each other.

"Okay, to make a long story short," KiKi began, "I met JuneBug in da club I worked at. I—"

"You a stripper?" Shella cut in.

KiKi's lightning quick comeback for that frequently asked question was, "An exotic dancer. My stage name was Rhapsody."

"Alright," Shella said dryly. "Continue."

"Like I was sayin', me an' Bug ran into each other in Studio X almost a year an' a half ago. Well, it was mo' like him steppin' to me at the bar after my shift ended. I was in a shitty mood but Prince Charmin' here got me to talk, an' befo' I knew it, we were havin' a deep conversation. Don't ask me how we got on the subject of pills becuz I honestly don't rememba how. But once I let him know I popped them periodically, he gave me a few Roxys he had on him to give me peace of mind from what I vaguely told him I was goin' through. Da convo trailed off then, so he gave me his digits an' left.

"I can't lie. Da feelin' those few pills he gave me got me hooked on 'em fast. I hit Bug up fo' mo', an' he became nothin' but my pill man. Then, I hit rock bottom. I had to quit dancin' becuz I had a serial stalker followin' me. That left me wit no money ta feed my addiction. I was so desperate to get high one night that I called Bug an' asked him to credit me some pills. He said yeah, so I went to his homeboy's house to pick 'em up, an' that's when things shifted from bizness to us makin' love that night. Bug invited me to spend da night wit him afterwards. That one night turned into five or six days. Otha than da night that the police raided da place an' took us to da station fo' questionin', I had a fun time wit Bug. It was like I was in a fairytale when I was wit him."

Her face suddenly contorted.

"That all ended, tho', da night Bug called me while I was out handlin' some bizness. He called an' told me to meet him at a park fo' a late night surprise. I made it to the park an' called him back to get directions to where he was. While followin' his directions, my…Da person that was stalkin' me miraculously saved my naïve ass from bein' killed by Bug an' his homeboyz. They wanted me—" she fought back tears "—dead becuz they assumed I had somethin' to do wit a murder that had been recorded an' released on DVD. I had absolutely nothin' to do wit none of that, tho'. I dunno what made Bug an' them think I did."

In truth, she knew what made Bug think she had something to do with the murder of Bizzy's father. She'd not only met both Bizzy and his father, Demetrius, she indeed had a hand in helping her former lover murder Demetrius. So, when Bug unexpectedly asked her if she knew a Beauti or a Demetrius, it eventually dawned on her that it was her bizarre reaction to his questions that gave her up.

From Bug's perspective, looking back, he honestly didn't want to expose her for the barefaced lies she'd told him; he was really feeling her energy at that time. He felt forced to tell Chad what he'd suspected about her, especially after Solo, a nigga he barely knew but became cool with quickly, was killed.

Rhapsody continued, "Befo' he set me up, I was startin' to… I had strong feelings fo' him. I knew he had some feelings fo' me, too, becuz he catered to me like I was a queen instead of treatin' me like a strung-out fiend." She wiped away her tears. "So, that's it."

Shella's nares were flaring prominently with every inhale she took. She was breathing fire and seeing red.

It was understood that Bug and she weren't together during that period. Yet, hearing how lovingly she spoke about her husband, and how generous he was with his drugs, dollars and dick, cut her down to size. If she hadn't been thirty-eight hot right now, she would've took what she'd just heard hard and wound up crying... over spilled milk.

Only the sounds in the background could be heard. The blowing wind, chirping birds, rustling trees, and the distant babel of parkgoers at play filled their ears.

"What now?" Cam broke the silence with his jarring voice. "Because I have a training session in a few, KiKi."

"How'd ya find me?" Bug finally asked the question he'd been longing to know.

"It was easy, to be honest wit'cha,' KiKi professed. "Durin' those nights we pillow-talked, you told me everything about you. I had no plans at all of seein' you ever again once I discovered you survived that night. But a series of events, like me findin' out I was carryin' ya child, fo' one, left me no choice but to move to your hometown an' look fo' you."

"What do you want from me?" was Bug's next question.

"I need protection from da person that's out to kill me...an' ya daughter," KiKi overexaggerated. "You owe me that much after you set me up fo' somethin' I had nothin' to do wit. I really need your help. I don't feel safe."

"Who wants to kill you? And why?" was what Shella wanted answered.

Even though Rhapsody had rehearsed for this moment, she seemed unsure about how to answer.

Rhapsody knew exactly who wanted to take her life and why they wanted to take it. After her partner-in-crime had been killed, she had been living with the constant tension of not knowing when she'd face the music for orchestrating her damning act of betrayal.

Rather than await her fate in PBC, Rhapsody fled south to a relative's house in the city of Lauderhill in Broward County. Her stay there wasn't long because news of what she'd done traveled quickly. Consequently, due to the person she betrayed knowing most of her family, she was forced to hit the road alone. With no destination in mind, she drove north on I-95 in a panic until she was near hopelessness.

Then Rhapsody saw a sign... a highway sign with "Orlando" on it. Almost instantaneously, JuneBug popped up in her head. She hated JuneBug's guts, yet her vulnerability drove her toward that sign.

Rhapsody was no stranger to Orlando. It didn't take her long to find out Bug was locked up in PBC. Low on cash and with meager belongings, she chose to lie low and survive by any means necessary until JuneBug was released. She had no outline whatsoever of how to convince JuneBug into helping her. Her solution came soon, however, when she discovered she was with child, and her intuition told her the child's father was JuneBug.

Rhapsody made the smart, yet hard, decision to keep her unborn child a secret from family and friends. She had acquired a few supportive sugar daddies in O-Town to help with day-to-day expenses. However, she ended up struggling badly with homesickness and trying to manage the morning sickness that seemed to constantly plague her. She gave birth to Daylonna a day before JuneBug was released. Afterwards, postpartum depression caused her to nosedive. She was unfit to be a mother. And she was certainly not ready to confront JuneBug. She became so unstable that she ended up calling her mom for the first time in months. During that emotional phone call, she accidently revealed her location. When she realized her mistake, her mom swore not to tell anyone where she was. But she knew that lady couldn't hold water.

With the help of her sugar daddies, Rhapsody shaped up enough to finally confront JuneBug. She needed his help ASAP since her mother had likely outed her. When she learned JuneBug was on house arrest, instead of disturbing his peace at home, she followed her intuition again. It prompted her to approach JuneBug the night of his wedding.

"Anotha stalker has been threatenin' to kill me becuz I refuse to be wit him," Rhapsody eventually answered Shella's questions with lies.

"Why didn't you go to the police?" was Shella's next question.

"I did," Rhap lied some more. "But that ain't enuff. I need Bug's help since I know he's cold-blooded an' connected to notorious gangstas."

Bug didn't hear anything that was said after Rhap mentioned that someone wanted to bring harm to his alleged daughter. Learning that triggered him to say, "Where she at now?"

"Where who at?"

"Who else? My daughter, hoe!"

Cam stiffened. He wanted to speak up for Rhapsody being called out of her name. He quickly decided against it, however, because the gun Bug was packing flashed back into his mind.

"At Cam's grandma house," Rhap replied, letting the slur slide to keep the peace.

"Go get her an' brang her back here now. I'll... Me an' my wife will shelter her."

"Huh? An' what about me?" Rhap asked, appalled by his proposal.

"What about you? Ta keep it a buck wit'chu, I hope whoeva it is that's tryna kill you succeeds. I might'a framed ya by mistake, but'chu got yaself in some shit I ain't puttin' my life, or da lives of my family, on da line fo'. Yo' rotten ass mo' than likely deserves what'chu have comin'."

"Damn, playboy, you don't have to be so cold-blooded," Cam interjected. "Have some respect for your baby mama."

"Stay in ya place, big dawg. You got no right bein' all up in mines. I damn sho' ain't up in y'all bizness." *Pause.* "As ah matter ah fact, you need to distance yaself from this unlucky black bitch befo' you get caught up in some shit you wished you hadn't. You heard da four-one-one wit'cha own two ears. Trouble an' death follows this bitch. She bad bizness an' needs ta be on all niggaz' blacklist."

The entire time Bug was talking, Cam and he had been staring each other down. By the end of his statement, Bug observed the venom that was once in Cam's eyes had vanished. He sensed that Cam wasn't cut out for dealing with these types of problems. Cam was conflicted and unsure about what steps to take next.

"Ahem," Cam cleared his throat. "Well, it's approaching the hour, KiKi. I got to go. So, do you need me to go with you to get your daughter from my grandma place? If not, you can drop me off at the gym so I can prepare for my client's arrival."

Rhap couldn't win for losing. She'd hoped against hope that she could persuade JuneBug to shelter both her and their daughter. But since her tactical plan didn't work on Bug, she was now forced to solicit Zip, her backup plan, for assistance. Lucky for her, Zip wasn't present to hear Bug's last remarks because he, too, might've immediately cut ties with her. *Something has to give because I swear all men are turning out to be cold pieces of shit!* she gathered secretly as her core heated up. *Here I am, thinking that Cam would have my back. That he really loved me like he said he did, with his quick-nutting ass*

Rhap looked at Bug with a fierce gaze. "Gimme a hour. I'ma drop him off at da gym first, pick up Daylonna an' bring her back here. She'll be safer wit'chu than wit me...at least until I handle this." She pivoted and stormed off. Cam was close behind her.

Yes, Zip must be the one that helps me make it through this safe and sound, Rhapsody concluded. *And once I no longer have to look over my shoulder, I'll get my baby back...*

and I'm going to live the rest of my life doing unto others before they do unto me.

"I'm tired of bein' played fo' a fool," Rhap mumbled to herself as she climbed into her car.

Chapter 6

December 9, 2011/ 5:01am/ Hialeah, FL

"Alright, my friend, everything is in place. You two are ready to head out now."

T.A.B. Trucking was open for business at last. JuneBug prayed that naming the company after his mother, Tessemera Augustus-Black, would bring him luck.

While Blue lent a hand loading palletized crates into the refrigerated trailer with a motorized dolly, Bug was on the dock overseeing the process with Adrian.

"You one hunnid percent sho' ya people in Palatka gon' be on point?" Bug inquired. "I don't wanna roll up into a country-ass town I dunno nuttin' about an' ya people be on some bullshit. Cuz I'ma tell ya now, I ain't da one ta try ta run game on or jack. I'ma have mo' than just words fo' they ass if they think we're easy come-ups."

"My friend, I need you to stop being pessimistic and looking at things from the dark side. Have a positive outlook for once." Adrian took a moment to see whether his bit of unwanted, yet useful, advice had registered. When it seemed like Bug could care less about what he'd just said, he added, "On a serious note, I need you to fully grasp the true weight of this rat race you and your *compadre* have joined. My *people,* as you called them, and I do not do this for kicks, especially since cocaine consumption has fallen fifty percent over the last six years. My people and I are components of a world-renowned drug cartel. We're on all the U.S.

government agencies' radar, of course. However, we're not scrutinized as intensely as the Mexicans and Columbians because everything we do is delicately arranged. So, with that said, my people will adhere to all protocols…unless they are threatened. The real question is, will *you* be loyal?"

"What'chu gettin' at?" Bug wanted to know. "You tryna insinuate that I'ma be on some creep shit? You think we gonna run off wit'cha measly fifty keys? Rememba, you only put me on becuz my loyalty to Kilo has been proven."

Adrian belly laughed, then said, "I know you're not crazy enough to do such a thing, my friend… because you're a cherisher of invaluable things."

Bug gritted his teeth at the subliminal remark. He knew very well that people who double-crossed the cartel faced capital punishment, so he didn't appreciate the redundant dig aimed at his family. Not once did he consider playing dirty with them. All he ever did was fixate on getting rich quick by working with them. To that end, Adrian's sideways comment about harming his loved ones was uncalled for.

After he let his words sink in, Adrian continued, "I understand, my friend, why you're apprehensive. This is your first run, your test, so wanting to play it safe is wise on your part. But I vouch for my people. We're all structured, by-the-book professionals, not some local bush league trappers. As long as you and your colleague are reliable and honest, you two have nothing to worry about. And I assure you, my friend, your sixty-two thousand, five-hundred dollars will be waiting for you in Orlando upon your return."

"This trip shouldn't take long at all. I'ma drive us there an' Blue gonna drive us back home. I don't think it'll take us long to unload da shit, so we should be back in O-Town, at the latest, two this afternoon."

"Homes, yo' ass ain't gonna hang out an' do nuttin' when its time ta unload in Palatka," Blue interrupted the convo between Bug and Adrian. Despite it being a nippy morning, he was perspiring. He wiped beads of sweat from his forehead with the back of his hand, then said, "Da truck is locked an' loaded. We ready ta clear it."

Bug peeped at his modest Seiko watch. "Already? Then, we outta here, blood."

"Befo' we go, tho', I wanna ask buddy sumthin'."

"What would you like to know, Señor *Azul*?"

"It's about da dope in da crates. Is it *in* da fish?"

"No, my friend. The yayo is in the middle of the frozen fish."

"Oh. I thought y'all were mo'… What's da word I'm lookin' fo'…Creative. That's it."

Adrian grinned. "Simple is better in most cases, my friend. In this particular case, you're only driving a couple hundred miles, so we didn't need to waste time stuffing those keys into tires or putting them into secret compartments or liquefying it and pouring it into cosmetic bottles. Does that make sense?"

"Ten-four," Blue said. "Now, can I ask one mo' question? I swear this da last one."

Adrian nodded.

"I know most of these crates are filled wit nuttin' but fish. So, I wanted ta know, outta curiosity, what'chu do wit the ones that don't got blow in 'em?"

"We give it to the hard-working, needy immigrant families in the area. Why do you ask?"

"Umm… Neva mind. I feel bad askin' since ya said that."

"Do you want some fish?"

"Hell yeah! I seen that it's Halibut. I neva had it. But I heard its good eatin'."

"Yes, it's delish, my friend. Both of you can take a box once you unload. How about that?"

Blue smiled. "*Gracias.* I appreciate it."

Bug wasn't keen on eating fish. His mother loved it, though. He'd just give the free box to her.

"Ai'ight, blood, let's be out. We can avoid most of da early mornin' rush hour on I-95 if we leave now."

They affixed a seal to the trailer's door, then inspected the truck and trailer again. Once they completed their inspection, they hopped into the cab of the 2009 Freightliner Cascadia with seventy-one-inch sleeper.

Appearing unexpectedly right outside of the driver's window, Adrian issued his final reminder before they took off. "Remember, my friend, do not cut off that satellite phone I've given you. Answer it whenever it rings. A lot of bad can transpire if you turn it off or fail to answer it. *Comprehende, my friend?* Now, drive safely."

When Adrian gave Bug the untraceable phone shortly after his arrival this morning, he told him the phone was only to keep their communications private. Adrian deliberately refrained from telling Bug the phone's true purpose.

Bug didn't have to be a genius to know the phone was also equipped with GPS to keep tabs on their every move. Hell, he suspected the crates with the coke in them contained tracking devices as well. He couldn't put anything past Adrian because he barely knew the guy.

And odds were favorable that Adrian had dangerous people keeping an eye on his wife and kids for insurance.

Bug and Blue made good time reaching the drop-off spot, a discount grocery store. They parked in the alley behind the market. Just as they were getting out of the cab, a crew of Latinos emerged from the store. They were approached by a lean, clean-shaven individual while the others headed for the back of the trailer.

"Which one of you is JuneBug?" asked the thirty-plus-year-old man who was of average size, red-skinned like a Native American, and had on a white du-rag with one long sleek cascading braid on each side of his head.

From the thick urban NYC accent, Bug recognized this was the man he communicated with twice on the satellite phone en route. "I am," Bug answered.

"Ai'ight, ai'ight. I'm known as Da Jackal, y'heard." He extended his hand out. Once he shook both Bug's and Blue's hand, he said, "Let's get down ta bizness then. I got otha goings on ta see about after this, y'heard."

It took ten minutes for the team of *pacos* to move the goods out of the trailer and into the store.

"Hold up," Blue abruptly called out as a stubby hombre was wheeling away one of the last two crates.

The worker kept pushing the hand truck because he didn't understand English.

"What's wrong?" Da Jackal asked.

"I almost fo'got that Adrian said we could keep two boxes of fish fo' ourselves."

Without delay, Da Jackal whistled. On cue, the worker halted. He said something to the worker in Spanish. After he finished speaking, the worker nodded and rolled the crate back inside the refrigerated trailer. He turned back to Blue and Bug and said, "Lemme check both boxes real fast, y'heard, ta make sho' they not none of ours."

"Do you," declared Bug.

The trio stepped lively inside of the cool trailer. Bug and Blue watched Da Jackal use a little crowbar to pry open the lid of the first crate. He cleared away the iced fish on top. Very carefully Da Jackal rummaged through the fish in the center. Once he verified the box was drug free, he replaced the lid and nailed it down with a couple taps of the crowbar's heel. He took off the second lid and repeated the process.

"Cono!" Da Jackal exclaimed, stepping back from the crate. "Y'all can't take this one, y'heard." He then hollered something in Spanish. A worker showed up in the blink of an eye. He spoke briefly with the scrawny man. The worker vanished, and he continued, "He'll be back wit anotha crate, y'heard. Y'all clear ta take off after that."

"Damn, we woulda came up if buddy ain't check that shit," Blue said playfully to Bug.

"I doubt y'all can get rid of what's in this box, y'heard."

"Maaannnn, there ain't shit unda da sun I can't move," Bug bragged because he honestly felt he could sell whatever came into his hands. His curiosity caused him to gravitate toward the crate to see why Da Jackal said what he said.

"If y'all can sell this shit, then y'all supreme hustlas an' should come work fo' us full time instead of bein' transporters, y'heard."

Bug glanced into the box. The contents in the middle of the frozen fish was indistinguishable to him. "What da fuck is that?"

Interested by Bug's puzzled reaction, Blue walked over and peered into the crate. He saw an indeterminate amount of Ziploc bags filled with what looked like red meat. He leaned in to get a better look at the bags, then said, "Why would they hide some beef in da middle of da fish?" He straightened up. "This gotta be some of that Japanese... What's it called... Oh yeah, this some of that Kobe beef, I bet. Adrian must be smugglin' it cuz it's illegal. Fuck, we fa'sho woulda made some money an' ate good if buddy wouldn'ta shook down this box."

A worker rolled into the trailer with another crate. He set it down and removed the other without tacking the lid back on.

"Ai'ight, ai'ight. We done here, y'heard," Da Jackal said, declining to give away what were in the bags. "It was nice meetin' y'all. I'll tell da big homie y'all were on point, y'heard."

This our first delivery and something... fishy... is already going on, Bug thought as Da Jackal strolled away. *I'm going to get to the bottom of this shit ASAP.*

Phone rings

Bug withdrew his phone from his pocket. The caller ID displayed a name that made him groan. "I'm leavin' outta Palatka now," he said immediately upon answering. "I should be home in a bit."

"The itinerary you provided me with, Mr. Stubbford, says you'll be back by three," Mr. Vickers reminded Bug. "I've been quite generous with you. I've allowed you and your mother to talk me into letting you work for her new company instead of an established trucking business. I've given you enough wiggle room. Therefore, if you're one second late arriving home, I'll violate you with no remorse, understand, Mr. Stubbford? I'll gladly throw you back behind bars where you belong. So, don't let anything hang you up. Or you'll make my day."

Bug couldn't understand why Mr. Vickers had it out for him. Since day one, he'd never failed a drug test, had never been where he wasn't supposed to be, and at no time had he disobeyed one of Mr. Vickers' many rules. He felt that Mr. Vickers only caved in to his petition to drive trucks for his mom out of Orange County because Mr. Vickers wanted him to fuck up. *One more year and I'm done with this hating-ass nigga,* he concluded before swallowing his pride once again and politely responding to his probation officer.

"Well, I'll be home befo'... Hello?"

Bug quickly realized he was talking to the dial tone.

Chapter 7

December 16, 2011/ 1:33pm/ Trujillo, Peru
The City of Everlasting Spring.

Located on the banks of the Moche River near the Pacific Ocean, Trujillo was a coastal metropolis in northwestern Peru. The predominant Roman Catholic city was the third most populous in the country. The city has a dynamic arts community, and it sponsored various domestic and international cultural events, with the International Book Festival being one of the most notable artistical events in Peru. The heart of the city has many buildings and structures of colonial and religious architecture. The city also contains suburbs and a central business district. Trujillo is exquisite, glorious, and utopian.

Just about everything in this equatorial foreign place was remarkable to Bizzy: The immaculate air, brilliant sunshine, picturesque backdrop, and the neighborly locals. What he found most phenomenal were the coca plants that offered him a life of luxury. *My pops told me to never respect material things that I could buy,* he thought as he jumped out of the taxi and sauntered to the downtown tavern a block away to do lunch with the man that changed his life. *But how can I not appreciate all the glamorous trappings of success I've been given access to since my arrival?*

Bizzy had been in the radiant city two months shy of a year now. He arrived by hopping from island to island in the Caribbean Sea before travelling through Venezuela and

Columbia. After he was picked up at the Columbian-Peruvian border, he was escorted to the severely earthquake-damaged city of Callao—pronounced *Kah-yah-oh*. He was awestruck when he finally arrived at the tremendous estate that looked out over the Pacific Ocean. And it was there that he met one of the world's largest cocaine producers for the second time.

Cesar Vargas DePalma reached out to Bizzy, a troubled but promising entrepreneur, on two accounts. The first reason was because of Bizzy's father's reputation in America's underworld. And the second reason was because Bizzy owed him ten million dollars.

Bizzy's first month in Peru was spent practically glued to Cesar's hip. Every place Cesar went, he went. And whenever he congregated with Cesar's contemporaries, Cesar introduced him as his protégé, which both flattered and amazed him. He didn't have much trouble interacting with non-English speakers, either, since his father had urged him to learn some Spanish.

Although Bizzy wasn't privy to any strategic planning sessions, he proceeded to soak up as much as he could. By the third month his Spanish had gotten better, and he absorbed more than he could've imagined about the global game of illicit drugs. And soon he had acquired the nickname of *El Hijo del Diablo*: The Son of the Devil.

A month later, Cesar took the leash off. Because he was recognized as a member of Cesar's network, he was free to roam the country solo without worry. However, he mainly travelled to take care of whatever he was told. His first tasks called for him to collect money from different locations and ensured it was safely transported to where it needed to go.

One day, he was put to the test. He was ordered to kill the next person he picked up money from. Without hesitation, he dutifully executed the woman.

Following that successful assignment, he'd murdered numerous people without knowing why. The *why* was of no concern to him. He did contemplate, though, what was really behind Cesar employing a raw nigga from overseas. Cesar ultimately informed him that it was his fearlessness and "uniqueness" that led to him being auditioned for a role in the organization. Cesar added that it was his readiness to act on short notice without complaint, as well as the originality he brought to the table that qualified him to try out for a position.

Most importantly, though, Cesar told him the ten million dollars owed would be reimbursed through the duties he performed.

Bizzy's natural ability and ingenuity helped him to pay off half of that debt in no time. And with Cesar's blessing, he was able to save significant funds for when he was ready to pick up his life in the U.S.

Currently, Bizzy was a broker. He oversaw exporting loads of drugs out of Peru. He was using owners of small planes to fly loads to Guatemala. From there, the work was either flown or boated through the Caribbean and into the U.S.

Bizzy refocused his thoughts as he made his way to the Chelsea Tavern, a customary business meeting place of his. He eased into the classy establishment, greeted the staff and familiar faces, then located Cesar in their reserved spot in the thick of the place. He took the only other chair at the table and got straight to business before Cesar got to running off at the mouth.

"Da loot from those guerillas has been dropped off hassle-free, jefe," Bizzy affirmed. "An' that *chivato* from Arequipa has been dealt wit."

"Did you do as I asked and made him squeal like a stomped rat?"

"Did I?" Bizzy answered boastfully. "After his face beat da shit outta my brass-knuckled fists, I put a gasoline-soaked tire on him an' barbequed that ass. He screamed so much that

I'm mo' than sho' that muthafucka still hollerin' in hell as we speak."

Cesar smiled at the mental image. *"Bien hecho.* Great job."

Because it was just another day on the clock, Bizzy didn't gloat. "Also, da shipment touched down safely in Guatemala. Howeva, I took it upon myself ta send it a diff'rent way to America from there. I did so wit da intention of developin' a new line. If it makes it, we'll have anotha route locked up. If it gets seized, I'll pay fo' da whole load."

"Okay," Cesar simply said. He had supreme confidence in Bizzy's judgment and foresight, so there was no need to question his tactics. Cesar knew his small five-million-dollar shipment would be safe because he was perfectly aware of the Bizzy using the route he relied on for emergencies only. Locating and utilizing this reliable route without getting a stamp of approval was more proof that Bizzy wasn't scared of taking risks. That demonstrated to Cesar the qualities Bizzy needed to be a top dog in his organization. *This young gent will go very far,* he concluded. *I wish he was of my blood.*

Over the years, Cesar became astute at judging one's character. He unquestionably favored Bizzy out of all his new underlings, so much so that he was already considering promoting him. Bizzy had proved himself beyond the shadow of a doubt. He truly felt that Bizzy had mastered his realm of responsibility and could run the operation from the bottom up. He thought Bizzy was that special.

Hell, he believed Bizzy, who had a knack for the game like his late father, could run his entire enterprise better than himself.

But he wouldn't dare tell Bizzy that.

"Are there any new assignments you got fo' me, jefe?"

"Not at the moment. Why do you ask?"

"Becuz I wanted ta ask ya if it was cool fo' me ta take some R an' R. I wanted ta take a trip ta Rio de Janeiro. Since a youngsta I wanted ta go there. An' since you don't got nuttin' new fo' me, I wanted ta know if I could shoot ova there fo' a few days ta kick back an' dick down a couple of them bad Brazilian mamacitas."

"You know you don't have to ask. You have the authority to go as you please when you're off duty. Just keep your phone on in case I need you."

"You should know me by now, jefe. You know I gotta ask. I don't get down like that. Yeah, I know I gotta pass ta come an' go when I'm in neutral. But becuz I'm goin' on da other side of South America, I had ta get'cha permission first, jefe."

"How many times must I tell you? You don't have to call me boss."

"A thousand an' one times, jefe." Bizzy grinned. "I respect a person that respects me. An' becuz I respect ya status, its only right I pay homage to you. You showed me that'chu run shit like a cartel kingpin oughta, so I call it how I see it."

Yes, handpicking him not only diversified my organization, but it has also been the best decision I've made in some time, Cesar reflected. *And my once skeptical colleagues now agree with my choice.*

"Tienes hambre?" he asked Bizzy.

"No," Bizzy fibbed.

"Well, that's too bad… because I already ordered for us."

Bizzy's grin grew. "I know you got me da monkfish then. No doubt wit my favorite Peruvian beer, Pilsen Callao." His dry mouth watered. "I'ma crush that shit as soon as it touch this table. This fuckin' Peruvian bud gimmie da munchies an' cottonmouth like a muthafucka!"

"I knew you were hungry, you red-eyed devil."

They laughed mutually.

After their food was served, they chitchatted while dining. Well, it was more like Bizzy listening to Cesar go on and on about this, that, and the third. Bizzy had grown accustomed to listening to Cesar spew needless facts he cared nothing about. Still, he hung on to all Cesar said perchance he needed to use it someday.

"Have you spoken to your *abuela* lately?" Cesar asked.

Bringing up his grandmother, Louise, caused Bizzy to frown slightly. "Yeah. She's... good. She's still battlin'. She's da strongest person I know." *Pause.* "I miss her. I can't wait to see her again."

"You will soon. Until then, you don't worry about her. I'll continue to pay to make sure she gets the best care. She's my responsibility now."

"Gracias, jefe. I-I... I can't thank ya enuff fo' footin' all her medical expenses."

They chatted some more until, after thirty minutes or so, Cesar stood up. To be damn near sixty years old, he was in great shape. He didn't look a day over forty. His bronzed skin and well-groomed, mostly gray curly hair were conspicuous in the laid-back restaurant.

Cesar straightened his handcrafted peach colored silk dress shirt and khaki slacks. He then placed a foot in the chair and wiped invisible dust off his python skin boot. After he cleaned the other boot and took a step to leave, he suddenly exclaimed, "Oh, it nearly slipped my mind."

"What?" Bizzy said, still seated and enjoying the remainder of his meal.

"As you know, I don't sit on any news I receive that pertains to you. I told you right away when your former homeboy, JuneBug, contacted Adrian looking for employment. Adrian has subsequently hired him and his pal Blue as transporters. Now, I'll inform you of what Adrian relayed to me during our most recent phone conversation."

Bizzy swallowed the food in his mouth and put the fork down. He leaned back in his seat and anxiously waited for Cesar to continue. He didn't care much about hearing what Bug was up to. However, every time Cesar brought him fresh news about JuneBug, he tuned all the way in just in case he needed to take immediate action against the backbiter.

"You know firsthand that we secretly follow new hires when they're off the clock. The tail on JuneBug notified Adrian about an unusual run-in JuneBug had with a female on the day of his wedding. After JuneBug was observed meeting up with that same female and others at a park the next day, Adrian soon identified the female. Adrian did additional research and learned two things: one, she's allegedly the mother of JuneBug's youngest child and two, she's someone you intended to kill for being an accomplice of your father's murderer."

The bombshell instantly filled Bizzy with fury. It consequently caused him to gnash his teeth. While he couldn't recall the female's name, he sure knew who she was.

A day after Bizzy was rescued from certain death by his sister Devon, whom he formally met on March 14, 2009, she bravely admitted to murdering their father out of vengeance. Within her confession, she revealed that a lot of her close friends helped her dismantle Demetrius' empire and pull off the murder.

With grudging consideration, Bizzy deemed Devon's actions to be justifiable and he quashed the vendetta with her. But hearing about Devon's bitch-ass accomplice upset him mightily. What upset him most was the lowdown bitch somehow turned the tables and got his cousin, Chad, killed the night she was supposed to die. And because he felt the cunning, poisonous bitch was on the hook for Chad's death—in addition to helping Devon kill his father—he was compelled to exact retribution on her. *I might've resolved to let bygones be bygones with Devon, but I'll be a pussy if I didn't see about her accomplices when I get word of their whereabouts,* he thought as his fury surged.

"Jefe—"

"I know. I can see it on your face," Cesar broke in. "Although I strongly advise against you handling the matter personally, I'll call Adrian and arrange for you to be picked at Miami International Airport. Safe travels." With no more to say, he headed for the exit.

A pair of sizeable men in black suits arose from a table not too far away and surrounded Cesar as he walked out of the establishment.

Chapter 8

December 16, 2011/ 10:09pm/ Orlando, FL

They rolled up to the House of Dolls and pulled the Chevy Malibu into a vacant parking space. Instead of exiting the vehicle and going into the gentlemen's club for a night of clowning and cutting up, they sat tight. At present they weren't interested in throwing bucks at bouncing tits, swaying hips, and vibrating asses. They were more interested in finding a particular well-proportioned hoe to throw in their trunk.

"I pray she shows up here. We been up here almost two weeks now an' this bitch nowhere ta be found. I'm ready ta smack her an' dip back ta Palm Beach."

"Rah, have you eva heard that patience isn't simply da ability ta wait, it's how ya behave while you're waitin'?" Devon asked her brother.

"Hell naw."

Devon rolled her eyes. "Did Fiona sorry ass eva hit ya back wit anythang new?"

"Nope. An' I'm thinkin' 'bout slumpin' that busted hoe when we get home if it turn out she gave me false info on her cousin. No bullshit."

"Patience, bro. Patience. Just becuz none of da strippers at any of da clubs we went to have recognized her from her picture doesn't mean she not here. We gotta couple mo' spots ta scope out after this one. I gotta good feelin' we'll soon cross paths wit da bitch. Cuz just like you, I'm ready ta get back to my boo Miracle, wit her aggravatin' ass. Me an' her will prolly pack up an' move ta Mobile as planned once I get back. Studio X will be all yours then."

RahRah sighed. Every time Devon threw Miracle's name out there, which was a lot, he was taken down a notch. The skeleton in *his* closet had been eating at him since day one.

"Ummm… Yo', Dee."

"Wassup, bruh? Don't tell me you ready ta haul ass. We just got here."

"Naw, it ain't that. There's… There's sumthin' I been meanin' ta holla at'chu about."

From the tone in Rah's voice, Devon knew that whatever it was he had to tell her was serious. She slightly turned in the driver's seat to face him.

Rah inhaled noisily through his nose, then exhaled slowly through his mouth. "Dee, I shoulda been told ya this as soon as it happened but…Please, don't be… too mad at me. I didn't—"

"Ronell, you neva been shy wit words, so spit da shit out already," Devon snapped. "You gettin' me mad by tryna tap dance around da shit."

"I was there when Miracle got shot."

"Huh? Run that back," Devon queried because she wasn't sure she'd heard correctly.

Rah repeated himself.

"What'chu mean you was there when Miracle got shot?" Devon asked, still not fully comprehending.

Rah swallowed the lump in his throat, "I mean I was there, on da scene."

Devon slowly registered what was said, and it crushed her.

A mental picture of Miracle being ambushed by RahRah caused Devon to tremble. Her breathing quickened. She was on the brink of blacking out. Yet, she was conscious enough to clutch her trusty Beretta .380.

Through clenched teeth, Devon said, "What exactly are you tryna tell me, Rah?"

From the second she displayed the pistol, Rah's attention had been focused upon it. He observed the weapon shaking in her hand and her finger twitching on the trigger. He looked into Devon's flaming eyes and said, "In order fo' ya ta fully undastand, I gotta start from da beginnin'."

Devon didn't say a word. She was anxiously awaiting Rah's explanation. She prayed whatever it was he had to say was legit because she didn't want to be the one to end his life.

Rah proceeded. "Y'know that me an' my Triple S niggaz was beefin' hard wit Eddie G an' his clique in downtown last year. What'chu dunno is that once shit got outta hand, me, Bumper an' Skat decided ta duck off at PopTart Tina's crib. We fell all da way off da radar, only slidin' through da streets in da dead of night ta fuck hoes. We kept our heads down an' outta sight.

"One day, while we were chillin' an' playin' Xbox, I getta call. I answered without lookin' at da caller ID. On my line was a female whose voice I ain't recognize becuz, fo' one, she was speakin' fast as fuck. But I was able ta hear her say that Eddie G's brotha, Dex, was on his way ta holla at a bitch in Pleasant City. After I heard that, I ain't think, I just reacted. I grabbed a choppa an' struck outta da crib without sayin' nuttin' ta Bump an' Skat, but they were right behind me. We ended up takin' cover in some bushes on Beautiful Avenue an' waited. A few minutes later da whip da bitch on da phone said Dex would be in, rolled onto Beautiful. Da whip ain't look familiar at first. But by da time I realized whose car it might be, Skat an' Bumper jumped out an' started gettin' off. I ain't shoot, tho'. I hauled ass ta my BM, Quinterria, place. I ain't stay there long. I ducked off out west. I was sick ta my muthafuckin' stomach when I found out it was Miracle in that car. I swear I didn't know it was her."

The expression on Devon's face was unreadable.

"I put er'thang I just said on my Big Ma, Dee," Rah swore. "I *DID NOT* know it was Miracle until after I saw da shit on da news. Y'know me, Bump an' Skat would *NEVER* harm Miracle. Ta me, she like a sista."

Devon couldn't believe what just came out of Rah's mouth. Her facial expression hardened.

Rah continued to plead his case. "I woulda told ya back then but I didn't know how to. I was at a crossroads. I felt responsible fo' what went down so it was difficult fo' me ta tell ya. Real shit.

"Instead of comin' clean," he went on, "I ditched Bump an' Skat an' immediately got ta work tryna figga out on my own who that fast-talkin' female was that called me wit that bogus info. First, I called that number back, but it no longer was in service. I ran into dead end after dead end after that. But I vowed ta kill whoeva it was that tricked me into doin' that shit.

"When I finally found da guts ta tell ya, I wanted ta do it face-ta-face. I camped outside of Saint Mary's hospital waitin' fo' ya ta visit Miracle. You finally showed up, an' befo' I could say what I had ta say, you invited me in ta see Miracle. I planned ta tell after we saw Miracle, but she woke up from her coma. I didn't wanna overshadow that moment, so I held it in ta tell ya later. Tellin' ya was put off again when Miracle revealed that Rhapsody was da one who set her up. At that moment it was mo' important ta find that lyin' bitch an' kill her fo' finessin' me. But I apologize fo' not tellin' ya as soon as it happened, sis."

After carefully digesting Rah's story, Devon lowered the gun to her lap. She believed him. Likewise, she knew her homeboys Bumper and Skat wouldn't have done what they did if they knew Miracle was in that car.

"I'll… I'll let it go." Devon cleared her throat. "It's water unda da bridge now, bruh. *BUT* mark my muthafuckin' words, I'll sic ol' Barry here—" she patted her heat "—on ya ass if ya lie ta me or withhold info from me again. If it's sumthin' major that affects me, you tell me ASAP. No excuses, no coppin' pleas. Ya feel me?"

"I feel ya."

"You betta." Devon smiled listlessly. "Now, let's getta move on an' go in here an' see if anybody knows sumthin' or has seen this disloyal bitch recently." She got out of the car. As they approached the club, she said, "I swear I dunno why I took that hoe back after she ran off ta Georgia wit that black ass nigga. If I'd just cut her off an' left well enough alone, I wouldn't be in this shit."

As they'd done previously, they separated once they entered the packed club. They artfully interviewed the bouncers, bartenders and strippers they hadn't the last time they were here. After about an hour, they reconvened near the entrance and filled each other in on their mutually fruitless endeavor before agreeing to call it a night.

"Daddy, is that you?"

Rah looked at Devon immediately because he knew the term of endearment wasn't aimed at him.

"Oh my God, it is really you, Daddy."

It took Devon a second before the girl's name came to mind. "Jazmine, wassup?"

Clad in a catsuit, Jazzy went up to Devon and embraced her former lover and pimp.

Jesus, she smells good enough to eat, Devon thought, clinging to the statuesque beauty that smelled like a basket of berries.

Jazzy took a step back to acknowledge RahRah next with a simple "Hey." "What are y'all doin' in Orlando? Y'all ain't recruitin' new girls, are y'all? Becuz from what I heard, Studio X still closed. And if you did open back up, Daddy, and didn't call me, I'ma fly off the handle."

"Naw, we ain't scoutin' out new talent. But Studio X will reopen soon. Rah gonna run da show, tho'. I'm done wit that chapter in my life."

The news made Jazzy pout because she took home a ton of money while working for Devon. Every club owner she danced for after Devon had been hogs. Her earnings fluctuated between not too bad and pathetic. She longed for the day to work, and sell pills, for Devon again. *Maybe Devon passed the blueprint to RahRah and he'd be just as generous as she was,* she thought before smiling again. *He needs to reopen Studio X tomorrow!*

"Y'all just in town for fun then?" Jazzy asked.

"I guess you could say that," replied Devon. "As a matter of fact, have you by chance seen Rhapsody lately? I heard she might be up here."

"Yeah, I seen her."

Devon and RahRah were both shocked speechless by the quick response.

Jazzy noticed their odd reaction. Suddenly, her smile faded. "What's the matter wit y'all?"

Rah was the first to snap back. "Nuttin'. We straight. We just been lookin' fo' her becuz…becuz—"

"Becuz we in town fo' tonight only an' wanted ta see how she doin' befo' we leave," Devon chimed in. "So, when did'chu last see her?"

Jazzy breathed a sigh of relief. "I bumped into her in Winn Dixie about… Hmm, was it three weeks ago? Maybe it was two weeks ago. I can't remember exactly when. But she was with some guy wit big ol' muscles."

"Was da dude her man?" Devon probed.

"Well, she claimed he was her neighbor." She paused. "Seriously, you didn't know that? I thought you, her and Miracle couldn't be divided. Unless that stankin' heifer done run off on you like she did before, but with this big guy this time."

"You got her digits?" asked Rah.

"Yeah."

"Give 'em to me," Devon said so fast that it startled Jazzy.

"O-okay, Daddy." Jazzy pulled her phone out of her Coach bag. After she gave up Rhapsody's digits, she said, "Before you go, Daddy, I'd love ta give you a private dance…for old times sake. I miss you." She leaned toward Devon and whispered into her ear. "And my pussy misses that marvelous tongue of yours." She proceeded to delicately kiss Devon behind the ear before sucking on her earlobe briefly.

"Aahh… So sorry, boo, but…but I gotta take a rain check," Devon said, fighting the urge to invite her back to the hotel for one last freak-off. "But'chu might wanna give Rah yo' info. When he open Studio X again, I'm sho' he'll let'cha fine ass work da pole."

"Hell yeah, you can work *my pole* anytime." Rah winked.

Jazzy made a disgusted face. However, she gave Rah her number. "Well, it was nice seein' you again, Daddy. I gotta go. My shift starts soon." She hugged Devon again and vanished into the building.

"What's da play?" Rah asked as they walked back to the car.

"Da play is we come up wit a plan that'll get this bitch ta come outta hidin'. Then, we strike an' bounce," Devon said ruthlessly before they got in the car and drove off.

Chapter 9

December 20, 2011/ 3:06pm/ El Paso, TX
Parts.
No, not just any kind of parts… body parts.
To be more precise, not *auto* body parts.
REAL. FUCKING. *HUMAN.* BODY PARTS!
I knew I was out of pocket when I said I'd transport whatever, Bug reflected as he laid in the truck's sleeper berth playing PlayStation 3. *But I never expected that punk-ass spic would pull a fast one on me by stashing that horrendous shit on my truck.*

When Bug confronted Adrian about the peculiar packages in the crates, Adrian contended that neither her nor his men knowingly loaded that onto his truck. Still, Adrian apologized for bungling his inaugural assignment. To rectify the situation, Adrian terminated his probationary period, which was going to keep him in Florida with no more than seventy bricks until he completed his fifth delivery. Adrian also raised his percentage for transporting out of state to fifteen. Lastly, Adrian compensated him handsomely for the slip-up.

The compensation was so sweet that Blue pressed Bug for three days about hauling nothing but human body parts. Bug would've been a bold-faced liar if he said he didn't consider it. However, he ended up sticking to his guns and staying in his lane. Besides, in his mind, the risk wasn't worth the reward. It was one thing to throw rocks at the chain gang by transporting large quantities of coke. It was altogether another to be trafficking shit he had no clue what the penalty was if he got caught.

And he wasn't going to try and find out what the punishment was either.

Blue then pressed him about something else.

Instead of getting paid in money, Blue wanted their cut in keys because the juice wasn't worth the squeeze. Blue understood they'd make more bread breaking down those bricks. It was a great pitch, something Bug had once considered, but he said no…repeatedly. He didn't want to return to dealing hand-to-hand. He preferred to remain out of sight, out of mind, in the streets.

After completing their third delivery, and with much thought, Bug reconsidered Blue's pitch. He changed his mind because he wanted to reach his goal faster. Inwardly, he swore to himself that greed had no part in his decision. He promptly spoke with Adrian about the change in payment. Without conflict, they hammered out a new arrangement. Afterwards, he consulted with Blue. While he knew what Blue planned to do with his share of the bricks, he told Blue that he was going to wholesale all his work to Wes, a hustler from PBC he'd dealt with in the past and had established a measure of trust. He viewed Wes as his most discreet means of obtaining the additional money.

"We almost there, homes," Blue informed from the helm of the semi. "We a couple exits away."

This was their eighth delivery, but their first time riding together since the new arrangement was finalized. They preferred operating both semis independently, since doing so got them closer to their goal in a shorter period. However, Adrian insisted that they make this run together, the furthest trip for them both.

Two exits later, they got off I-10 West. They were in the western panhandle of Texas, about twenty-five miles from New Mexico.

"Move, Fry," Bug commanded the nine-month-old French bulldog that was curled up in the passenger seat. When the all-white pup didn't budge, he picked him up, sat down and placed him in his lap. "They should be callin' in—"

Satellite phone rings

Fucking GPS, Bug said to himself. "We just got off exit twenty-three a second ago," Bug told the caller. "Yeah… From da GPS, we'll be there shortly."

"No bullshit, homes, I used ta fuck wit a chick that was stationed at da Army base in El Paso," Blue declared once Bug got off the phone. "I even lived here wit her fo' 'bout five months."

"Oh, yeah?" Bug said, intrigued. "You ain't neva tell me 'bout any of that."

"Fo' real? I thought I told you 'bout Wanda."

Bug shook his head while petting Fry.

"Okay then. It was 2000, an' I just came home from prison. I was cruisin' da city wit my cousin Pookey one day when he stopped at one of his broads' crib. We went inside ta chill an' there was a thick red chick chillin' wit my cousin's female. We started choppin' it up, an' that's when I learned she had just returned from Germany. She was on leave. So, I got her info that day, an' we became real close real fast.

"After we spent a couple of months together, she had to go back ta da base. She said she liked me a lot an' wanted me ta go wit her. I was on my dick at that time, altho' me an' you hit one or two small licks ta put a few racks in my pocket. Once I told her I had no money, she told me outta da blue that befo' me an' her started kickin' it, she'd been approached in Fashion Square Mall by two guys that wanted her to make—you won't believe this shit—a porno."

"You lyin'."

"I ain't. But check it, she asked me what I thought 'bout her doin' porn. I told her straight up that I wouldn't look at her any diff'rent if she did it. My response had her walkin' on air."

"So, you let'cha girl do porn?" Bug asked, enthralled now by the story.

"She wasn't my bitch, homes. But anyway, she decided ta do it becuz she wanted ta make a few bucks befo' she went back. She hit da niggaz up an' they had a shoot at a fancy hotel downtown. She asked me ta go wit her ta da shoot becuz she didn't wanna be alone wit niggaz she ain't know. I said yeah, then I strapped up an' went wit her. When we got there, inside of da suite was four or five otha bad bitches, a few niggaz, finger foods, an' bottles of liquor an' cases of beer. Once da action got goin', I caught a cut wit Wanda an' we smoked da trees I brought. All da while, we watched those hoes walk in an' out of da bathroom an' bedroom butt naked. After an hour or so, they told Wanda she had a shower scene. When she went ta do her thang, one of da niggaz approached me an' asked if I wanted ta put a few bucks in my pocket."

"What da fuck he meant by that, blood?"

"Homes, I said da same thing!" Blue chuckled. "But da nigga asked if I wanted ta fuck one of da bitches an' get paid."

"Did ya do it?" Bug was all into the story now.

"Naw."

"Why not? You said you were on ya dick at that time. You shoulda put one of them hoes on ya dick an' got paid. That's what I woulda done, stupid nigga."

"Fuck you, nigga. I didn't do it cuz that ain't sumthin' I wanted ta do. But back to da story…When da cameras stopped rollin', they paid er'body. They gave Wanda an envelope wit what was supposed ta be eighteen hunnid dollars. Instead, them niggaz gave Wanda twenty-six hunnid. They said she did a excellent job an' wanted ta work wit her again. But guess what she did wit da bread after we left?"

"What she do, blood?"

"She took 'bout five hunnid out da envelope an' gave da rest ta me."

"You bullshittin'."

"I bullshit you not. I told ya I'ma pimp, homes. Hoes be choosin' me even when I'm down." Blue cheesed. "Anywayz, she said she gave me da money ta help me keep my head above water 'til I found a job once she left. After she told me that, I decided ta go ta Texas wit her. I ain't tell nobody…not you, my mama, or my brothas an' sistas. I just got ghost."

"Oooohhh, I rememba now when you up an' disappeared. So *that's* where yo' ass was all that time. I rememba you told me you was wit a bitch in Tampa when you suddenly popped back up. You a ol' lyin' ass nigga." Bug shook his head. "How was it in El Paso, tho'?"

"Borin' as fuck. I ain't know nobody there but her. I lived wit her off da base. When she was workin', I hung out mainly in da rec center on da public part of da base. All I did was play pool wit some soldiers til she got off. Once she was free, we'd drive around da city an' I'd take in all da sights while smokin'."

"Y'know ya way around here then, huh?"

"Fuck no. I just told ya I stayed on base all day. I used ta be so fuckin' zooted when we slid through da city at night. I don't rememba nuttin' but seein' a handful of niggaz in this Mexican city. I *hated* it when I was here. When I couldn't take no mo', I told Wanda I was homesick. I got on da next Greyhound. *But* I almost ain't make it back ta Orlando."

"Why? What happened, blood?" Bug was happy there was more to the story.

"Da bus got pulled ova by fuckin' Border Patrol right outside of El Paso, homes. It was a random inspection. I had wrapped up da pistol I took wit me in a shirt an' put it in my duffel bag. When da agents got on da bus an' started pullin' bags outta da overhead bins, my heart started beatin' fast. Then, one agent started yellin' 'Who's green bag is this?' an' nobody said nuttin'. He asked again, an' again, nobody said nuttin'. In my head, I'm like, who's bag is that? Da agent said he was goin' ta ask one mo' time. Nobody still said nuttin'. He started pullin' da bag out an' that's when I saw it was my bag, so I claimed it. Da agent asked why I ain't say nuttin' until then. I told him I thought my bag was blue, becuz da bag was green an' blue. So, he asked if he could search da bag. Again, in my head, I said FUCK NO! But my mouth said, 'go ahead,' That's when my heart dropped ta my feet. I couldn't run, so as he searched my bag, I'm thinkin' 'bout goin' ta jail in *El Paso.* When da agent zipped my bag up an' put it back, I damn near cried tears of joy. I told myself I'd neva come back here again. Now, look at me. I pray that what I said back then don't come back an' bite me in da ass."

"You straight, blood. I don't believe in that superstitious, karma bullshit. An' neitha should you."

"Yeah, you right, homes. I'ma be positive." Blue paused. "I wonder if Wanda still there. I ain't talk ta shawty in 'bout... nine years."

"Blood, she ain't there. Soldiers don't stay on bases that long," Bug said.

"How y'know that?"

"I just do."

After a short pause, Blue said, "You could be right. *But* I still wanna see if she there after we deliver this shit. That thick, red bitch had some fiyah head an' good pussy. She had her pussy an' nipples pierced, too. She was a cold freak. I'm mad I ain't stay in touch wit her."

"Maaannn, we goin' straight home, blood, once we drop this load off. I'm halfway finished wit my papers, too. I ain't tryna kill that punk-ass P.O. of mines ova him violatin' me on some petty shit. So, we in an' outta El Paso like a robbery. Got me?"

"Yeah, I got'cha," Blue said, a little mad because he really wanted to find out if freaky Wanda was still at Fort Bliss. "I guess I'll take my frustration out on da next fuckable lot lizard we see at da truck stop."

Bug laughed before focusing on the handheld Garmin GPS device. He proceeded to give Blue turn-by-turn directions to their destination. After almost two days of driving, with short pit stops to eat, shower or refuel, they pulled up to, of all places, a body shop. *I see that Adrian got jokes,* he thought with a faint frown.

They came to a stop in front of Chaparro's Auto Body Repair. With Fry on a leash, they got out and spoke to a man called Pitufo. Once they greeted each other, they got to business.

"Where's ya help?" Bug asked after he saw that there wasn't anybody else around.

"Yeah, who's gonna help you unload this trailer?" Blue added. "Becuz I damn sho' ain't tryna do it in this heat after I been behind da wheel da last nine hours."

"Oh, no, amigo. The cargo no dropped here," Pitufo stated.

"What! What'chu mean cargo no dropped here? Where does it go then?" Bug inquired with a raised brow. "We were told ta come here. Da GPS led us *here.*"

"Si, you come to right place. But you drop off in El Paso del Norte."

"This north El Paso, ain't it, homes?"

"No, amigo. El Paso del Norte is across the Rio Grande."

"Across da Rio Grande! You mean across da border?" Bug nearly yelled. "I hope you ain't sayin' we takin' this into Mexico. Cuz if that's what'chu sayin', then I'm sayin' FUCK YOU!"

"But amigo—"

"But nuttin'. You heard my dawg. We ain't takin' that shit into Mexico," Blue declared.

Pitufo felt their fury. He was outmatched so he didn't say another word. He took a flip phone off the clip at his hip. He dialed a number while walking off a piece.

"Homes, Adrian is outta fuckin' pocket if he thinks we goin' across da border. I just told ya 'bout my bad experience wit Border Patrol. I ain't tryna deal wit 'em no mo'. I got lucky once. I ain't tryin' my luck wit 'em again."

"I feel ya, blood. We ain't—"

Satellite phone rings

"Wassup...? What'chu mean what's da problem? Da problem is you ain't tell me this shit was ta touch down in Mexico...How was I 'posed ta know that El Paso del Norte is also called Ciudad Juarez? You playin' too many bitch-ass games, Adrian...I don't care if you got people that work at da border crossin'. What if ya people ain't on point? Then what, huh...? Maaannn, I ain't takin' that chance. So, you might as well call ya people in Mexico, or whoeva, ta pick it up right here... I don't care 'bout—How much did ya just say...? Two hunnid thousand mo'...? Damn. Umm. Lemme... Lemme holla at my dawg real quick."

"Homes, no. No no no. Ain't nuttin' ta holla at me about," Blue said with conviction. "Just like how you stood firm 'bout not wantin' ta move body parts, I'm sayin' hell naw. Not even two hunnid grand is worth da risk of goin' to a Mexican jail fo'. An' I'ma greedy nigga. So, no."

"Blood, I'm wit'cha when ya right." Bug put da phone back to his ear. "You heard my dawg. We ain't doin' it, Adrian... Man, I dunno who ya think I am. I ain't no fuckin' peon. An' I damn sho' ain't a bitch... I don't give a fuck who you are or who ya work fo'. As a matter ah fact, I ain't fuckin' wit'chu no mo' after this. You tried me twice now. You won't get a third chance." He ended the call.

"What's next?" asked Blue.

"We gonna unhook da trailer, leave it right where it's at, an' we gonna bobtail it back home. Let that muthafucka figga out how ta get those gun parts ova there."

"I'm wit that."

Bug put Fry back in the cab of the truck. Blue and he then got ready to drop the trailer, which consisted of disconnecting the air hoses, letting down the landing gear and unlatching the king pin.

Pitufo reappeared. "Amigo, soon your phone ring. You must answer."

"Fuck that," Bug said while lowering the landing gear via the crank handle. "This shit yo' problem now. We outta here, Jose." He stopped cranking. "Yo', Blue."

"What's good?"

"We got time now ta stop by that base ta see if ya broad still there."

"That sounds like a plan, Stan," Blue happily replied.

"Answer the phone, amigo," Pitufo advised Bug again. "If you miss call, you no like what happens next."

Before Bug could go ham about being threatened, the satellite phone rang. Impulsively, he answered. "What?!... I told ya we ain't goin'. We ain't changin' our minds, eitha... WHAT? Adrian don't fuck wit me! I ain't da nigga... FUCK YOU!"

"What happened, homes?"

Instead of answering Blue, Bug hurried back to the truck. He climbed into the cab and got his personal phone.

"What happened?" repeated Blue, climbing into the driver seat.

Bug pulled up his call history. In less than a second, the frequently called number was selected. He pressed the dial icon. "C'mon, c'mon. Pick up, bae. Please, pick up. Becuz I swear I'ma—"

"Hey, baby."

"SHELLA! Baby, you okay?"

"Uhhh, yes, Dayvan. Why you yellin' like that? What's wrong?"

"Where da kids?"

"They – They're... Deuce an' Trey are playin' the game. And Daylonna right here in my lap. I just fed her. Now tell me what's wrong. The tone of your voice about to trigger an anxiety attack."

"Listen, I need ya—"

"Hold on, bae. The doorbell rang."

"NO! Shella, listen ta me. Don't answer da door!"

"Why not? It's only the pizza man."

"Shella, no, listen ta me, goddamnit! Don't answer da fuckin' door. I need—"

"Who are you?" Bug heard Shella say over the phone. "No, you can't come in. I don't know—I said NO!... Wait, the baby about—"

The line went dead.

"Hello? Shella...? SHELLA!" Bug threw the phone out of the truck. "NO!" He pounded on the dashboard with the heel of his hands. "I'ma kill that nigga! I swear ta God I am!"

Once Bug stopped hyperventilating and regained some semblance of control over his emotions, he filled Blue in on what had just happened.

Blue didn't wait for Bug to finish speaking. As soon as Bug said that Shella and his kids were abducted by Adrian, he'd heard enough. He got on his cellphone and called the few people he truly loved. His grandma was the first person he called, then his mama and siblings. They were all safe. He didn't give two shits about his four baby mamas, but he hit them up just to check on his kids. And for the moment, everyone he cherished seemed to be in the clear.

Nevertheless, because Bug was in a bad situation, Blue was, too. They were brothers. Therefore, they did the utmost to ensure they made it through all plights together and unscathed. And when the smoke cleared, they further disproved that brothers had to share the same DNA.

With reality sinking in fast, Bug knew he had to get off the fence now. Seeing that Adrian was a capo in a dog-eat-dog cartel, he needed to pull himself together and resolve how to rescue his family. After weighing his options with Blue for a short time, he realized he had just one choice. He wasn't stoked about what he had to do. But he was willing to do just about ANYTHING to get his family back unharmed.

Bug called Adrian back. He strained to keep his anger in check as their conversation got straight to the point. Adrian guaranteed that his family would be returned safely once he completed this drop off in Mexico and two additional deliveries. Bug had no insurance that Adrian would keep his word, yet he headed for Mexico anyway.

Six-point-five million vehicles crossed the southern border at numerous border crossings every month. That equated to two-hundred-fourteen-thousand vehicles daily. Out of all those vehicles, only one percent of cars and six percent of trucks were searched. For all, passing *into* Mexico wasn't too nerve-racking. Reentering the U.S. from Mexico, however, could be stressful, especially for smugglers of contraband or drugs.

Because El Paso and Ciudad Juarez were connected by a pair of bridges that spanned the Rio Grande, Bug and Blue didn't have to travel far. They had no issues whatsoever crossing into Mexico. About fifteen minutes later, the GPS showed them the way to the Plaza de Las Americas Mall.

Still heated, Bug rang up Adrian. Adrian let him know who to look for and what to do next. The man they were expecting, Jorge, arrived in a big rig with a forty-eight-foot trailer. Bug wasn't in the mood to be cordial. He simply confirmed that the man was Jorge, then he and Blue swapped trailers with him. Jorge subsequently left with the unlicensed gun parts, while they rode off with the unknown.

To be quite honest, Bug didn't give a fuck what he was hauling now, as long as he got his family back when it was all said and done. There could be a nuke in the back; he was all in, which was a state of mind he had tried to avoid.

In under an hour, they'd doubled back to the border. Every single lane was jam-packed. Unlike the amount of time it took to get into Mexico, it took them considerably longer to get back across the border. The Border Patrol agent they came upon asked them a series of questions as two other agents with dogs circled their truck. The questioning process this second time was tense, even with them using the lane specified by Adrian.

Thankful to have made it back on American soil, they went back to Chaparro's Auto Body Repair as directed. Pitufo was waiting for them with a smile on his face. In his hand was a rugged army bag, which he handed over to Bug. Bug inspected the bag's contents, and it was stuffed with bills. Before this shit show went sour, Bug knew the arranged commission for this trip, which was four keys, awaited him in Orlando. He came to the quick conclusion that Adrian was honorable enough to pay them for the extra job.

Pitufo beckoned them with his arm to help him unload the trailer. Since they were in no position to protest, they didn't defy the order. Light of heel, the trio went to the trailer's doors. Bug popped the seal, removed the padlock and swung open a door. The hot stench that emerged from within the trailer hit them all with breakneck speed. It had no impact on Pitufo at all, but it caused both Bug and Blue to turn away and gag and gasp for fresh air. Once the light breeze dissipated the odor a bit, they turned back around.

What Bug and Blue saw was awful.

With Pitufo's assistance, they helped at least a hundred grungy men, women and children of all ages climb out of the ghastly trailer. Some of them had bags. The rest had nothing but the dirty, smelly clothes on their backs. All of them, however, wore a smile on their faces because they'd arrived safely in the land of the free.

Not smiling was Bug.

When all of the illegal aliens were removed from the trailer, Bug pulled out the satellite phone and contacted Adrian. "What now?" he curtly asked. "Yeah, we got da money... Maaann, gimme my family back. I'd appreciate that. Ya coulda kept them peanuts... San Diego... Ai'ight. You'll know when I get there, of course."

Damn, this some bullshit me and my family have to deal with five days before Christmas, Bug thought, climbing back in the truck. *I have to be the stupidest nigga for putting myself in this position.*

Chapter 10

December 20, 2011/ 9:56pm/ Orlando, FL

Being in possession of Rhapsody's cellphone number should've been advantageous. But Devon had yet to think up a surefire way to use it to get Rhap to break cover. Neither Devon nor anybody associated with her could just phone Rhapsody out of the blue. Doing so would certainly raise a red flag and spook her into taking flight, possibly out of state. Devon didn't want that to happen, so she had to carefully consider what her next move would be.

RahRah came up with a reasonable solution. His quick fix was manipulating Jazzy. He believed using Jazzy was their best chance of pouncing on Rhap. After giving the notion some thought, Devon believed so, too. However, she didn't want to involve Jazzy. She didn't want to have to cover their tracks by killing one of the most loyal bitches in her bygone harem.

After deciding to not exploit Jazzy, Devon's next course of action became clear: reverse lookup Rhap's phone number. She tasked Miracle with the special project since one of Miracle's sisters worked at T-Mobile. It didn't take long for Miracle to find out that the number was registered to Keema Langston, Rhapsody's real name. But the listing indicated the address of Rhap's mother in Palm Beach County. It was unpleasant news, yet it didn't deter Devon.

Thinking back on their conversation with Jazzy at the club, Devon remembered that Jazzy had bumped into

Rhapsody while shopping at the Winn Dixie in Pine Hills, aka Crime Hills. RahRah and she camped out in the parking lot and watched for their target. At the end of their first day of surveillance, Rah recommended they cruise through all the neighborhoods and apartment complexes in a three-mile radius of the grocery store. He theorized that Rhap, being skittish and careful, would rather shop in the vicinity of her hideout in case of an emergency. Devon concurred.

The following day, instead of staking out the Winn Dixie, Devon and RahRah began exploring hoods and complexes nearby. They were specifically looking for Rhap's purple Altima because they both doubted that Rhap, who was addicted to Roxicodone when she fled PBC, had the money to buy another car. And even if she did have the money, they sensed she wasn't clever enough to switch whips.

They were currently in the process of searching their sixth neighborhood when a fatigued RahRah said, "I'm tellin' ya, Dee, we gotta stop perkin' an' use Jazzy." Rah yawned. "She coulda been got this bitch ta come ta us without knowin' what we up to. We coulda been aired both of them hoes out an' been home, gettin' ready fo' Christmas. I still gotta go shoppin' fo' my jits, so let's stop bullshittin' becuz we open ta get shot at while slidin' through one of these hoods we know nuttin' about."

"You blood thirsty, bro," Devon said, taking issue with Rah's proposal once again. "You fuckin' wit Bumper an' Skat done made you a savage." She expelled a breathy sigh. "But lemme emphasize it this time... If I can go without Jazzy's involvement, I'ma do my all ta keep her outta this. I don't wanna kill her cuz I actually like her. She been a good bitch ta me, an' y'know she has."

"I thought I raised you betta than this, Dee. You actin' soft. Niggaz like you an' me from around our way ain't soft. You *shoulda* been fuckin' wit me, Bump an' Skat – rest in peace, my nigga – when Tripled S was warrin' wit Eddie G. That woulda been ya refresher course. You woulda remembered then that collateral damage is part of da game. You gotta have a killa instinct when ya gotta get'cha man. It's no holds barred, anything goes, when you gotta settle a score. You know this, so stop bein' a pussy."

Devon sucked her teeth. "Look... You right, bro. But... but..." She paused to really consider what Rah had said. "We'll take advantage of Jazzy if what we doin' now doesn't pan out. An' if it doesn't, I'll buy Sierra da new Elmo doll and Callero a IPad fo' ya when we get home."

"Peep game, Dee, if we don't find her between now an' tomorrow evenin', I swear on er'thang I love I'm goin' ta call Jazzy myself, set da shit up without you, an' off both of 'em myself without blinkin'."

Well then, that's that, Devon thought. *Sorry Jazzy.*

Rah yawned again. His mouth opened wide enough to catch a dozen flies. "We burnt up anotha day doin' this stupid shit. I dunno what da fuck I was thinkin' when I came up wit this dumb idea. Drivin' here an' there in these unfamiliar streets tryna find this bitch ain't only dangerous, it's like tryna find a fat bitch at a salad bar."

"Patience, Rah. Patience," preached Devon, cautiously optimistic that their endeavor wouldn't be fruitless. "No way was this a bad idea. We'll come across her any minute now. Ya wanna know why? Becuz her goofy ass is in line ta fuck up. An' when she does, we'll snatch her black ass up and torture her bald-head ass ta death fo' havin' us go through all this shit."

Rah had drifted off. He was dead asleep.

Devon sneered while she continued the search.

A short while later, she was driving out of the Stella West Apartments. Instead of calling it quits for the night, she drove to the next complex. She began perusing the parking spaces of the Hibiscus Place Apartments. Since Rah was in la-la land, she attentively swept the surroundings. Mere minutes into her quest she became lost in thought. Images of home and how much she missed Miracle and Kamani ultimately commandeered her thoughts. Even Bizzy crossed her mind. She yawned.

"What time is it?" she said to herself aloud. She looked at the time displayed on the Panasonic CD player, and it read *10:41PM*. "Fuck, my eyes gettin' heavy. Soon, I won't be able ta focus on da road. I might as well take it ta da house like Trick Daddy said." After another long yawn, she declared, "But first, I'ma hit up Denny's. I ain't eat all day."

About twenty minutes later, Devon was parking at the Denny's on West Colonial Drive.

"Rah?"

Light snoring

She nudged him. "RahRah?"

Rah grunted. He then turned his head toward the window and resumed sawing logs.

Devon shrugged. "Yo' loss, nigga. An' ya greedy ass ain't gettin' none of my shit eitha, so ya might as well keep sleepin' when I come back."

She left the car running while she went inside. She waited in the short line, yawning twice. When it was her turn to order, she could've sworn she heard a familiar voice calling her name. Rather than turning to locate the voice, she blamed her sleepiness for hearing things and kept ordering her food.

"Devona?"

Ok, that's somebody that knows the real me, Devon shared to herself, turning away from the cashier to see who was calling her by her government name.

When she laid eyes on the person, she no longer felt sleepy.

"I knew you'd turn around when I called you that."

"What're you doin' here?" Devon asked. "I was literally just thinkin' 'bout you."

"So was I! An' on some kinda law of attraction type shit, our thoughts of each otha drew us to our favorite spot. Ain't that some wild shit?"

A short distance away at the West Oaks Mall…

"I dunno how I let'chu set me up like that."

"I got'chu good, didn't I?"

"Yeah, you did. You lucky, tho', I ain't storm outta there on ya ass!"

"I'm glad you didn't. I had a good time comfortin' you."

"Yeah, I must admit your cologne did calm me."

"Ha! It wasn't my cologne that had you all up on me. You wanted me ta caress you. That movie wasn't all *that* scary."

Rhapsody playfully punched her wannabe black Albanian paymaster as he steered the Audi R8 GT down West Colonial Drive. "I dunno what'chu talkin' about. Scream 4 was scary as hell. I told you I don't like scary movies." *Especially since my life has now become like a "I know what you did last summer" flick*, she concluded as the hairs on the back of her neck stiffened.

"Well, you don't have ta worry 'bout anything ever happenin' to you. I'll hold you all day an' night. I won't let nobody... cut you up!" Immediately, with his left hand on the steering wheel, he reached over with his right hand and slashed at her with his index finger.

"Boy, stop! You so silly." She giggled. "Well, I wish I could stay anotha night wit'chu in that big ole house of yours, Shane, but I can't. I have ta leave town in da mornin'," she lied.

"Oh. Okay. Cool."

She picked up on the sadness in his words. "I'll be back soon, tootsie. I promise."

"When? Becuz lately you only come around ta see me fo' a couple days once – twice, if I'm lucky – a month."

Rhapsody juggled several sugar daddies in Orange County, each bringing something a bit different to the table than the other. Yes, all of them were infatuated with her, with most of them splurging cash on her for the time she spent entertaining them. For instance, her buster, Shane, came from a prominent family with deep pockets. He didn't mind being played like a video game. As long as she indulged in his weird fetishes, such as giving him golden showers and rim jobs, he'd do anything for her. Often fronting like he was a gangster, in private settings, he manifested very little in the way of toughness. She used him to keep a low profile in one of the multiple homes he owned in the suburbs around Orlando. She felt safe and secure shacking up with him. And she would've stayed with him long-term if not for her fear of going out for the obligatory public outings with him during daylight hours. Therefore, after a few days with Shane had elapsed, she manufactured an excuse to leave to hook up with Cam.

Muscle man Cam was her designated protector. Since she preferred his protection capabilities over his money, she turned to him when she needed to go out in public. Cam wasn't to be confused with a thug or a roughneck. But she assumed that if a threat were to arise, they'd think twice about attacking with his hulking ass in her company. And until recently, she had relied on his grandmother to babysit her daughter when needed.

After she handled her business in the streets and spent some quality time with Cam, she'd briefly fool around with her other admirers: Zip, Diego and Lonnie.

Zip was a substantial player in the nefarious activities in the city of Apopka. He was an arrogant hustler, a point-blank killer in the streets. But behind closed doors, he was Romeo to Rhapsody. The reason she hardly ever spent more than five or six hours with him was because his better half was the game. She explicitly kept him on hand for unforeseen events that required immediate action. She knew all it took was one call and he'd slay anything that threatened his access to her superb pussy and exquisite head, which is why she wisely chose to take humble Cam with her to meet Bug in the park.

Diego was her married Latin lover that lived in the predominately Hispanic city of Conway. At forty-six, he was the oldest of her sugar daddies. Odd as it was, though, she called upon him for sex only. The three hundred dollars he paid her for an hour of her time was good. However, what was even better than the money was his mastery in the bed, the car, the laundry room… Hell, wherever they did it, he put it DOWN. His wife's libido had decreased drastically over the last five years, according to him, while his sex drive remained the same. He gladly took his sexual frustration out on Rhapsody, which didn't bother her one bit. No lie, she looked forward to seeing him the most and would see him more if he was able to get away from his clingy wife more often.

And Lonnie, who lived near the University of Central Florida, was a loner and the one she had deep conversations with. Though Lonnie catered to her, too, sex didn't define their relationship. Ultimately, she ran to Lonnie when she needed to be herself. Talking to Lonnie was therapeutic for her. Lonnie reminded her so much of the relationship she had had with Devon, not just because Lonnie was a good-looking butch, either. Like the Devon of old, Lonnie was respectful, considerate, easy to please, and dependable.

Why did you have to burn me, Devon? Rhapsody thought. *I would've walked to hell and back for you. We could've been an unstoppable duo. But no, you had to choose that worthless hoe Miracle over a go-getting bitch like me. Oh well, your loss.*

"I wish we could spend mo' time together, baby," Rhapsody fibbed blithely. "I swear I do. But'chu know I have ta take this show on da road ta get my coins."

"Boo, I tell ya every time I see you that I'll take care of ya. You don't ever have ta strip again if you settle down wit me. Why won't you take up my offer?"

"Becuz I'ma IN-DE-PEN-DENT bitch, that's why. I don't need no man ta take care of me. I take care of my man, tho'. An' I'ma make this all up ta you now."

"You comin' back ta my place then?" he asked full of hope and excitement, taking his eyes off the road to look for her response.

"Yes... ta get my car." She giggled. "But I'll give ya sumthin' ta rememba 'til I see ya again." Rhapsody pulled down her Baby Phat halter top. With her full thirty-six double D's exposed, she leaned over and began unfastening his YSL belt. Throughout the process, she peered lustfully into Shane's wide eyes, which were shifting back and forth from watching the road and looking at her. She licked her succulent lips as she unzipped his pants. She reached into his jeans and pulled out his uncircumcised little man. A crafted expression of awe occupied her face as she lowered her gaping mouth onto his shrimpy manhood.

The car suddenly swerved hard to the right.

"Boy, I ain't even start yet an' you already 'bout ta crash," she shrieked, holding his stiffening five-inch cock tightly.

"My bad, boo. I- I- I won't crash." He placed his right hand on her head and guided her back to his dick. "Oh shit, yo' mouth wet an' warm."

She sucked and swirled her tongue around the crown of his dick first. She moaned theatrically while doing so. Once he was fully hard and pulsating in her mouth, she began to move her head up and down in short quick movements. It wasn't difficult for her to deepthroat him; she needn't worry about her gag reflex.

The car veered harder.

Before Rhapsody could pull away, Shane pinned her head down to prevent her from moving. "It won't happen again. I swear. Just don't stop, boo."

Though steamed and aggravated, she kept at it.

This was her first time slobbing on Shane's nub while driving. She never had an issue giving mouth service to other niggas as they drove, so Shane's abrupt swerving threw her for a loop. She had it in her mind to shine him up all the way to his place but cancelled that plan. Instead of giving him a performance worth writing home about, she decided he had nothing but a short skit coming.

She bobbed up and down like an engine piston. She hoped to make him nut before his crazy driving killed them both. She moaned louder. She immediately noticed how the sound incited him. She became overjoyed when he began pumping in and out of her mouth, an indication he was two shakes of a lamb's tail from blowing. She stopped bobbing but kept sucking on his pink helmet. She jacked his little leprechaun dick crazily. She kneaded his balls not as fast. She even purred, sending deep vibrations into his loins. And she got her throat ready to swallow his customary huge load.

"Oh shit… Aahhh," he howled as his eyes rolled backwards.

Hurry up already, she said to herself as she gulped, *so you can focus on getting me to my car sa—*

TIRES SCREECHING

The sportscar careened off the road.

"OH SHIT!… AAHHHH!" Shane yowled as his eyes locked onto the concrete light pole.

Meanwhile…

"Why didn't you call me? Since Miracle snitchin' ass told you where ta find me, you shoulda just called me. Y'know I don't like surprises," Devon admonished, exiting the Denny's with her order in a bag.

"I ain't spoke ta ya in ova six months, so I *wanted* ta surprise ya," Bizzy replied as they came to a stop not a dozen feet from the entrance.

"Well, you did that," Devon admitted. "So, what hotel you in?"

"I ain't get one yet cuz I planned on droppin' by my BM LaShawn crib tonight. I wanted ta spend some quality time wit my son BJ while I'm in town." He paused. "Oh, I wanna thank you fo' takin' care of BJ an' my otha son, Bilal, in Tally while I was gone."

"I told ya I'd keep my word. It was yo' money any—"

"OH SHIT!" Bizzy yelled, reacting suddenly to the collision on W. Colonial he saw in his peripheral.

Devon saw it, too. But she was struck silent.

"Call 911!" someone shouted in Denny's parking lot.

A person responded, "I'm calling them n—Yes, 911? There's been a bad accident on Fifty in front of the Denny's. Send an ambulance now, please. Hurry!"

"Tell 'em that somebody flew out da car when it rolled over!" a different person reported. "It looked like a woman."

"Anybody gotta extinguisher?" someone asked the bystanders. "The car on fire!"

Chapter 11

December 21, 2011/ 5:49am/ San Diego, CA
Eleven plus hours later, Interstate 8 was still unreeling before them. Gucci Mane's *Return of Mr. Zone 6* was spinning in the deck.

"Aye, homes, can I tell ya what's been on my mind without you gettin' mad?" Blue asked from the sleeper berth behind the front seats of the truck.

When they weren't talking casually, Bug spaced out. At times he was so lost in his thoughts that unknown miles were driven in an absolute blur. If not for Blue's timely interruptions, there were occasions where he forgot he was driving.

Bug lowered the volume on the music a tad, then replied, "I hate when you say that dumb shit, blood. Y'know I can't guarantee that. Especially not right now. I been past thirty-eight hot hours ago. I'm hella tight, an' it got my stomach hurtin' like a bitch. It feel like sumthin' might be wrong."

"This whole situation has been a super heavy burden fo' ya ta come ta grips wit, Bug. It has personally affected me, too, so I know this can't be good fo' ya health. You still recoverin'. But ta keep it real, it could be much worse, homes."

"Blood, I know you just ain't say that bullshit. Becuz da only thang that can be worse than this is—" he sighed, afraid to speak into existence the worst possible outcome "—If that muthafucka harms my family."

"That's what I wanted ta talk about. I wanted ta tell ya that Adrian has been… As fucked up as this is goin' ta sound, Adrian has a heart."

"He has a *heart!* What da fuck you mean by that, blood? Spell that shit out fo' me, please, becuz you… you 'bout ta make me spazz da fuck out."

"Look, I mean…" He paused to think over how to say what was on his mind. He wasn't going to harbor any regret about what he was about to say. He just wanted to be exceedingly clear so as not to offend his suffering homeboy. "Look, JuneBug," he began as he ran a hand through his wavy hair, "Adrian playin' a real dirty game by takin' ya family an' usin' them as leverage ta make us do this shit. He crossed da fuckin' line, an' he has hell ta pay fo' what he did. That's a fact. *But* Adrian ain't as cutthroat as he portrays ta be. I say he has a heart becuz he's bein' hospitable wit'cha family. Besides da undastandable looks of uncertainty on their faces, you seen wit'cha own eyes on da video he sent you that he got'cha fam in a nice home. He coulda had 'em chained up in a dungeon or some shithole. But he didn't. Then, he's lettin' ya talk to Shella an' ya sons every couple hours. That's fair. An' I overhead Shella tell ya er'time you asked that they're bein' treated like honored houseguests. She said there are friendly women watchin' ova them an' makin' them feel as comfortable as possible. Now I ain't sayin' Adrian ain't vicious, but at least he ain't violatin' ya fam. How he treatin' them says a lot ta me. It tells me he's a man of some honor. Becuz on GP, if da shoe was on da otha foot, y'know damn well we'd have Adrian's wife an' kids tied up in a traphouse guarded by predatory niggaz. So, I honestly feel nuttin' bad gonna happen ta ya family."

Though Blue's outspokenness could be both untimely and offensive most of the time, Bug didn't find what he said out of order. All things considered, he knew that Adrian considered him a nonentity, an expendable. It was hard for him to fathom why his kidnapped family was getting the royal treatment. Whatever Adrian's reason, or reasons, for not mishandling his family, he *was* grateful for it. Nevertheless, Bug did feel like Adrian's hospitality towards his family was an act of flim flammery. He presumed that Adrian's leniency was to give him a false sense of security. Adrian needed him to be at ease until the job was done, he concluded. *When all this is over, me, my family and Blue may be done for,* he thought.

"Bug?"

"Huh? What?"

"Damn, nigga, I called ya name 'bout six times. You zone out like this often when ya drivin'?"

"What'chu want now, blood?" Bug replied, ignoring Blue's last question.

"I was tryna let'chu know it's 'bout time fo' 'em ta call."

"Good. Cuz we almost there. I can find out where in San Diego we goin'."

"Aye, homes—"

"What?" Bug cut him off, slightly annoyed.

"I ain't tryna get on ya nerves, homes, but—"

"If ya keep on wit'cha borderline offensive questions an' shit, you won't be tryin'; you'll be succeedin'. You just barely slipped through da crack wit da last shit ya said. So, I'm givin' ya fair warnin'. If ya keep teasin' these waters, you gonna eventually drown, blood. So, wassup?"

"Bug, you gonna kill me?" Blue asked, playacting with a hound dog look on his face.

"Maaannn, say what'chu gotta say befo' I kick ya out da truck... while it's movin'."

"Neva that!" Blue chuckled, and his chuckling caused Bug to crack the tiniest smile. "But anyway, I been meanin' ta ask if you talked ta ya newest BM yet. I noticed you ain't call her, an' she ain't call you, this whole time. Unless y'all have talked an' I ain't know 'bout it."

Bug gnashed his teeth. "I'ma give it ta ya blood raw. That black bitch da furthest thang from my mind right now. She been irrelevant, an' she still is. All she eva will be is an eater that I fucked around an' accidently blowed up. So no, I ain't call or hear from her. I been focused on Shella, my two boyz, an' that baby that might be mine. Fuck that hoe!"

"You wouldn't care if Adrian snatched her up, too, then?"

"You said it yaself: Adrian has a heart. He woulda told me he had her if he did. But if he tells me later that he do got her, I'll jump fo' fuckin' joy. Point blank, I *pray* he yanked her ass up… an' merked that slut."

Blue stared at Bug slack jawed. When Bug met his gaze, he looked away and said, "Homes, you… you clearly ain't gotta heart. I hate my baby mamas. But I don't *really* wish they die."

Bug reflected on Blue's words. By his own reckoning, he considered himself a generally good guy, someone who never looked for trouble but didn't duck it. Life experiences and circumstances had, on numerous occasions, caused him to act in a heartless manner. The current situation with Adrian and his family was a case in point. The men that played fair in this dirty game were at a disadvantage. He had to become like all the other depraved motherfuckers in the game: no humanity, no soul, no fucking heart!

Bug made the scheduled call. He talked to Shella briefly before getting the address of where they were to go. A short time later, they pulled their tractor unit up to a second-rate gas station. They met their contact, Santiago. Santiago had a Marlboro parked in his mouth, a standoffish demeanor, and leathery features that made him hypnotically ugly. He hurriedly provided them with paperwork for the load they were to pick up at another location. Next, he gave them directions, and they went on their way.

They ended up at the Port of San Diego. They didn't know what lie ahead since they were fresh in the trucking industry. They got in line with the other queued trucks. Approximately thirty minutes later, they handed the port clerk the paperwork Santiago had given them. Soon after, the clerk provided them with a paper that directed them to two separate areas. They went to the first area for a chassis for the shipping container they were picking up. At the next area, they waited for the crane to load them up. As soon as the container was locked onto the chassis, they took off without the required inspection.

Despite the load manifest indicating they were hauling sunflower seeds, Bug had no idea what was *really* in the sealed container. However, all that really mattered to him now was making it safely to the drop off location. Adrian swore to him that his family would be released immediately once he reached Buffalo. *This nightmare should be over by Christmas Eve,* he assured himself as he relaxed in the passenger seat with Fry on his lap. *Then I have to carefully figure out how to get Adrian back for taking the wrong family hostage… that's if his ass don't kill me first.*

***

Back at the Port of San Diego…

"…*Nyet*, Yuri. It's not here. Vee search thorough," Arkady briefed his Russian superior over the phone. "I apologize for being behind schedule. Vee have small issue on the vay here."

"This is the second time this has happen," Yuri Komarov reminded his minion. "However, this theft is different."

"How so, Yuri?"

"On that container is our biggest shipment. I vividly express to you, Arkady, our urgent need for this container. Vee need it to advance our mission. Your inexcusable tardiness maybe set us back hundreds of millions of American dollars. So, you must find it… or I'll remove you all. Understand?"

The shipment in question was *krokodil*. Krokodil, a Russian drug confirmed by the Department of Justice in 2004, meant crocodile in English. It was a heroin knockoff with nicknames like "Russian Magic" and "Poison." It was a form of desomorphine, a drug three times more toxic than morphine. It also contained codeine. The drug's appeal was it could be made at home, and the high was better than heroin, though it didn't last as long. Addicts loosely described the high as a feeling of a "warm wave rushing over you."

The downside of krokodil was its adverse effects on the body. It was contaminated with heavy metals that wreaked havoc on the nervous system. It ultimately dissolved the nerves, in addition to causing the death of soft body tissue due to loss of blood supply. Addicts of krokodil lived on average two to three years. Russian authorities considered the drug to be the hardest addiction to overcome, and, because of that, it became the most hated drug in Russia. Yuri and his cabal wanted to get daft, yet arrogant, Americans hooked on krokodil. They sought to corner the market and kill as many Americans as possible before the calamity could be brought under control, hopefully leaving the USA in a tenacious state of social and political disarray.

"*Da*, Yuri, me and the boys find it."

"Be quicker than quick. And I'll find out how this happened."

In the meantime...

"...Yes, Haverty, the usual suspects are here: Maksim Belav, Arkady Rostropovich, Ivan Ivanoff, Misha Zhukovsky and Pyotr Mendeleev," Homeland Security Agent Murray updated his supervisor over the closed comms connection. "No, they have yet to procure the shipment. They seem to be searching for it still... I agree. But our source was only able to provide intel that the Russians were importing something extremely important. The source claimed he never came by any info that gave an exact fix on the container. We're ready to move in and take them down, though, the moment they claim it... I understand how important this is bu—Wait a second, Haverty. Rostropovich and Mendeleev have separated from the others… No, sir, I absolutely will not stand for any one of these commie bastards lamming it. The endless hours of legwork won't be in vain. The last act is today, Haverty… Okay, let me report back to you in a second. I have to tail these guys."

Agent Murray proceeded to instruct the other disguised G-men and Port Authority police to keep an eye on Belav, Ivanoff and Zhukovsky while he went after Rostropovich and Mendeleev. Blending in with the port activity, he followed the Russians from a safe distance to the port clerk booth. There he found a place that provided sufficient cover and monitored them closely. He noticed the pair having words with the clerk and becoming more irate by the second. Once they left the booth arguing with each other, it became clear to Murray that the Russians didn't know where their container was located.

Where's that container? Because we surely have no idea of its whereabouts, Murray wondered. *Maybe our source was incorrect.*

"Haverty, we have a problem," he said. "There's a possibility our source made a mistake, sir… You suspect someone may have swiped the container from under their noses… I think not, sir, because I don't know who would have the courage to steal from them. However, I do know they have tightened up their operation after we confiscated that container nearly a year ago with the fifty keys of krokodil… Uhhh, no sir. Working alongside the CIA won't be a problem for me. Where will I link up with him…? *She,* sir…? No, sir, that won't be an issue… Yes, sir, we'll track it down and get it before the Russians do."

Chapter 12

December 22, 2011/ 6:58pm/ Orlando, FL
No way. Couldn't be done.

Sometimes karma was instant. When it wasn't, outrunning it forever was simply impossible.

As a result of the universe being balanced, every evil deed perpetrated bore with it the seeds of retaliation. Karma doesn't bother itself with a person's beliefs, either. No one was exempt from karmic payback. And it most often rear-ended both believers and nonbelievers when they least expected it. Essentially, karma was universally undefeated.

"Why you sweatin' so bad?"

"You havin' second thoughts or sumthin'?"

The questions from the vehicle's other two occupants weren't rhetorical, yet Devon disregarded them for the moment. She found herself preoccupied and so emotionally distraught about what they were planning to do that she couldn't think straight, let alone have second thoughts. She hadn't been this nervous since January 3, 2011, the night she planned to kill one of the men who was now in the same vehicle with her. And just like that night, when her plan misfired spectacularly, she was ready to get this one over with.

"Naw, I ain't changin' my mind, RahRah," she finally declared. "An' Biz, I'm sweatin' so bad cuz it's D-Day fo' this bitch. I'm just hella impatient right now, y'all. I'm ready ta go. I'm ready ta get this shit poppin'."

"Oh, what happened ta all that patience is good bullshit ya been preachin'?" Rah wisecracked.

Rah's witty remark made Devon smirk. The smirk was short-lived, though, because the situation at hand was serious.

"What if someone knows we don't belong there?" Devon asked again. "What if they call one-time befo' we can pull this off?"

Instead of discounting her nervousness, Bizzy chose to reply to those hypotheticals. "Da bravest, most fearless muthafuckas are also da most nervous, most anxious muthafuckas, lil' sis, believe it or not."

"What? That philosophical shit ain't answer her question," Rah retorted. "Cuz on da real, except fo' in da movies, I ain't heard of no hood niggaz tryin' what we finna do. This guaranteed plan of yours looks good in a movie script, but I'm wit Devon. What if—"

"Doin' this kind of shit is how I earn a livin'," Bizzy interjected. "This a cup of tea compared to what I done pulled off. But if *you* havin' second thoughts. I undastand. This real gangsta shit ain't fo' er'body."

"Nigga, y'know *personally,* I'ma bona fide gangsta," Rah boasted. "Fo' da right cause, I'm all in. But makin' sho' Dee makes it through this unharmed is my main priority. It's kill-or-be-killed when it comes to my sista." Too much testosterone and pride caused the van to fill with a tense silence.

Prior to them meeting for the first time two days ago, Bizzy and RahRah only knew of each other through conversations with Devon. They had neither disdain nor admiration for each other. A mutual wariness instantly developed between them. Their demeanors gradually improved, however, after hanging out in Devon's hotel suite for a few hours. They both mellowed while bantering and fogging up the suite with high quality grass.

Everybody was good and high after the first blunt. When the second one got fired up, Bizzy and Devon proceeded to recap the last six months of their lives. Rah, on the other hand, mainly daydreamed in between listening to them catch up with the times. The merriment and good vibes did a quick one-eighty the moment Demetrius was brought up.

Having been quiet up to that point, RahRah hastily jumped into the conversation. Without thinking, because he was high as fuck, he bragged about jacking Demetrius for over three hundred keys with his Triple S homeboys. He also affirmed that, after Demetrius' death, he and those same homies clashed with Demetrius' flunkies for control of West Palm Beach.

Once Rah finished shooting off at the mouth, an enraged Bizzy acknowledged it was him and his team that Triple S had been engaged in hostilities with. There, the friction sparked.

Bizzy and RahRah were prepared to dump on each other then and there if not for Devon stepping between her blood brother and her foster brother. Devon turned to her talent of inducing people to bend to her will. She urged them to squash their beef since what happened in the past was no longer an issue. Amazingly, her tact convinced Bizzy, who idolized Demetrius, to live with what couldn't be undone. And she made Rah swear on their grandmother's soul to never speak about Demetrius in Bizzy's presence again.

Regardless of the truce between them, their attitudes toward each other soured, becoming noticeably cold and reserved. But they were committed to playing nice until they blotted out their mutual enemy. However, after they completed this mission, there was a good chance they'd shoot it out if they ever met again.

"I think da shift finally 'bout ta change, y'all," announced Devon. "Is it go time now?"

Bizzy peered out of the backseat window. He saw several individuals attired in scrubs and lab coats exiting the

Orlando Regional Medical Center—ORMC. He checked the time on his Hublot watch. "Yeah, it's that time. Make sho' y'all got'cha fake ID badges displayed, ya gloves, an' ya cannons. Nuttin' else should be on y'all."

"Be easy. Take a deep breath. Hit that emotional kill switch in ya head," Rah counseled Devon, noticing how fidgety she was.

"You don't have ta come, sis," Bizzy let her know. "I told ya I fo'gave you, but I ain't sparin' none of da muthafuckas that helped you kill our pops. That's why as soon as I got word where this bitch was, I came here ta handle it personally. Runnin' into you, tho', an' eventually learnin' that y'all also lookin' fo' this bitch is fate. She tried da three of us, so we all have da right ta cash in on this bitch well-earned karma. It's a reason why she crashed in front of us. It's a reason why she was thrown from da car befo' it exploded. It's a reason why da crash was on da news while Devon was watchin' TV. It's a reason why Devon heard her name an' we learned where she was at. It's fate. So, y'all can just chill in da van an' I'll take care of her fo' all of us."

There was no way Devon was going to sit this one out like a scrub on the bench. She considered herself pivotal in this scheme, likening herself to the sharpshooting Ray Allen during the 2007-2008 Boston Celtic's run to the championship. She started this game and intended to stay in it until this bitch's clock expired. Since their freedom was riding on them being organized and cool-headed, Devon needed to pull herself together. First, she cocked her head hard to the right and cracked her neck. She repeated the motion on the other side. Next, she cracked her knuckles. Lastly, she took a few deep breaths. "Ai'ight, let's do this like Brutus."

They double-checked themselves before getting out of the hot Chrysler minivan. They left the van running with the doors unlocked for a quick getaway if needed.

RahRah walked off first, initiating the mission.

Thirty seconds later, Devon followed.

And Bizzy was thirty seconds behind her.

Once everybody was inside the ten-story, 808-bed ORMC, they tried their best to look like they were employed there. They discreetly moved through the 345,000 square foot private hospital, concealing their profiles from cameras as much as possible.

Pushing an empty wheelchair as a decoy, Devon arrived at the sixth-floor room first. As previously planned, she posted up in the empty, antiseptic smelling corridor. To keep calm while waiting for her brothers, she admired a few of the more than seven hundred pieces of artwork that hung on the interior walls of the hospital. It felt as if a century had passed before Rah showed up. He, too, had a decoy, which was a laundry cart. But, in her honest opinion, he didn't look like he worked there. He may have been dressed in scrubs like the other ORMC workers, but he still looked out of place for some reason.

Rah looks like a nigga with an ulterior motive, a nigga on a high-level mission, Devon thought as RahRah sidled up beside her.

Bizzy appeared some seconds later. He had no decoy. Truth be told, he didn't need one because, despite the pressure, he moved with style and grace.

Biz moves like a seasoned killer on a small-time assignment, Devon surmised after Bizzy sauntered over to join them.

At the moment, there wasn't anyone in the stretch of hallway that they occupied. Before someone came along and thought they looked suspicious, they put on latex gloves, drew their guns and barged into the room.

Their victim was alone, which was unfortunate for her. But for them, Lady Luck continued to be on their side.

Rhapsody's bruised eyes enlarged at the sight of them. She shrieked. She would've screamed louder and longer if her jaws weren't wired shut. She then tried to reach the call button that summoned a nurse.

She moved too slow, however.

Rhapsody's broken, stiff and burned body allowed RahRah to grab the device nestled beside her. "Nice try, hoe," Rah said, his voice full of hate.

"Keema Keema Keema. From da look on ya face, I can see you're surprised ta see me," Devon sneered. "Y'knew ya couldn't hide from me fo'eva. You still stupid as fuck if ya thought you could."

Rhapsody broke down.

"We ain't fallin' fo' those crocodile tears, bitch," Bizzy spouted. "Ya ass 'bout ta hook up wit punk-ass JJ real soon."

In tears, Rhapsody mumbled something unintelligible.

"What's that?" Devon asked.

"Please, no," Rhapsody managed out the side of her mouth clear enough to be understood this time. "I have a daughter now, Dee."

"What?" Devon exclaimed. "Play that shit back."

"I have a daughter. She only seven months old."

"Where she at?" Devon asked off-the-cuff.

"Dee, we ain't got time fo' this shit," Rah interjected. "Let's slump this bitch an' be out." He placed the cold barrel of his throwaway .25 against the flattened space on the side of Rhapsody's forehead.

Before Rah could squeeze the trigger, Devon said, "I got it, bro. I know you wanna do it cuz she tricked ya into ambushin' my baby. An' I also know Biz wanna do it cuz she helped me set up Demetrius. But I gots ta be da one do it cuz her love an' hate fo' me is behind all this. This is my responsibility."

Rah lowered the weapon. "Hurry up then an' make her an afterthought."

"One shot ta da head will set this dirty hoe on her way, sis," Bizzy recommended. "Any mo' than that an' we'll definitely alert sumone."

115

Bizzy's remark about one shot to the head awakened Devon's memories. She suddenly heard the loud, ringing boom of her mother's fatal gunshot. The memories of the woman she barely knew were gone in a flash, though.

"I ain't gonna shoot her," Devon declared, tucking away her disposable heater. "She gotta suffer fo' what she did. She gotta experience real terror." She subsequently went over to Rhapsody's bed. She locked eyes with her former friend and lover. Rhapsody's watery and blackened eyes expressed remorse, and Devon almost bought what she was selling.

Before Devon had been snaked by Rhapsody, she couldn't deny loving the ambitious bitch once upon a time. Following the ultimate betrayal, she concluded that Rhapsody fell victim to the deadly sin of envy. She recalled Rhapsody telling her repeatedly how Miracle wasn't deserving of being her number one. Even if that was true, she didn't think that Rhapsody would go so far as trying to kill Miracle just to be her main bitch. *When you think you know somebody to a T, you really don't know them at all,* she concluded before snatching the pillow from under Rhapsody's swollen, scarred head. *But now I see for myself that constantly disregarding a lovestruck and jealous person can lead to a crime of passion.*

"If you'd just loved me like I loved you, none of this woulda happened," Rhapsody murmured. "I never stopped lovin'you, tho'. Even to this day, I love you, Devon." She sniffled, then turned her head aside slowly and sobbed. "Oh, my baby, Daylonna. Please, my baby, Lord. JuneBug, please watch ova my baby girl."

Devon's eyes moistened. Rhapsody's genuine pleading instantly brought back thoughts of her mother. She wondered if her mother called out for her before being murdered by Demetrius.

"Hold up. Who name ya just said?" Bizzy asked.

Rhapsody didn't respond. She just cried while mumbling incoherently. She knew it was curtains for her.

"Dee, stop thinkin' 'bout it an' get this shit ova wit befo' sumone comes," Rah said firmly.

Reliving the day that Demetrius shattered her life angered Devon. She placed the pillow over Rhapsody's head and pressed down. She imagined she was killing Demetrius again. Rhapsody squirmed a bit. She began to groan. Her heart rate increased, causing the machine that was displaying her vital signs to start beeping faster. By the time her heart rate had reached 120 beats per minutes, she was thrashing wildly. She soon went limp. And her heart rate dropped dramatically.

Some seconds later, Rhapsody flatlined, and the machine shrilled.

"That's our cue," Bizzy stated the obvious before concealing his pistol.

RahRah pocketed his gun and said in parting, "Good riddance, hoe. Enjoy Christmas in hell."

Devon hastily put the pillow back under Rhapsody's head.

They removed their gloves and pocketed them. One by one, they filed out of the room. Devon and Rah grabbed their decoys before they split up again. As they navigated their way out of the hospital, they heard dismayed nurses saying that a patient had coded red. Unperturbed, they kept their course until they were outside.

Bizzy made it to the van before Rah and Devon. Just as Devon slid the rear door closed, Bizzy pulled off. They rode in silence until they were in traffic.

"I swear I heard her say JuneBug name," Bizzy blurted out. "I wonder why she said that nigga name."

"Huh?" Devon said, finally scanning the streetscape and currently feeling rueful about her last act.

"She said, verbatim… 'JuneBug, please watch ova my baby girl.' Why would she say his name when she 'bout ta—" A lightbulb switched on in Bizzy's head. He remembered now. "That's right. Cesar did just tell me JuneBug gotta baby by that bitch. An' that nigga from Orlando."

"Who da fuck is JuneBug?" Rah asked with irritation from the passenger seat. "An' why ya worried 'bout that nigga anyway?"

Disregarding Rah's spitefulness, Bizzy answered, "In short, JuneBug was my cousin Chad homeboy. They grew up together in Orlando. They both used ta hussle fo' my pops befo' they hussled wit me."

"And?"

Bizzy scoffed at Rah's persistent sideways remarks. "From what I was told, JuneBug met da bitch in Devon's club an' became her pill man. He took a likin' ta that hoe quick-like. His tender-dick ass eventually had her layin' up in my crib. The one that he, Chad an' Solo was lookin' after when I went outta town. Solo, my pops' bodyguard when he died, knew Rhapsody, too, an' he soon suspected da bitch was shady becuz of how strange she was actin'. He told Chad an' JuneBug 'bout her odd behavior. JuneBug liked her so much that when he found out da bitch was flaw, he was slow ta expose her. When I got word of it all, I hurried back from outta town just ta personally deal wit her. After JuneBug tricked da bitch into meetin' him at a park that me an' Chad had set up as an ambush, shit didn't go as planned. Chad ended up dead, JuneBug got shot an' went ta jail, an' da bitch... I dunno what happened ta her that night.

"Now, I ain't sweatin' that nigga at all, altho' I wanted ta kill him fo' puttin' on FaceSpace he wanted ta kill me fo' callin' him a rat. I only labelled him a snitch, tho', after two feds that were lookin' fo' me told my Aunt Sheryl that he mentioned my name da night Chad was killed. Once I found out da feds lied to my aunt an' he didn't in fact rat on me, instead of cleanin' up his name, I simply pardoned him an' tried ta dismiss him."

"Wait a second. You slung mud on that nigga good name an' *you* da one carryin' a grudge." Rah said. "That's flaw-er than a bitch, champ."

"Look, green-ass nigga, da night Chad died still eats at me. How shit unfolded that night, I suspected JuneBug double-crossed me an' saved that bitch somehow. He mighta got shot that night, but I feel like that was a accident."

Rah burst out laughing. "You really think that nigga put himself in da line of fiyah ova a bitch? Who ya think he is, Suge Knight?"

Bizzy had had just about enough of Rah's disrespect. He was almost to the point where Devon would just have to forgive him for killing Rah; just like how he forgave her for killing their father.

RahRah observed Bizzy's jaw muscles clench and unclench rhythmically. The menacing gesture didn't faze him, though. Yet, he decided to quit provoking him. "Now what? You gonna merk JuneBug?"

Bizzy could tell Rah wasn't being sarcastic with the question. He pondered for a couple of seconds. Then, "Since I'm already here, I might as well get him befo' he gets me. I know he wants to kill me, so I'll beat him ta da punch."

Rah shook his head in disbelief. "What about da baby she claimed she got?" he asked.

"What about it?"

Rah could tell Bizzy wasn't being sarcastic.

And Devon knew it, too. *I won't take issue with Bizzy wanting to kill JuneBug,* she thought. *But damn, we might end up at odds with each other again if he's straight up with causing harm to that motherless child.*

Chapter 13

December 22, 2011/ 7:31pm/ Yukon, OK
Envy – Lust – Pride – Sloth – Wrath – Gluttony – Greed
Being resentful about another's advantages or assets is *envy.* Having an uncontrolled sexual desire is *lust.* Possessing an exaggerated sense of self-importance is *pride.* Unwilling to do any kind of labor is *sloth. Wrath* was having a violent temper. *Gluttony* is overeating. And having a hoggish appetite for riches and possessions is *greed.*

Those are the seven deadly sins that are viewed to be fatal to spiritual progress. For that reason, they are highly offensive to God.

The foundation of all reprehensible actions is said to be greed. Yes, an insatiable desire for wealth beyond reasonable need is the root of all evil. Avarice, a synonym of greed, has caused a significant percentage of people to either go bankrupt, do time in prison, or worse, be buried six feet deep. The world is driven by greed. Indeed, it is the most destructive of sins.

JuneBug could attest to greed's detrimental effects. During his time of living high on the hog, he saw, as well as experienced, how gold fever laid waste to lives. He kept grinding, though, just like the other self-willed hustlers he knew. And just like them, he lacked a coherent rationale for why he chased the almighty dollar so relentlessly. Reflecting on the choices he'd made in the past, often fueled by greed, JuneBug questioned his decision to pick up his first pack. It not only flipped his world upside down, but it was also probably going to cause him to expire before his time. Since the day he was diagnosed with colon cancer, his time left on earth had become his most unfathomable unknown. The doctors may have detected his cancer in its early stages, but there was no telling if the cancer would return. It was because of that uncertainty that he let greed get the best of him.

This latest scheme he'd concocted wasn't devised to demonstrate his genius at playing the game. Personally, he'd already proven his mettle in the streets. He now put his freedom and health on the line for his family. He simply wanted to make sure his wife and kids were in a great financial position for a long time, should his cancer take him out. So, this time, his motive backed up his play. The greed component only entered the picture because his stomach issues were worsening, and he wanted to accumulate as much cash as he could.

Before this ordeal with his family ensued, Bug only experienced a sharp pain in his repaired intestines now and then. But minutes after all this began, the discomfort in his gut intensified. He hardly had an appetite, so he dismissed the additional pain for hunger pangs. When the pain became too much for him to cope with, he relinquished the driver seat for good and curled up in the sleeper berth. The pain became so unbearable, however, that he begged Blue to find the nearest hospital ASAP. Off I-40, Blue located the INTEGRIS Health Canadian Valley Hospital just outside of Oklahoma City.

Before admitting himself, Bug asked Blue to do him a major solid: continue the mission without him. Physically, he might be unable to go on, but rescuing his family was still his main priority. So, commissioning his right-hand man to complete the mission solo didn't require a lot of thought. What other alternative was there?

Before Blue went on without him, JuneBug called Adrian and explained what was going on. Indeed, Adrian had a heart and extended the scheduled delivery by twenty-four hours, not a minute more. Adrian also reassured him that his family would be freed upon delivery as promised. Then, unexpectedly, Adrian wished him a speedy recovery. He hit up his mother next, and she said she'd be by his side soon. He finally bid Blue safe travels and checked into the hospital.

Bug remained hopeful that nothing major was wrong with him. He prayed that the doctors could get him into a better condition fast. He needed to get out of there and catch a flight to Buffalo right away.

Following some tests and imaging the doctors ran on him, they discovered a blockage in his large intestine. He requested the least invasive procedure so he could be on his way. The doctors gave him a mild laxative to begin with. It had no effect. They recommended surgery after that, but Bug was unwilling to be operated on because that would leave him bedridden for a while. And so, he negotiated with the doctors, promising to have the surgery if they gave him a stronger laxative and it didn't work.

While laid up waiting for the effects of the stronger laxative, a pair of unexpected visitors dropped in on JuneBug.

"Dayvan Stubbford?" the white woman said moments after walking into the room with a biracial man.

Bug sat up slightly. "Who y'all? Cuz neitha one of ya are dressed like da doctors I seen so far."

The two uninvited guests assembled bedside.

The man replied, "No, sir, we're not doctors. My name is Dylan Murray, and I'm with Homeland Security."

"I'm CIA. Lane's the name."

"CIA an' Homeland Security. What da fuck?" If Bug's colon hadn't been blocked, he would've shitted on himself. He knew what the Central Intelligence Agency was about…

kind of. But he had no fucking clue what Homeland Security handled. His best guess was terrorists. *Maaannn, what in the fuck did I get myself into now?* he wondered. *When will this nightmare stop getting worse?*

"I don't know why you're making as if you're surprised we're here," Murray said. I'm sure you know the reason for this visit."

"Ummm… Yeah… I'm… I'm fucked up. I'm-I'm in hella pain rite now."

"Yes, you are fucked up," Lane jeered. "You'll know what *real* pain is after I'm done with you."

"We learned what's going on with you from the doctors caring for you," Murray interjected. "We were told you'll likely need surgery, but you're refusing it so far."

"I wonder why that is?" added Lane. "Could it be because you have something important to do? Like catching up with your accomplice who has helped you steal a container from the Port of San Diego."

"What? Maaannn, I ain't take nuttin' from nobody since I was a jit. Y'all got me mixed up wit sumone else."

"Let's not play fuckin' games, *JuneBug,*" Lane said, stepping closer to the side of the bed. "You're the real owner-operator of T.A.B. Trucking, correct?"

To keep his mother out of this, JuneBug nodded in a hurry.

Murray picked up from there. "According to the records and surveillance footage, you and Gabe Erickson gained access to the port by means of a doctored shipping document yesterday at 7:04am. About an hour later, you two left there with a container I was… excuse me, *we* were interested in. Because you slipped through our fingers, we launched a search for you and Mr. Erickson. We carefully scanned our networks for your names. Then, *viola,* we were alerted when you checked into this hospital, hence this visit."

JuneBug was feeling cornered. So, in order to not incriminate himself further, he demanded, "I need ta call my lawyer."

Lane leaned forward, inches from his face, she said, "You're not getting shit. You're going to call your pal and get his location right now. We're not going in circles with you, scum."

"Bitch, you crazy as fuck if you think I'm sayin' anotha word witout my attorney. So, back da fuck outta my face."

Murray pulled Lane away. He then stepped forward. "Mr. Stubbford, whether you know it or not, what's in that container is a danger to society. And whether you stole it or not, the CIA, the FBI, and other agencies, we were keeping tabs on that container for a reason. Once you took it, for whatever that may be, you put yourself in the middle of a years-long investigation." He sighed.

"I'm going to level with you, Mr. Stubbford," Murray continued. "You're not the prototypical person that would be allied with the people who that container supposedly belongs to. So, turn it over to us, get yourself out of this situation before it's too late, and I guarantee you and Mr. Erickson will face minor penalties."

"And before you speak too soon... or remain silent, you piece of shit," Lane jumped in, "Just know that you've violated your probation. So, if you don't give us that damn container, I'll slap you with kingpin charges. And I guarantee you'll spend eternity and a day in a federal supermax prison."

Before Bug processed the rude agent's ultimatum, he asked, "Who did I steal from? And what did I steal?" *Please, don't let it be human body parts in there,* he prayed as he awaited their response.

"We're not at liberty to let you know any more than what we've already disclosed," Murray said. "Now, what's it going to be? Play ball with us..."

"Or stick to the worthless G-code you *people* live by." Lane finished snidely.

To tell or not to tell? That was the fateful question Bug had to answer. He had proved that he wasn't a hot nigga not too long ago. In this case, though, he'd be a genuine snitch if he decided to break his silence and tell the whole truth.

Opening his mouth wouldn't ensure his family's safety, either, because the US government may be unable or unwilling to help him to recover them. He'd cooperate with a written guarantee from the feds stating that they'd do their best to retrieve his wife and kids, though. Damn his good name in the streets. Provided that the streets knew about his current predicament, he'd be let off the hook for squealing by the rational street niggas. As for the street hawks, the ones who didn't condone gangstas singing under any circumstances, he'd tell them straight up that abiding by the G-code became highly questionable when his innocent loved ones got entangled in his shit.

True enough, I did wrong. But the fact of the matter is, if niggas have never walked in these shoes, they can't badmouth me, he deduced as his stomach bubbled. *I can't think like a gangsta when I'm in this position, so niggas will be entitled to their own opinions for what I'm about to do.*

"If I'ma help y'all wit this, I'ma need y'all ta help me wit sumthin'," Bug finally spoke up. "An' if we come ta a undastandin', I'ma need our agreement in black an' white. We ain't shakin' hands on this becuz I know how y'all crooked muthafuckas play."

"You need our help?" Lane laughed at his straightforward request. "What more do you want than to not be punished to the greatest extent of the law?"

"Let's hear what you need help with," Murray said, intrigued. "And depending on what it is you seek will determine if you get anything in writing."

The whole good cop, bad cop routine didn't shake Bug up one bit. The dirty tricks the law used to get what they wanted had him leery, though. He knew he couldn't bet on them outright. But he'd chance it this time. *Won't be no turning back once I get going,* he thought as Shella and his kids flashed in his mind.

"Ai'ight," Bug began, "I need ta tell y'all first that I just can't turn ova that container ta y'all. It must reach its destination safely by Christmas Eve mornin'."

"What's this bullshit you're trying to sell us?" Lane asked with irritation. "We want that container... Now!"

Reserved, Murray said, "Just tell us what's going on."

"Okay, check it. Da person I work fo' is holdin' my wife an' two kids... I mean three kids... They all bein' held hostage until that load makes it ta where he said I need ta take it."

"Who do you work for?" Murray followed up.

This is the point of no return, Bug said to himself. "I only know him by da name Adrian. I dunno his last name. He from Miami... at least I think that's where he from. That's where we meet ta do bizness."

"That's it?" Lane said mockingly. "That's useless."

"I concur," Murray added. "That's not enough info to warrant our help."

"LOOK, they... they got my fam—" Bug broke down. "They got my family. I just want my family. That's all I know."

Murray and Lane looked at each other quizzically. In sync, they stepped away from a weeping JuneBug and huddled up.

"Does the name Adrian ring a bell in your agency?" Murray asked Lane. "That name, I don't recognize."

"I'm on it. The CIA has an unmatched criminal database," Lane said before pulling out her phone and posting up in the nearest corner of the room.

Murray returned to the bedside. "So, this guy Adrian, why did he take your family in the first place?"

"Becuz I didn't wanna complete a job he fooled me into doin'," Bug replied, relaxing some.

"How did he fool you?"

"I agreed ta go one place. But when it was time ta drop off an' go, he said I was ta go another place. I refused, so he took my family."

"So, Adrian is using your family as leverage. How long has he had them?"

"Two days now," Bug answered. "That's why I need y'all—"

"Adrian Edouard Mendoza," Lane interrupted, rejoining Murray bedside after ending her brief call. "He's a key player in the Atahualpa Cartel. And Cesar Vargas DePalma is the one who calls the shots for that organization."

Murray whistled in amazement. "Holy moly, Mr. Stubbford, you've hooked yourself up with a bad lot. I mean, Cesar DePalma has been on every agency's radar for decades. He's on Interpol's top ten most wanted list. Some consider him a magician or imaginary because he up and vanishes whenever—"

An idea suddenly struck Murray.

"Quid pro quo," Murray exclaimed unexpectedly.

Stomach rumbling

"What?" Bug said.

"A favor for a favor," Murray simplified it. "Something given or received for something else is called quid pro quo. It's Latin." He smirked. "It's evident what you need help with, Mr. Stubbford. So, we'll extend our assistance to help you get your family back… as long as you assist us with this case extensively."

"I'm all in now. I'm ready ta do whateva it takes ta get my family back," Bug professed while climbing out of the bed.

"We need you to call Mr. Erickson and get his location for us right now," Lane ordered.

Stomach rumbling

"Where do you think you're going?" Lane asked once Bug was on his feet.

"To da shitter if that's okay wit'chu," Bug replied snippily before farting. "All that talkin' 'bout jail seemed ta do da trick. I gotta take a mean dump." He then pushed past the mean white bitch and entered the lavatory. He removed his concealed phone from his waistband and texted Blue. While texting, he yelled through the door, "Tell da doctors I'm shittin' an' I'll be good ta go once I come out. Then, after I call my mama an' tell her to cancel her plans to come up here, I'll call my dawg, ai'ight?"

"We'll be right back, Mr. Stubbford. And you'll call Adrian, too, when we return."

The two agents left to inform the nurses about JuneBug's bowel movement and to deliberate further.

"What in the world is going on here, Murray? Why would a drug lord from South America meddle with the Russians?" asked Lane. "I believe this piece of shit is trying to outsmart us. I think he's lying through his bronze teeth."

Murray shrugged as they walked. "It seems to me that Stubbford is being truthful. I believe that he and Erickson aren't cognizant of what they've gotten themselves into. But, to be sure, we need to find out if this Adrian guy is linked to the Russians or not."

"Do you think the Russians are searching for these morons, too?"

"Without a doubt. And I daresay the Russians know where this guy is since we know where he is. But that's a good thing."

"Why is that?"

"Because we're going to use that container as bait to apprehend the Russians. Then, we're going to use Stubbford to nab Adrian Mendoza."

"And how do you plan to do all that?"

"First, we let them deliver that container."

"What? Are you shitting me?"

"Whoa, don't get yourself all worked up. Once we learn Erickson's location, we're going to have agents from the nearest field office apprehend him until we get there. We'll get Mr. Stubbford back in the truck, then we'll shadow them to their destination. We'll take in everyone at that drop off location. After that, we'll escort Erickson and Stubbford home. Then we devise a plan to collar Adrian. If we only arrest underlings at both sites, we'll wring as much info as we can from them and, hopefully, we'll take down two crime rings in good time."

Lane just smiled. "And here I am, all this time, thinking you Homeland Security guys were the dullest knives in the drawer."

In the parking lot of the INTEGRIS Health Canadian Valley Hospital...

"I hate Americans," Pyotr uttered while screwing the suppressor onto his Walther PP9. "Look at them, shiver and cover up from a little cold. They are useless. They vill not survive one vinter in Siberia. That's vhy I love killing them. Killing them is much much better than verking in Russian coal mine."

"Are you positive this is the hospital?" asked Misha, paying Pyotr's rambling no mind. "I don't see big truck anyvare."

"*Da,* Maksim say he check in hours ago," Arkady answered.

"Vhat's the plan?" Misha asked next.

Arkady said, "I go in there vith Pyotr and vee make him tell us vare container is. Once vee get container back, vee kill that nigger. Then, vee take container to Houston as planned."

"Vait a second," Pyotr declared, aligning his gun's sights on a man exiting the hospital with a woman. "I see that man before recently."

Arkady and Misha took notice of the man in a trench coat and the cigarette-smoking woman.

"Da, I see him before, too," Arkady affirmed. "He was at port in San Diego."

"He's police," Misha asserted.

"Are you going to call Yuri and let him know vhat is happening?" Pyotr asked.

"Da, you must call Yuri at once. He expects container to be in Houston tomorrow," Misha said.

"Not yet. Vee see vhat happens first."

Chapter 14

December 22, 2011/ 9:06pm/ Orlando, FL

Motherhood... Something that nearly all women looked forward to experiencing.

Devon, however, would never experience it. There was no chance of her ever bearing a child of her own. Despite putting on an act like her life was a bed of roses, she was figuratively and literally empty on the inside. Because she lacked a womb that could bring a new life into the world, she felt less than a woman. True, she had Kamani, Miracle's now nine-year-old son whom she helped to raise since 2004. But she knew the love she had for him would never compare to the love a mother had for her own flesh and blood. Devon had every right to be bitter about her impotency. But that didn't stop her from having a soft spot for kids. She loved all kids, especially those without parents.

"I'm sorry, bro, but ya gotta turn around. I can't just up an' leave now. I need ta know she'll be safe. So, you can drop me off at da same hotel an' you go on home without me. I'll be home soon, hopefully."

RahRah looked over at Devon in the front passenger seat. It took him only a second to see she wasn't playing. He turned back to look at the onrushing pavement of I-4. He let out a deep, frustrated sigh. "Devon, you need ta tighten up. You're way too invested in this baby ya neva laid eyes on a day in ya life. That's gonna eitha land ya silly ass in da joint or a pine box."

Nonplussed, Devon shrugged. "So be it. But I'm gonna do whateva I can ta make sho' that lil' girl, if she really does exist, is good. I won't be able ta live wit myself if I found out sumthin' happened ta her an' I coulda prevented it."

"Goddamn, Dee, why you gotta be fuckin' Superwoman? We came up here fo' one thing, an' one thing only. We put a handle on that. Now, we need ta put as much distance as we can between us an' this body we just caught." Again, Rah sighed. "I know ya like da back of my hand, Dee, so I know ya ain't changin' ya mind. An' as bad as I wanna leave ya ass up here ta be a hero, y'know I can't do that."

"Bro, I tell ya time an' time again that'chu don't owe me nuttin'. Yeah, I saved our lives, but that was a fluke. Even befo' that fateful day, you've been goin' hard fo' me at every turn. You freed yaself up at da drop of a dime er'time I was in a jam. I truly appreciate ya, bro, but—"

"Do ya really appreciate me, Dee?" Rah interjected because she hit a nerve. "I say that becuz these days I feel like ya been stopped appreciatin' me. Me ridin' fo' ya without discussion, I feel like, has become an expectation."

Devon was thrown by his statement.

In part, there was truth in what he said. She couldn't think of a time when he'd left her hanging out in the cold. She could, however, recall distancing herself from him when he went to the panhandle to do a three-year bid. She had visited him and kept his books straight early on, but she ended up giving him less and less attention the closer he got to being released. Overlooking him was inadvertent, because she had a ton on her plate around that time. Instead of being heated and snapping on her about the situation, he kept his cool. And it was because of his abiding attitude that made her respect for him skyrocket.

"Rah, real nigga shit, I ain't merfin' when I say I do appreciate you. On er'thang, I love you an' I'll put my life on da line fo' ya as well. I apologize if I made ya feel some type of way lately. If it weren't fo' you, bro, I dunno where

I'd be in this life. I owe ya mo' than a thanks an' any amount of money. I'm—"

"Dee, stop wit all that mushy shit." Rah cut her off. "Y'know I ain't wit all that. I'ma just follow ya lead. So, let's do whateva ya got planned an' haul ass. Rememba, Christmas rite around da corner," he concluded as he changed lanes in preparation for getting off the highway at the next exit.

Devon hadn't looked that far ahead yet. All she knew so far was that she was going to call Bizzy and offer to help him take out JuneBug. She assumed she wouldn't have to convince him because of her intention to tell him that she felt an obligation due to his assist in the matter with Rhapsody. *Yeah, that should work,* she thought before calling her brother. *Then I'll make my moves as I go.*

At the same time, in the notorious projects known as Beirut on the west side…

"Que pasa, jefe? You miss ya boy yet?"

"Hmmm, let's see… Margins are up. Money is steadily coming in. I have yet to take a major loss in life. So, what is there to miss about you, my boy?" Cesar chuckled.

"Oh, so that's how it is, jefe?" Bizzy laughed as he slowly paced back and forth in the small living room. "Anywayz, I called—"

"Daddy, when are we going to the movies? You said you'd take me to see Harry Potter. So, can we go now?"

Bizzy stopped in his tracks. He looked down at his six-year-old son and said, "I know what I said, BJ. You don't have ta keep remindin' me. I'ma take ya once I get off da phone, ai'ight?"

"Me, too?"

"You goin', too, Quez," he said to BJ's three-year-old brother who wasn't his son. "An' so is Spechul."

The saggy-diapered Jaquez jumped up and down with joy. However, Byron, junior, showed his displeasure with his father's evasiveness by thrusting out his bottom lip.

"My nigga, you betta stop poutin' like a lil' sissy. I said what I said, so y'all go on an' get ready."

Jaquez bolted, screeching happily on the way to his room.

BJ, on the other hand, stopped frowning. He then showed his contempt by curling one side of his upper lip. As he coolly sauntered off, he glared fiercely at his father until he was out of sight.

"Lil' nigga don't get fucked up! Mean-muggin' me like you want static," Bizzy said loudly before putting the phone back to his ear. "Cesar?"

"I'm still here."

"Mala mia. My fault. My bad ass son an' his lil' brotha fuckin' wit me 'bout takin' 'em ta see that nerdy, wizard-boy flick."

"Kids. I love kids. They're so energetic, as well as funny and naïve." Cesar thought twice about what he had just said. "Well, they're naïve until they find out on their own that the world is cruel.

"For instance, I gave my ten children the best of the best until each one could set off on their own. I spent a bankroll on their passions and hobbies as adolescents. I did all I could to shelter them from my life's work. But I fell terribly short with all of them. All my children are adults now, and all of them are different from each other. But every single one of them – my four spoiled daughters and six sons – are integral figures in the family business now. So, enjoy your little ones before they grow up and become like you... or worse. You just can't assume they're going to turn out the way you expected."

A tingle ran through Bizzy's spine. He could attest to what Cesar said. His father, Demetrius, also tried earnestly to keep the street life out of his sight.

Throughout elementary school, Bizzy assumed that the cash flow from Demetrius' successful laundromat, convenience store, and other personal businesses in Tallahassee were the reason he got the princely treatment. It wasn't until the sixth grade that he got a glimpse of what his pops really did. Once he learned that Demetrius was an infamous gangsta, he sought to become a gangsta, too. He subsequently transitioned from a temperate child to a temperamental one almost overnight. Demetrius, who wasn't much of a hands-on parent, simply chalked up his sudden behavioral change to puberty. But then he got caught flaunting a deuce-deuce in school in the eighth grade. And that finally caught his father's attention.

Rather than straightening up after that incident, Bizzy went further off course. He was hung up on becoming a G.

When he moved on to high school, picking up his diploma wasn't on his mind. Instead, he picked up a pack. He then piggybacked off his father's name to get rid of the mediocre work he copped from a local dealer. By the time he was in the eleventh grade, which nobody expected him to reach, his name was ringing throughout Tally's streets. Surprisingly, he secured enough credits to graduate. But, above all, he secured the street credit he sought.

At no point in his quest for hood fame did Bizzy consider getting his life back on the straight and narrow. He knew that he wasn't living up to Demetrius' expectations. He didn't care, though, because his father was a long way from being an ideal role model. He also didn't give a rat's ass that Demetrius had spent a fortune keeping his criminal record clean when he fucked up. On the contrary, he *did* care when Demetrius' big-faced bills couldn't save him from doing a short bid at Coleman Low for something his pops did behind his back. After he did his time like a man, Demetrius, who was going through a bad break, accepted his lifestyle and hustle because he was needed to help keep the RockBottom Family from literally hitting rock bottom.

From there, Bizzy sunk deeper and deeper into The Game. He went in over his head after Demetrius was killed, though.

"I hear ya, jefe," Bizzy finally said. "Anywayz, I called ta let'cha know I'll be back wit'cha after I handle one mo' thing."

"Let me take a wild guess… You want to take care of your pesky Bug problem."

Bizzy smiled because nothing seemed to get past Cesar. Still, he asked, "How'd y'know?"

"Let's just say that your Bug problem has the potential of becoming *my* problem. Instead of putting Adrian on him like I normally would have, I'm giving you a blank check to take care of him. You'll be contacted with the essential information that'll help you with your extermination."

Before Bizzy could subtly ask Cesar how JuneBug could become a concern in *his* orbit, his phone beeped. He looked to see who was waiting to connect. Once he saw who it was, he said to Cesar, "Ai'ight, jefe. I'll call ya when I'm ready ta come back." Then, without a concluding remark, he answered the other call. "Wassup…? I'm at my baby mama crib. I ain't gonna be here too much longer, tho', cuz I'm takin' my lil' man an' his brotha an' sista ta da movies… After that, I gotta do some homework. I told ya that befo' ya peeled… You turned around! Fo' what…? I mean, I ain't trippin'. Just be sho' it's sumthin' y'all wanna do becuz I dunno where we can end up or how long this'll take… Say less. I'll meet ya at my hotel in about three hours or so… Already."

He ended the call with Devon.

"Unh unh, nigga, what hoe you meetin' at'cha hotel?"

"Bitch, stay in ya lane an' outta my bizness," Bizzy said to LaShawn, his crass and silly baby mama. "I don't question you 'bout all da niggaz I know you got comin' in an' outta here."

"Oh, hell naw, Byron! I keep tellin' yo' punk ass don't be callin' me a bitch – *BITCH!*"

"Whateva, bitch," he replied, unruffled.

LaShawn, who resembled Regina King in *Boyz n the Hood,* flared up. Just as she commenced her hysterics, Bizzy yelled, "BJ, Jacquez, Spechul, come on if y'all comin'. Y'all got one minute ta be in da car." He walked out of the apartment with his rod clutched. *Damn, I must get BJ out of this fucked up hood that LaShawn refuses to move out of,* he said to himself while guardedly strolling to his rental car. *This time last year I said that I'd have BJ and Bilal in my custody in three years tops, so I must stick to my program and be on time for them.*

Chapter 15

December 23, 2011/5:47am/Somewhere in central Illinois
A goon at heart, twenty-four-seven, three-sixty-five.

A perpetual outlaw that hadn't kept his nose clean since learning how to walk. Blue wasn't even slightly ashamed about being a career criminal. He was extraordinarily proud about being a menace that never had to bust his ass for an honest buck for a single day in his life. Dirty, dishonest work was his niche. And it was the prospect of making easy, illicit dough that originally captivated him about Bug's plan. However, Blue felt that it was a blessing to have become a truck driver. He quickly became fascinated by the freedom he felt operating an eighteen-wheeler.

Rolling through open country and scoping out the scenic landscapes were unexpected treats he came to highly enjoy. Even when the scenery became blurry, being on the road had provided him with a piece of mind that he'd never experienced before. True, he and Bug blew beaucoup herb on the road, but he was placed on a unique cloud nine while barreling down the highways and byways. For once in his life, he sincerely thought he'd made a sound decision, although it was still rooted in criminality. He'd become absorbed by this occupation that was camouflaging his ongoing dirty deeds. It astounded Blue that he'd found his true calling while making a killing flipping his portion of the bricks.

Then, the unfortunate situation with JuneBug happened, which activated Blue's sixth sense of premonition. He felt the return of the circling black cloud over his head. His blessing appeared to have been short-lived – the story of his life. Nevertheless, he remained confident that he'd be on the up-and-up again after the affair with Adrian was settled.

Presently, Blue was furious. The reality of being a big rig driver had gotten to him yesterday. Before Bug got played by Adrian, he had no complaints about the trucking industry because he didn't look at himself as a typical trucker; he considered himself a street nigga from the trenches masquerading as a driver. The payoff also made it hard for him to see the harsh realities of hauling goods. But now he understood why three hundred thousand truckers, give or take, left the industry annually.

Besides haulers being pressured by employers and shippers to burn up the road seventy hours a week just to pull in fifty grand a year, the truckers-only area of truck stops was a world of their own. Because truckers were required by federal law to end their shift after fourteen hours of working, with no more than eleven of those hours behind the wheel, a majority of drivers spent their ten-hour break at one of the mainstream truck stops strung out along every major highway in the U.S. But first, they had to find one that's not at capacity.

By and large, truck stops were crawling with prostitutes, sex traffickers, robbers and hijackers. And it was entirely possible for a trucker to be snoozing in his rig next to a serial rapist or murderer. Those were all reasons why women made up a very small percentage of the four hundred thousand people that earned a CDL yearly. And, consequently, why the trucking industry had a retention issue. On the whole, there was more to being a big-rigger than what met the eye. It wasn't an easy way to make a living.

Blue pulled into a Love's Travel Stop. He'd exceeded the number of hours he was legally allowed to drive by an hour.

He cruised the lot, praying that he wouldn't strike out a third time trying to find an empty space.

No luck.

"Arf arf!"

"Yeah, I know, Fry. I'm sick of this shit, too. But don't trip, lil' buddy. I'm 'bout ta go ta da nearest motel an' we gonna crash there. An' I'll shoot da manager a stack if they gotta problem wit our truck bein' there."

"Arf arf arf!"

"You got it. A big, juicy T-bone an' fried eggs fo' both of us. I'm hungry than a muthafucka."

Blue exited the truck stop, got back onto I-70 and continued east. Day was just about to break. He proceeded to watch the road ahead for signs that displayed exits for upcoming lodging, restaurants and gas stations. His eyes were dry and burning. He couldn't wait to get out of the truck and into a real bed, and into some pussy, if he was lucky.

A sudden flash caused Blue to check the side mirror. What he saw instantaneously made him break out in a cold sweat. *What the fuck? I didn't do nothing wrong.*

In the back of Blue was a vehicle with its lights flashing. *I swear I'm going to see a witch doctor as soon as I get back to O-Town because I have to be cursed and I want it removed,* he thought before looking at the speedometer and seeing that he wasn't speeding. He checked the mirror again to verify that the vehicle behind him was DOT, and he confirmed that it was.

Since this would be the third time he'd been pulled over by DOT, the first time by himself, though, he knew the procedure. His anxiety kicked up a notch as he pulled onto the shoulder. Once he came to a complete stop, he began to retrieve the three things the prior DOT officers had always asked for.

From the sideview mirror, Blue watched the officer approach the cab. With every unsteady step the officer took, his anxiety stepped up, too. However, he felt poised enough to breeze through the impending interaction.

"Top of the morning, sir," the silver-haired white man said after he stepped onto the running board and clung to the grab bar of the cab.

"Mornin', officer."

"Well, I'm not going to hold you up. I pulled you over for speeding. You were eight miles per hour over the speed limit according to my radar gun. Now, please, pass me—"

In a flash, Blue presented his CDL, medical card, and insurance.

The deadpan officer grabbed the documents through the window. "Your logbook as well," he said, instantly noticing that the book wasn't offered.

Neither of the past DOT officers that Blue had encountered had asked to look at the logbook, so the request was new to Blue. But it wasn't an order that would cause him to panic. He just prayed the officer was like the others and didn't ask to go into the trailer.

After Blue surrendered the logbook, the officer said, "Sit tight, sir." He then retreated to his cruiser.

"*Arf!*"

"Who ya tellin', Fry? But this shit should be ova quickly." Blue reached over to the passenger seat and patted Fry's abnormally big head.

Every now and then, Blue used the driver's sideview mirror to spy on the officer. Since it was still quite gloomy outside, he couldn't see what the officer was up to. All he knew was the officer was taking an unusually long time, and the suspense only made his anxiety worse.

"What da fuck takin' this old cracka so long? I know he ain't trippin' 'bout me drivin' a hour ova da—"

What Blue had just witnessed in the mirror caused his words to catch in his throat. He did a doubletake to be sure his fatigued eyes weren't playing tricks on him.

Oh no, his eyes weren't.

Two distinct vehicles had pulled up behind the DOT cruiser. The DOT officer got out of his car and hobbled toward the four individuals that exited their vehicles. The quintet shook hands. They then gathered in the grass and conferred. Blue's mind raced while he looked in on the group in the truck's right sideview mirror. He was beginning to settle into the conclusion that his luck had finally run out.

About ten minutes later, the assembly broke up. Blue observed two of the men head toward his passenger door. He looked in the driver's side mirror again and saw the other three, including the DOT officer, walking in line toward him. Their suspicious maneuver raised the hairs on his neck. Now, he definitely knew what time it was.

"Mr. Erickson," the DOT officer said, reappearing at the driver's window, "Would you step out—"

Brrrraaatttt

The three-round burst from the AR-15 ripped through the door with ease. The 5.56 rounds hit the old officer square in the chest. The force caused him to fly off the running board. He landed hard on his back in the middle of the interstate's slow lane.

"Shots fired! Shots fired! Officer down! Send back up! NOW!"

Like a piece of food lodged in one's throat, Blue wasn't going down without a fight. Today was the day he held court in the street.

Blue stuck the AR out of the window and let off at the two fleeing men. He hit one in the leg, tearing a chunk of meat from his hamstring. He then opened the door and jumped down from the cab. He aimed at the DOT officer who was moaning but not moving. He was about to officially retire the man but…

Car horn blaring

A SUV travelling in the right lane tried to swerve around the "obstacle" in the road. Unfortunately, the DOT officer was run over. His crushed body rolled down the interstate like tumbleweed. There was a lengthy trail of blood left on the crumbling asphalt.

The spectacular incident fired Blue up. The kill merely whetted his appetite. He now craved more.

Like a wolverine that had just consumed a bag of cocaine and was thirsting for blood, Blue crouched slightly and sought out the others, not sure what branch of law enforcement they were. He crept alongside the trailer, frequently glimpsing underneath it and behind him. Near the end of the forty-eight-foot trailer he spotted blood. He cautiously followed the splotches of red until they disappeared behind the trailer.

"Hey, pal! I need your help! I just ran over—"

Blue spun around and opened fire without hesitation. He wasn't fucking around. His fuse had blown, and now he was quick to pick off anything that moved.

Once the civilian was dispatched, Blue forged ahead. With his back against the container, he peeked around the rear and laid eyes on a wounded man. The whimpering man was sliding on his belly away from him. Again, he wasted no time approaching the man and honeycombing his back.

Two down, Blue confirmed to himself with a menacing look on his face. *Three more to go.*

Out of nowhere, a hailstorm of bullets flew in Blue's direction. One of them ate up the divide in an instant and struck Blue in his right shoulder. He dropped his high-powered killing machine.

"SHOW YOUR HANDS AND GET ON THE GROUND," a distressed man called out from behind one of the vehicles.

Blue tuned out the directive. Instead, he picked up the rifle and started busting erratically. He emptied the fifty-round magazine. He ducked and took cover in front of the cruiser and reloaded. Although his extra clip was attached to the empty one, he had some trouble swapping them with his now disabled right arm. The men continued to yell orders in between shooting at him. When the other clip was finally locked in, he took a deep breath, smoothed his wavy hair down with his functional hand, and sprung back into action.

Knowing instinctively that his chances of surviving this episode were slim to none, Blue advanced toward the concealed men carelessly. It took him mere seconds to get a fix on someone. The man popped his head up in what appeared to be an attempt to locate him. But that was a critical mistake. Since aiming with precision was now complicated, he blitzed the man, who was pinned down between the second and last vehicle. He intended to nail his next victim at point-blank range.

When Blue confronted the man, it didn't surprise him much to see that the man wasn't hunkered down alone. Due to his bloodlust caused by his manic state of mind, Blue didn't balk. He discharged his weapon. The AR was like a coupon, knocking off half of the closest man's head. The other man, however, unloaded the remaining rounds in his service pistol into Blue's torso. As Blue was falling to the ground, he squeezed the trigger. By chance, he struck the second man in the neck. After that final, reflexive action, Blue slammed onto terra firma with a thud, knocking the wind out of him.

"Move a fuckin' inch and I'll end your life, shitbag," the third man materialized and shouted. He hurriedly kicked the AR-15 away from Blue. While keeping his firearm trained on Blue, he looked over at his downed partners. He gasped at the sight of his nearly headless associate.

"Br-Br-Brad... help me!"

The third man looked over at his other partner. He saw that there was a gushing hole in his neck and foamy blood around his mouth. He desperately wanted to tend to his partner's severe wound, but he had to handcuff Blue first. "Hang in there, Mitch," he urged the partner who was on the brink of dying. "Let me cuff this piece of shit first and I'll be right with you, buddy." He looked down at Blue again. His nose turned up in an instant, and his face reddened.

Although Blue was bleeding profusely from several holes, he felt like adding a hole of his own right between Blue's eyes. "You black stupid bastard," he began as he reached down and flipped Blue onto his stomach and cuffed him, "We're the FBI agents sent to locate you and fuckin' help you."

As Blue lay there dying, the man's last statement abruptly brought something back to his mind.

Blue had spoken to JuneBug briefly one time on the phone during his solo journey after leaving Bug at the hospital. But he'd forgotten about the text Bug sent shortly after he hit the road. No lie, he'd pushed the text to the back of his mind because it sickened him. He had a difficult time collecting his thoughts after he read that Bug had cut a deal with some pigs. He was all for helping Bug to whatever degree. However, he wasn't with helping Bug do the law's work because doing so was shameful to a real G like himself. Yes, he had sympathy for Bug's desperation to get his family back. But he had to draw the line somewhere. Therefore, he thought little of the text and pressed on with the mission.

Look at me now, Blue thought as his life dwindled. *I'm all shot the fuck up by the same motherfuckers my dawg made a deal with. Ain't that a bitch?*

"Fo'give me, blood. I failed ya," Blue muttered softly. "But at least I'll fo'eva be rememba'd fo' takin' four pigs out wit me." He then cackled like a lunatic. His demented laughing soon led to him hacking up blobs of blood. He continued cracking up and coughing up blood until he expired.

Blue happily lived by the gun… And happily died by the gun.

Chapter 16

December 23, 2011/6:37am/Coles County Memorial Airport, IL

"...I'm past desperate right now and depending on you because time is of the essence," Agent Lane said testily. "...I'm giving you a hard time because I don't see why calling AG Eric Holder and asking him to have all news media to sit on this for a day is so impossible... As if I care that he's new to his post. Only he has the authority to issue the nationwide gag order I require this second. Hell, I'll settle for him having the media omit certain details from their report... That's right. Murray's also harassing his supervisor to reach out to the Secretary of Homeland Security to do the same as we speak. Two heads working on this should get through and pull it off..." *Sigh of frustration.* "You've never known me to beg and pray, director, but I'm praying and begging you to do this for me ASAP. It'll prevent this joint case from going belly up..." *Sigh of relief.* "Was that so hard? Thank you. I know you'll get this done before seven because you're the greatest... Yes, I know. I owe you big time. And good morning by the way."

Feeling prouder than Mother Mary, Lane ended her call with the CIA director with a faint smile. Agents Murray and Lane and Junebug had arrived at the small airport via a Cessna 182 ten minutes ago. Before they left Oklahoma City, the agents calculated where Blue would stop for his ten-hour break if he couldn't be located on the road. They wanted to get Bug back in the truck pronto so they could move forward with their planning. Close to the end of the four-hour direct flight, though, they learned about Blue's rampage. As soon as they landed, the agents began making high-level calls.

The unexpected turn of events left both Lane and Murray scrambling for a quick fix. They were worried that the debacle would be broadcast on every news channel in America this morning, ruining what they had planned. If they got the band-aid they urgently requested from their superiors, they could resume. Of course, they'd have to go forward at breakneck speed. But the risk would be worth it. If they didn't receive the help they'd asked for, however, the fallout from mishandling the multi-agency case could cause them both to be demoted or, worse, pink-slipped.

Lane was confident that they'd get what they sought. Often, she threw her weight around to get what she needed, anyway. With no margin for future errors, Lane, a fussy woman by nature, was now paying excessively close attention to all that was connected to the case. Until this shit-show was over, she was triple-checking everything. She was prepared to take whatever steps were necessary to prevent a complete failure. She aimed to keep her boss happy by any means.

"Are you sure the container is secured?" Lane asked Murray as soon as he reappeared.

Murray hadn't known Lane that long, but he had become irritated by her commanding ways. "You're not in charge, annoying bitch," he whispered to himself. Then, aloud, he responded to her. "For the third time, yes. It was moved off site immediately and placed in a safe, secure location. And before you ask again, the agents safeguarding it have been instructed to not tamper with its contents."

"Did your supervisor, Haverty, budge this morning?" Lane fired off the next question.

"He's more than likely on the phone with Janet Napolitano, and she'll call Eric Holder at once. I have a lot of faith in my colleagues. They'll get the job done."

"Okay. Now what about—"

"A chopper pilot was recommended to us, and he said he'll fly us to the nearest major airport, which is Decatur. He's fueling up now. We'll be set to take off in the next ten minutes or so."

All of what Lane just heard was sweet music to her ears. "Great. Is the lowlife ready to go?"

"He's still in the restroom. That laxative is still at work. And the news about Mr. Erickson has made him extremely queasy."

Lane sneered. She hated all levels of criminals. But she particularly hated those like JuneBug: a puppy playing with the big dogs. She was in the business of taking down kingpins, not lending a helping hand to a small-timer. She couldn't harbor any empathy for lawbreakers. Therefore, she didn't feel bad in the least about Blue's untimely demise or JuneBug's kidnapped family. She deduced that Blue would still be alive, and Bug's family would be home safe if they hadn't been involved in lawlessness. And, quite honestly, she wouldn't lose a wink of sleep if Bug's *innocent* family got killed. All she cared about now was collaring whoever was in charge at the predetermined delivery spot with JuneBug's help.

"Did he call or get a call from Adrian Mendoza lately?"

"He said he last spoke to him right before we left Oklahoma City. When he exits the restroom, I'll tell him to call Mendoza. We'll find out then if Mendoza is aware of what has happened."

"More importantly, we'll find out if our communications tech has properly hacked his satellite phone in the little time that he had. We need his true whereabouts falsified for the last few hours until we get him back in that truck." *Pause.* "He has to get moving right now."

As if on cue, JuneBug popped up. He wore a long face.

"Call Mendoza," Lane barked unsympathetically. "Let him know you'll be joining your accomplice soon and that everything is going as planned. Then fulfill your obligation. Or the next flight you'll catch will be on Con Air." She subsequently stomped off. She had to start building up her unit for Bug's arrival in Buffalo... and his ensuing, fateful ending.

"Maaannn, this bitch... I swear on my momma I'ma cuss that dog ass hoe out da next time she disrespects me."

"Don't mind her, Mr. Stubbford," Murray advised, although he'd revel in seeing JuneBug challenge Lane's mean-spirited arrogance. "Make the call so we can, one, get you back to that container and on the road ASAP and, two, pinpoint Mendoza's location. Remember, your family is depending on you."

Bug didn't need to be reminded of that, but it instantly moved him to action. He took the re-engineered satellite phone out of his shoulder bag. "Did ya contact my P.O. Vickers yet?" he asked before calling Adrian. "He been on my ass threatenin' me in da worst way becuz I told him I had ta tweak my travel plan a lil' bit. He said if I don't make it home as scheduled... Put it this way, he talkin' 'bout doin' me way worse than what that bitch Lane said she gonna do ta me. I told him ta expect a call from someone important that'll explain why my itinerary changed."

"I'll contact him as soon as I land in Orlando. Now make the call and let's be off. We have agents standing by waiting for you in the parking lot. They'll take you to the container and the truck you're driving, and you all will drive in a convoy to Buffalo. Soon, all will be behind you. Just don't lose faith."

Bug refused to give up hope. He just hoped... No, he prayed Murray tracked down his family and rescued them sooner than soon.

"Tell me you'll find my family and save them," Bug implored, looking into Murray's warm baby blues.

Unlike Lane, Murray somehow felt pity for JuneBug. He, too, couldn't stand lawbreakers. But when a minor player like Dayvan Stubbford got their loved ones entangled in their illegal affairs, he exerted himself trying to help the innocent. He was innately interested in the safety of the righteous.

"No promises, but I'll do my best," Murray replied, locking onto Bug's sorrowful gaze as he prepared to place the call to Adrian Mendoza.

***

Moments later, in the Isleworth community in Orlando…

"…Well, because your family's well-being rests in your hands, I hope you don't experience anymore setbacks… Good. No more stopping means you'll get there earlier. And the earlier the better… Now, before we disconnect, this will be the last check-in call. You should know by now that your family is good. I'll call you once I've seen you've arrived… Okay, my friend."

Adrian ended that call and immediately got on his cellphone.

"El Hijo del Diablo, your target is en route. He should be there approximately eleven hours from now… You have a blank check, so, yes, doing it up there would be perfect. You're a clever and instinctual killer, so I'm sure you'll pull it off with ease… Ha. You're quick. The catch is, you're still a wanted man here in America. I don't think it's wise for you to be travelling about. You could spend all the money you want but you still could compromise your identity. If it were me, I'd save myself money and a headache by remaining in the area and wait for him to return home, then stick it to him. But ultimately, the choice is yours… Good choice, my friend. I see you've learned how to play chess. Patience. Foresight. Checkmate… We'll play one day. Now, I'll keep you posted… Sure. What's your favor...? That's fine with me. In fact, I'm glad you asked. You coming to relieve us will allow me to get back to my order of business in Dade County. I'll text you the address."

**

Occurring at the same time in St. Petersburg, Russia…
"Vas attending this meeting in person necessary? I vas very cozy in Barbados."

"*Da,* Vlad, this is important," Yuri Komarov replied to his comrade before scanning the patriotic faces seated around the ornate hardwood table. "I vanted to inform you all face-to-face about the minor interruption vee are encountering in America."

Yuri wittingly assembled his cabal in Russia's second largest city, situated about four hundred miles northwest of Moscow at the head of the Gulf of Finland. With a population of nearly five million, and an average December temperature of about twenty degrees fahrenheit, this ordinarily bustling port city was perfect for this clandestine session.

In attendance were Vladimir Moussorgsky, Oleg Baryshnikov, Rurik Karamzin, Aleksei Lvov, Leonid Yeltzin, and Yuri, the chairman of the secret group. These chosen men had colluded with Yuri for more than a decade. They were all either ex-KGB, producers of raw materials, or related to one of the leaders of the USSR from generations past. Self-made or bequeathed, each man was a billionaire. They were a visionary oligarchic group that managed numerous enterprises together. And they carried a grudge. They all had a bone to pick with the United States of America for past transgressions perpetrated upon their Mother Russia and the current sanctions levied against them.

Yuri liked to credit his outfit's growth to his ability to pull off a hard sell. However, the trust that quickly developed within the group was what truly laid the foundation for their prosperity. Yuri made sure that trust, not just patriotism, was their guiding principle, because a strong foundation kept the house from toppling. So, Yuri was befuddled when the most reserved member of the group recently began asking him a lot of questions during their special sessions about their cached currency and cloaked financial accounts. That humble associate seemed to be fishing for something, and Yuri had yet to figure out what that something could be. Initially, the questioning didn't seem out of the ordinary. He merely thought the group had finally touched on something that really interested the man. When he was asked the same line of questions at the last council meeting, though, he wondered if his leadership was being questioned. He hoped that wasn't the case because he didn't want to deal with a mutiny inside of his group... at least not at this crucial period.

With their container now missing, Yuri suspected that the member's abrupt inquisitiveness might somehow be behind it. Yuri inconspicuously watched his associate's face for a few seconds before he finally addressed the group. He searched for any condemning sign. He thought he detected a smug look that exposed the truth and made a mental note of it.

Maintaining his usual even disposition, Yuri began speaking to his comrades. He opened with the theft of their container. The stark news caused some members' eyes to widen and glare with shock. Before they could besiege him with legitimate questions, he continued by assuring them that their subordinates were on top of it. He purposely left out the unsettling parts of what was happening since he controlled the narrative. In his view, the others needed to know that the container with their drugs had been taken. He felt they didn't need to know the FBI and Homeland Security were onto it all.

More importantly, the others don't need to know that the finishing components for my "gift" to America are on that container as well, Yuri contemplated.

"How did… whomever it vas… know vhen to steal our shipment?" asked Leonid, who was a relative of Boris Yeltsin, the first president of post-Soviet Russia.

"Da, how could this happen?" inquired Rurik, the most intrepid of the group. "Did you not put homing devices in all shipments after first theft?"

Yuri slumped in his chair slightly. His distinctive Cro-Magnon facial features hardened as if he'd eaten something rotten. "There v*as* a homing device in the shipment. But it either malfunctioned or vas detected and deactivated. Still, I sense Sergei Glinka is to blame." With that statement, most of their facial expressions matched Yuri's. Inwardly, they, too, feared Glinka was to blame.

Sergei Glinka was a former Russian intelligence officer. His grandfather was a member of SMERSH, a short-lived Soviet-era counterintelligence unit renowned for its brutal tactics. He defected and resettled in the USA in 1998. Ever since then, he'd helped U.S. intelligence agencies track the dealings of shady Russians that harbored ill intent for America, especially those that had the means to act on their inclinations. He used secret contacts in Russia that relayed classified intel to him. How his operatives came by the inside information had yet to be revealed. And the unsuccessful attempts to assassinate him on U.S. soil only made him work harder on taking down his former countrymen.

"Is our money safe still?" Oleg, their newly inquisitive peer, wanted to know.

Ugh, not this routine again, Yuri thought as a hint of hatred flashed over his ugly face. *If he follows up this question with the same ones he's already asked, then he's definitely up to something dubious.*

Yuri wanted to ignore Oleg. Better yet, he wanted to throttle Oleg until Oleg confessed the true reasons for his probing and repetitive questions. Nevertheless, he remained diplomatic and despotic. He needed to stay above suspicion for the others. *I only have to keep them in line a little while longer, then I'm one step closer to becoming the biggest arms dealer in the world,* he said to himself.

Yuri smiled at the prospect. *"Da,* our dark money is still safe," he finally responded to Oleg. "According to my contacts, the American government has yet to detect our shell companies."

"That's good," Rurik said.

"Da, but today is the day vee finally discuss transferring our money to other shell companies or into several offshore accounts, like in Panama or Cyprus," Oleg proceeded. "No more putting this issue off."

Oleg had brought up moving their dirty U.S. currency elsewhere the last two meetings. Yuri rescheduled having that discussion both times because, in truth, he'd borrowed and spent their money without their consent. He'd bought troves of weapons, some of which were capable of mass destruction, to sell illegally, mainly to countries embargoed by the United Nations.

Hoping to put this issue off once more, Yuri looked around the table at the others. It was vital that he kept them focused on the small picture. "Brothers, you have nothing to fear. I assure you all that our twenty billion dollars is safe. My contacts vill inform me ASAP if othervise. Continue to trust me, brothers. I promise you all that vee vill become absolute rulers in the underworld thanks to our krokodil. Remember, the deadlier the drug, the more it's vanted. And due to that reality, nothing vill deter our plan, brothers."

"If the American government intercepts our container, unlike the metric ton of krokodil that vas seized last time, the *ten* metric tons in *this* shipment vill cause them to investigate thoroughly," Oleg insisted. "Who knows vhat that investigation vill uncover. So, I say damn your contacts and vee move the money now before it's too late."

Yuri regarded the others with a faint smile before speaking. "Besides Oleg here, does anyone else vant to move our money? *But,* before you all answer, I vant you to know that moving that much money all at once vill surely cause an investigation by the Americans. Now, vhat say you?"

The men looked at each other for a few moments. Nobody said anything in the end, for Yuri had never misled them.

Oleg frowned.

Yuri grinned, however. "Good."

They then talked about scaling up their production of krokodil should everything fall back into place, followed by new methods of smuggling it into America, and ended their agenda with the settlement of minor issues. Afterwards, Yuri asked if anyone had a matter for discussion before they broke up and returned to their warm-weather habitations.

"Yes," the tycoon Aleksei spoke up. "There's something I'm curious about."

"Vhat is it?" Yuri replied.

"Is my new three hundred ninety million dollar, three hundred thirty-five-foot vessel the most luxurious in our yacht club now? It has a helipad, big swimming pool, and two bowling lanes."

The quirky inquiry sparked a frivolous debate among them. All the while, Yuri leered at Oleg. *It is imperative that I find out why he's inquiring about our money,* he said to himself. *I need just a little more time to achieve my vision. I need that container.*

Chapter 17

December 23, 2011/ 6:58am/ Orlando, FL

Surprisingly, the wish she'd asked for had been granted. But now what?

"Here we are," RahRah whispered to Devon shortly after they were invited into the two-story home in the upper-class community of Isleworth. As they kept in step behind Bizzy and a well-built Latin guy, his low voice imparted how ready he was to set it off when he said, "What's da play, chief?"

Devon didn't respond. She still hadn't figured that out.

Realistically, she couldn't have planned for this since she didn't know exactly what they'd be walking into. She had no choice but to wait and see what they were up against first before drumming up a plan. Now that she was on site, the first thing she had to do was take a head count.

"My, my, my, you've changed quite a bit since we first met over a year ago. You resemble your father even more now than you did back then," Adrian stated, descending the stairs. "I miss my dear friend, Demetrius." He sighed. "I'm pleased to see you again, Señor Bizzy."

"It's good seein' ya, too," Bizzy replied as he shook Adrian's hand for the second time ever.

Though they'd developed somewhat of a rapport over the past eighteen months through several important phone calls, their introductory meeting in Miami Beach was an occasion Bizzy would never forget. He was in the process of resurrecting RBF when Adrian unexpectedly contacted him and requested that they meet. He knew diddly-squat about Adrian at that time, yet he decided to meet him because he suspected that Adrian would have something significant for him. That something ended up being a small package, and its contents were things that he was grateful Adrian had given him. Thereafter, in his book, Adrian became a reliable associate. As for reciprocation, Adrian only accepted Bizzy after Cesar had vouched for him.

"If my memory serves me correct, you said your sister and *compañero* would be accompanying you, my friend," Adrian said, looking at the people behind Bizzy. "Where's your sister?"

Bizzy turned a bit and brought Devon forward with his arm around her shoulder. "This is my sister, Devon."

"Wow. She... she must be confused for a man all the time," Adrian said to Bizzy before addressing Devon. "Have you ever been mistaken for a man? I'm sure you have."

Devon flippantly replied, "Naw. Have you, tho'?"

The cheap shot didn't fly over Adrian's head. He wasn't an easily offended type of guy, so he laughed at her clever comeback. "I don't know why but I've always liked those who hit back with subtle disrespect." He laughed some more. "Well, I apologize if I've insulted you, Devon."

"Er'thang fifty-four."

"I take it that means all's forgiven." Adrian then eyed the person next to Devon, who was unmistakenly a man. "What's your name, my friend?"

"RahRah," he said while stepping forward fearlessly.

Following the awkward introductions, Adrian asked Bizzy to go with him to the kitchen for a private chat. Once there, he didn't dilly-dally. He summarily laid out the two rules of the house. His first, and most important, rule was that no harm was to befall JuneBug's family unless he personally authorized it. And rule number two was to do nothing that would draw unwanted attention to his home away from home. Bizzy didn't object. He gave Adrian his word that he'd abide by his simple rules.

Adrian moved on. "I already know the answer to this question I'm about to ask but I must ask anyway, my friend," he said with a serious visage. "Do you trust them?"

Bizzy needn't ask who *them* were. "They wouldn't be here if I didn't," he asserted.

Chilling silence ensued.

"Very well then," Adrian finally said.

"Ai'ight. Now I need ta ask you what do I do if ya call an' tell me ta off 'em?"

"I don't want you to kill them here, that's for sure. So, if I call and give you the kill order, you tell the young lady that her husband came through and she and her kids are free. You'll then tell her that you'll chauffeur them home. You'll get them in the SUV that's parked in the garage, engage the child safety locks, and... Well, what you do with them once they're out of here is up to you, El Hijo del Diablo. Just make them disappear forever." He winked.

"What I'd prefer ta do is kill two birds wit one stone," Bizzy said.

"What do you mean, my friend?"

"Once you lemme know when JuneBug is back in town, you'll tell him to retrieve his family at da place I choose. I'm gonna make that fuck nigga watch me kill his family befo' I chop them all into gator bait." *Pause.* "Man, ya made my day when ya said ya got that nigga family."

"I'll let you know when JuneBug arrives in Orlando, and I'll do as you said. Once again, just make sure they disappear forever."

"I got'cha."

"Okay, before I leave now to head back down south, do you want one or both of my men to stay behind? I can install them outside as sentinels until this is all over."

"That ain't necessary. I got this."

"I know you do, my friend. Cesar speaks highly of you." Adrian patted Bizzy on his back. "See you sooner or later. And at that time, we will see if you've learned how to play chess."

"I'll checkmate you in six moves."

"In your dreams, my friend."

They laughed mutually.

Once Adrian exited the house with two men and two women, Bizzy said, "It's just da three of us now. Let's go check on da hostages."

Devon frowned when Bizzy referred to Bug's family as hostages. Nevertheless, she was thrilled Adrian had left with all his personnel. She could now explore the spacious house without looking suspicious.

They marched upstairs. At the top, they realized they could either go left or right. They looked and saw all the doors in the hallway to their left were wide open. To their right, at the end of a short hallway, was a single door that was shut. Common sense prompted them to head toward the closed door, which was likely to be the master bedroom. Bizzy opened the door without announcement, and they immediately sighted a woman huddled on a massive bed with a baby and two boys on the floor in front of a big flat screen playing an Xbox 360.

The new faces at the bedroom door struck Shella with blind fear. Still, her reflexes moved her to sit up and scoop the baby off the bed and hold it close. With a faint heart, she asked, "Who are you?"

"We're da new babysittas," Bizzy responded sarcastically, walking into the cavernous room. His size and intimidating voice caused the boys to drop what they were doing and scramble onto the bed with their mother. "We're just checkin' y'all out ta see what condition y'all in." He took a few seconds to give them a visual examination. "Y'all seem ta be in good health, an' y'all will stay like that if y'all stay in line. If y'all decide ta take me fo' a fool an' make a scene or try ta run off on my watch, tho', I won't hesitate ta… Let's just say it won't be pretty. Now stick ta da protocol by doin' what y'all been doin' an er'thang will be fine an' dandy. Ya hear me?"

Shella didn't procrastinate. She nodded in compliance.

"Bet." Bizzy smiled comically, then he turned to Devon and RahRah, who were both standing just inside of the room's doorway. "Watch 'em fo' a sec while I confirm that da house is locked tite." He slid past them.

Devon moved towards the bed. She glimpsed at Shella and the boys. However, she honed in on the adorable baby with frizzy locks in Shella's arms. Devon took a shot at the infant's age; she guessed the baby was no more than six months old. The baby girl looked nothing like Rhapsody to her. But she did notice that the child had inherited Rhapsody's Hershey-chocolate skin tone.

"What's y'all names?" Devon asked, trying to ease the tension in the room. "My name is… Call me Dee."

Shella turned away slightly in a futile attempt to shield the baby and kept silent.

"Look, whetha you believe it or not, I'm not here ta hurt y'all," Devon said, getting straight to the point. "I'm here ta… ta take good care of y'all."

Shella remained apprehensive, of course. How could she believe this person named Dee when she felt like she was stuck in a recurring nightmare?

"What's her name?" Devon asked as she stood next to the bed.

Although Devon's tone was the friendliest she'd heard since this all began, Shella's guard stayed in its place. But she meekly said, "Daylonna."

"That's unique. Does she have a nickname yet?"

Though she considered the question to be strange, Shella said, "Ummm… My oldest son calls her Tootsie."

Devon smiled. "She sho' does look like those lil' chocolate candies." *Pause.* "Can I hold her?"

After Daylonna was briefly taken from her after they were kidnapped, Shella had declined to let anyone touch the baby thereafter. She wouldn't even allow Deuce or Trey to hold her. In the case of something threatening suddenly taking place, she wanted to be ready to protect the baby with her life.

"Please," Devon implored sweetly, just above a whisper. "I swear I won't hurt her."

Shella looked at Devon intensely. Through Devon's eyes, she didn't detect any desire to cause harm to the baby. For that reason, she slowly handed Daylonna over to Devon.

Devon gently took the little one out of Shella's trembling hands. She carefully cradled the child in her arms. She couldn't remember the last time she'd held a baby so small and precious. She instinctively rocked the content baby while Daylonna and she stared at each other. Before long, tears formed in Devon's eyes. She began to fantasize about a life she would never have, a life where she was married to a loving man with kids of their own.

"Dee, you straight?"

Devon's fantasy was interrupted by Rah. She looked at him and snuffled. "Yeah, I'm—" Her voice cracked. She cleared her throat before continuing. "I'm good." She handed the baby back to Shella and wiped her eyes with the back of her hand.

With God as my witness, I will NOT let ANYTHING happen to that little girl, Devon concluded as she walked out of the room.

***

Meanwhile, outside of the house…

"Francisco, I want you to stay here," Adrian instructed his henchman.

"Regreso para dentro de la casa?"

161

"No. Don't go back in the house. I want you to park there." He pointed to his other home directly across the street. "I want you to report back to me if you see any unusual or unexpected activity."

"Esta bien."

Chapter 18

December 23, 2011/ 8:51pm/ Buffalo, NY
"Better late than never."

That excuse was used regularly.

When JuneBug became hip to the saying, he used it every time he was late. He hardly ever got chewed out for using it, either. He felt like it couldn't be overused.

Today, Bug prayed his tardiness hadn't gotten his family killed. He tried more than a few times to contact Adrian once he knew he'd be late. But Adrian answered none of his calls. He worried more and more about Shella and his kids after each unanswered call. The mental distress also triggered shooting pains in his stomach.

JuneBug hit New York's second largest city an hour behind schedule because he had encountered sporadic snowstorms along the way. Being a rookie truck driver, driving through the stuff while constantly looking out for patches of black ice was grueling and scary. The escorting agents often instructed him to get off the road when driving conditions got treacherous, but he disregarded them. He drove slowly instead. No matter what lay ahead, be it a blizzard, tornado outbreak, or the ending of the world, he wasn't stopping. The continued wellbeing of his family propelled him forward in his sturdy Peterbilt tractor unit.

It was now dark, and the weather conditions were horrendous. The view of the majestic cityscape, especially of downtown, from I-90 was obscured by heavy lake-effect snowfall.

"I dunno how we made it, but we finally here, Fry. You can come out from unda da bed now," Bug said with a sigh of relief. He looked behind him and saw the wide-eyed puppy in the same place he'd been for last twelve hours. He knew the shootout that Blue had engaged in with law enforcement had left Fry shellshocked. He felt sorry for Fry because this situation had afficted him, too, and potentially ruined the rest of his own dog ass life. "Sorry, lil' buddy. I'ma make sho' ya live da good life when we make it home." He then retrieved the satellite phone to prepare to call Adrian again. Before he could place the call, the satellite phone rang.

"I'm here," Bug said as soon as he answered. "I mean, we here. Me an' Blue."

"You're late," Adrian said matter-of-factly.

It was the ominous tone of Adrian's voice that sent chills through Bug's body. He wasn't sure if Adrian was saying he was too late to save his family or stating the obvious.

"We got held up by da on an' off snowin'," Bug contended, remaining optimistic. "I tried ta call ta let—"

"I know, my friend. I took the bad weather into account."

Adrian's response caused Bug's apprehension to ease a little. He then got straight to it. "Where this shit goin'?"

Adrian gave Bug an address. He swiftly entered the data into the Garmin GPS device. As soon as the drop-off spot was displayed, he said, "Tell ya people I'll be there any minute now."

"Okay. Once my colleagues call and tell me all is good, I'll release your family as promised, my friend."

Bug hung up abruptly because no more needed to be said.

The next thing he did was get on the horn with one of the agents behind him. He relayed the latest to the agent. He heard the agent radio in the location to another agent, presumed to be Agent Lane. Before ending the call, he asked if Agent Murray had located his family. When he was told Murray hadn't reported back yet, he disconnected the call and got off the highway at the next exit.

***

Not too far away from Bug's I-90 exit…

Pyotr told the caller to hold on a second. He then broke the news to his fellow countryman in the driver's seat. "Viktor said the truck got off the interstate."

"Vhich direction is it heading?" asked Misha.

Pyotr went back to talking to Viktor. Seconds later, he said to Misha, "Vest."

Misha crunk up the sedan and stepped on it.

Once JuneBug hopped on a small plane in Oklahoma City with the agents seen outside of the hospital, Arkady had no choice but to call Yuri. After Yuri learned about the wrinkle, he berated Arkady, then he made a vital call of his own. Though his call was on short notice, he found out where Bug and the agents had flown to. He then ordered Arkady, Ivan and Maksim to fly to Orlando and Misha and Pyotr to fly to Buffalo.

Misha and Pyotr arrived from OKC the next afternoon. They were welcomed by a couple of local Russian mobsters. They gathered at a safe house. With no time to waste, they formulated a sufficient plan to recover the shipping container, then they mobilized to assume tactical positions and awaited JuneBug's arrival.

"Vhen did vee become cat's paws, Pyotr?" Misha blurted out, skillfully steering through the snowstorm. "Yuri used to inform us about all proceedings. Nowadays, he tells us vhat to do vithout explanation. For instance, how did he know the container vould turn up in Buffalo, out of all places? And how did he know vhare to send Arkady to find the guy's family? Doesn't that seem odd to you? Don't you think vee deserve to know the truth about how he finds out these things?"

"Quit your complaining," Pyotr retorted while inspecting his Walther PP9. "Let's face it, Misha, vee are tools. And because I know vee are tools, I don't really care to know how Yuri gets info. All I care about is getting this container back." He shrugged. "But I vill remind you that Yuri is very powerful. He knows many shakers and movers worldwide. He can find out virtually anything he vants. Now, speed up. Vee need to intercept that truck before it reaches destination. Vee also need to bevare of police. Vee vant to have the advantage by seizing the container on the road and not at the designated area."

Some minutes later, Misha came upon their collaborators. "There's Viktor and Pavel."

"And there's the truck," Pyotr said, pointing to the truck several cars ahead. He then got on the phone with Viktor. Because this was a coordinated operation, they all needed to be in their proper places when it was time to strike. They couldn't afford to mess this up. Their lives depended on them getting that shipping container back.

"Everybody in position?" Pyotr asked Viktor. "...Say vhen, okay?"

The Russian squad shadowed the truck closely. They were waiting for the golden opportunity. Less than five minutes after they were strategically arranged, the truck turned off Amherst Street and onto an unplowed side street. The blunder was fortunate for them. At last, they made their move.

But, little did they know that the two unmarked vehicles in close proximity of the eighteen wheeler would complicate their task.

***

Two miles down the road at the delivery location...

"I can't believe I'm working with *the* Stephanie Lane. This is surreal."

"Stop being a groupie, Watson."

Watson didn't stop, of course. "How are you not stoked, Lewis? She's a legend. I've heard she's psychic. She's known to bust a crook without doing a lot of legwork. She's—"

"She's coming, so pipe down," FBI Agent Lewis said.

"Okay, boys, get on the ball. It's almost showtime. The package should be here any second now," Lane announced over their secure communications channel.

Lane and two dozen other agents had the general store in Black Rock surrounded. From the "white chatter" over the comms system, she was able to discern enough about JuneBug's movements to prepare for his arrival in this largely Hispanic section of Buffalo. The outside temperature was low, but her impatience had her body heat high. She was raring to go because she needed to redeem herself for the fiasco earlier. "Are eyes still on secondary targets?"

"Roger that, subjects are visible, just barely," reported an agent. "They appear to be prepping for his arrival."

"Are all exits secured?"

"Affirmative," a second agent chimed in. "We didn't have adequate time to do recon but all visible escape routes are marked."

"It's a swirling mess out here but our fine training and perseverance will pay off, fellas," Lane psyched up her makeshift team. "After we've bagged these scumbags, we'll celebrate and formally get acquainted with each other in Buffalo's finest titty bar. Those of you who have better halves, they don't have to know. How about it?"

"As long as everything is on you, I'll gladly go back home to the missus covered in wet glitter and smelling like a two-dollar hooker," a third agent avowed over comms.

Although it was soon to be no laughing matter, imagining the team that she'd frantically whipped up at the last minute chuckling at the remark, like the guys next to her were, brought a rare smile to Lane's face.

Where is this fucker? she wondered, the smile fading.

Countless shots ring out in the distance

"That sounded fairly close by," Lane professed, her heart rate escalating.

"It sure did," Agent Lewis said beside her. "A little too close for comfort, to be honest."

"Relax, guys," Agent Watson asserted. "For all we know, it's just local gangs feuding, even in this shitty weather. Think back, we were informed in advance that Buffalo is overrun with gangs battling over drug turf."

Despite what the agent just said being accurate, Lane still felt bad vibes.

Phone vibrates

Lane answered her government-issued cell phone in the blink of an eye. "Hey, were those gun—" The blood chilled in her veins. "Where are you...? Hold them off. We're coming." She then yelled over comms, "We're moving out! Our primary target is under attack! I repeat; we're moving out because our primary target is under attack!"

"I can't believe this. This is about to get ugly," Watson said before hustling toward the sound of gunfire.

"Yes, it is," Agent Lewis said, checking his firearm on the run. "I wonder why she didn't see this coming, being psychic and all."

***

Back to JuneBug…

Never to suffer would mean to have never been blessed, the proverb Bug's late grandmother often recited popped into his mind.

One untimely or tragic event after another was making Bug a believer in superstition and karma. Forgotten in a flash were the countless days he rode on the gravy train. The beat-up SUV he'd just T-boned came out of nowhere. Visibility was poor but his intuition told him that the vehicle intentionally ran the light at the empty intersection. The two four-door automobiles that fishtailed to a stop and flanked him in an eyewink verified his feeling: He was being ambushed.

Thinking quickly and assessing the situation, Bug, uninjured in the collision, dove into the back of the cab. A second or two later, the mysterious assailants opened fire on his semi. Under different circumstances, he would've defended his life with an ill-gotten weapon. Instead, because he was unarmed, he grabbed Fry in an effort to protect the pup. *Where are those fucking agents?* he wondered.

Another second or two elapsed before Bug had a flashback. The deafening gunfire sounded like the night he was shot. It felt like he was reliving that night again. He began to tremble in unison with Fry. Despite being shook up, and the blasting sounding like it wasn't going to end soon, he remained attentive to the running battle outside the cab. *Whoever these foreign sounding motherfuckers are, it sounds like the police got them tied up now,* he deduced after realizing the cab of the sturdy tractor-trailer wasn't being struck as often as before. *I need them to keep blowing at each other so I can get the fuck out of here the first chance I get.*

While paying close attention to the concentration of fire, Bug crawled to the passenger door with Fry in the crook of his elbow. He estimated that at least a hundred rounds had been fired thus far. When he heard the gunshots letting up, he opened the door and listened for his opportunity to run for it. The moment the volume of shots decreased to his liking he jumped out of the cab with Fry in his arm like a football.

Satellite phone rings

JuneBug clearly heard the phone. There was no way he was turning around to go get it, regardless of what was at stake.

As Bug bolted, the shots suddenly multiplied, indirectly letting him know that he'd been spotted. Bullets whirred past him, kicking up snow around his feet. But, no matter what, he wasn't going to stop making tracks in the two-feet deep snow. He was determined to not feel the burn of hot lead tonight, so he tapped into his inner Usain Bolt and tried to run faster than the cold fifty-mile-per-hour wind was blowing. Not once did he lose his footing or look over his shoulder. The bursts of gunfire soon sounded like they were miles away. As soon as he felt he was a safe distance from the battle zone, he transitioned from running to speed walking. His thoughts, however, were still sprinting.

Bug made it out of there in one piece. But he couldn't count his blessings just yet. He was now lost. He was freezing and assed-out in an unfamiliar city. He had no money, no means of transportation, no friends, no family or affiliates in the area. And, perhaps most importantly, no way to directly contact Agent Murray to extract him from this predicament.

Bug's eyes became misty as he walked aimlessly. The biting breeze wasn't the cause of him becoming teary-eyed. He'd just about reached his breaking point. He was mentally torn up and physically exhausted by the succession of events that had gone awry. The once clear mental picture of his family was now fading into darkness. He had failed them, and that was the bottom line.

Low in spirit, with the temperature plunging, Bug bundled Fry up inside of his hoodie. He flipped the hood onto his tilted-down head and walked heavily in the convenient shadows. He was on the lookout for any safe shelter or open establishment to orient himself. He was also watchful for the presence of police. He might be in despair, but he couldn't afford being locked up right now. He pondered the futility of searching for a ray of hope during a blizzard. *If things don't get better from this point forward, me and my family are doomed,* he concluded.

"Yo', kid!"

Maaannn, it looks like karma ain't done fucking with me yet, Bug thought before trying to convince himself that all would be fine when he was actually F.I.N.E.—Freaked Out, Insecure, Neurotic, and Emotional.

"Yo'! I know you hear me, son," the passenger hollered as the Buick Park Avenue rolled parallel to Bug.

Indeed, Bug had heard the passenger in the car the first time. He kept his head down, though, and picked up his pace, on the brink of striking out like lightning.

The car pulled over just ahead of Bug. He stopped walking. He shifted, getting ready to run.

"Yo', you need to get in this car, kid, if you tryin' not to get bagged." The passenger stuck a blaring police scanner out of the window. "You hear that. You're a fugitive, and them boyz are gettin' ya description out there. We just happened to roll up on ya. So, do you want our help, son?"

This can't be another trap, Bug gathered, scrutinizing the three in the car as best he could through the falling snow. *But if they're thinking about robbing me, they'll see that it's an unlucky night for us all.*

Police sirens approaching

"Fuck that nigga, B," the driver said. "Da roads gon' be impassable soon. I'm outta here, B, befo' them people come, too."

"Wait!" Bug yelled once the car began moving. Because the police sirens were within earshot, and his sixth sense alarm hadn't gone off, he jogged toward the car. *These young* vatos *might rob and kill me, but it's a risk I must take,* he said to himself while climbing into the back seat. *Where there's a will there's a way, so I can't give up on saving my family. I must maintain a positive mindset to get through this shit.*

Chapter 19

December 23, 2011/ 11:29pm/ Orlando, FL
Question: Why are good women attracted to bad boys?

There were several acceptable answers to that question. An indefinite, quick answer was that bad boys exerted their masculinity with superior sexual performance. The most reasonable answers, however, were derived from polling women.

General studies suggest that a small number of women tend to date bad boys when they want a short-term fling. Moreover, the survey said that bad boys possessed qualities that women themselves wished they had. Women generally suppress the innate urge to exhibit their rebelliousness. The interviewed women determined that bad boys were typically fearless, aggressive, and ruthless, all of which increased their sex appeal. The truth of the matter, though, was just about all women craved someone with a rough edge, but who also had a soft side. However, being too soft is just not appealing to a significant number of women. Through the process of human evolution, roughnecks were naturally selected for their ability to protect and provide for a woman and her young.

Almost all women who have messed around with a bad boy have had their hearts ripped to shreds. Some of the brokenhearted women became addicted to the excitement and hopped from one bad boy to the next. A good many of the beleaguered women ultimately got over their bad boy infatuation and abhorred the assholes thereafter. The latter would usually go on to pursue a more stable, long-term relationship with a boring "Joe Schmoe" that will financially and mentally support them.

Brought up to be moralistic, Shella was a shining example of what a good woman should be. Her parents taught her at an early age to always be well-behaved and to shun wayward individuals, especially bad boys. By the tender age of nine, she possessed a high degree of self-worth and couldn't see herself ever being the girlfriend of someone out of her league, not in this lifetime or the next one. Thus, whenever she was approached by bad boys trying to "holla" at her, she shot them down with the cruelest words she could hurl at them – including JuneBug.

Shella had heard of JuneBug before he strutted up to her in a Jones High School hallway during her freshman year. Because the buzz about Bug was all bad, she had a narrow assessment of him. In addition to being a bonafide street nigga, she heard he was also a popular playboy. So, when he stepped to her in that crowded hallway between classes, looking and smelling like a billion bucks, she verbally attacked him on the spot. She thought the public humiliation would certainly run him off with his testicles tucked in his ass like the others before him. But what Bug did once she finished snapping sent an extraordinary sensation coursing through her body.

Rather than cussing her out for treating him like a simp, JuneBug just smiled at her. And it was that reaction that caught her totally off guard. His glimmering gold-grilled grin, as well as his pheromonal cologne, did something to her, something she'd never experienced before then. He winked at her and swaggered off without saying a word. His reaction had piqued her interest after that; she knew that she had to try him out… at any cost!

Hooking up with Bug would be dangerous, akin to playing Russian roulette. Still, she was willing to take a chance with someone who was her polar opposite. She harbored no expectation that she'd be able to change him from a bad boy to a gentleman. She just wanted to explore the electrifying feeling that Bug gave her.

Because Bug didn't go near her or look her way after the scene in the hallway, Shella set out to woo him. Even though it meant debasing her character, the campaign worked, and they hooked up just before the end of their freshman year. As expected, Bug was unapologetically himself. But he also showed her that he had a loving, kind-hearted soul. His charming, sweet ways had her sprung. She fell head over heels for him when he took her virginity. Not too long after that supremely intimate event the inevitable happened: Bug had been unfaithful.

Shella was always cognizant of what she'd signed up for. Bug often downplayed his infidelities and his activities in the streets by speaking to her with a forked tongue. She quickly became aware that he'd tell her whatever she wanted to hear just to defuse the situation at hand and keep her off his back… until he fucked up again. She appreciated that he went over and beyond to keep his personal life separate from what he had going on in the streets. Still, she complained day and night about him hanging up his player's hat. She wanted her righteous parents to meet a semi- honorable man when she finally introduced Bug to them.

Shella never got the chance for an introduction because, between then and now, she had suffered quite a few heartbreaks during their toxic "situationship." When her parents finally learned, on their own, that she was dealing with a thug, she withstood their justified criticism and toughed it out with Bug. She hoped that Bug would wake up sooner rather than later and see that she was a good woman, and not a doormat like her mother said she was. She had become the street's definition of what a good woman was, which was a helpmate that stood by her man through all the bullshit that she wouldn't have experienced herself if she'd remained single… or away from a bad boy. Looking back on her ugly, turbulent romance with JuneBug reduced her to weeping.

Devon firmly believed that ignorant people deserved what they got. However, she pitied Shella after listening to the moving story. Saving Rhapsody's baby was set in stone a day ago. The fate of Shella and her two boys hadn't been factored into the equation. Now, they were variables that would have to be part of the solution to the problem.

"Listen, girl," Devon began in an advisory tone, "you dunno me at all, but fo' some reason ya felt comfortable enuff ta vent ta me just then. You said a earful, an' I was able ta figga ya out from yo' story. Off da rip, I got da impression you were a intelligent sista. But I now recognize how wet behind da ears you are. You so green that'chu dunno you been dickmatized. An' even if you ain't been dickmatized, how do you stay in a lie of a relationship an' still love that nigga? Becuz from what'chu just told me… This is my honest opinion, by da way… After all you been through wit that triflin' nigga, this gots ta be da last straw. This gotta be da moment ya finally respect yaself enuff ta walk away. Again, this my standpoint… He neva served you, helped you grow, or made you happy. So, my recommendation is you leave him. It can be as easy as ABC. But'chu gotta be strong enuff not ta go back to him, regardless of what he says or does. You're a good woman. You can't let him walk all ova you eva again. You betta smarten up. He showed ya from da get-go he was fo' da streets. Let da streets have his ass. Y'all like water an' oil anyway. No matter what, y'all will neva mix an' grow together. Y'all ain't meant fo' each otha. You gotta wipe ya hands of him. Ya main focus should be on these kids now."

"He told me he wasn't in the game anymore," Shella uttered, her voice breaking. "He – he promised me he was goin' legit for real this time. He swore… he swore up and down that jail and his cancer scare had changed him. But—"

she broke down "—it was all a lie. I believed… I believed he finally would put me and his kids first. Instead, he put our lives in danger. Like da fool I am, I – I – I thought he changed because he loved me. I believed all his BS when I knew it was bullshit." She was crying inconsolably now.

Devon was further moved by Shella's emotional awakening. It moved her so much that she saw this occasion as her opportunity to atone for all the wrong she'd done in her life. It also moved her to clasp Shella in her arms. As Shella bawled in her embrace, Devon looked at Deuce, the baby cradled in his arms, and Trey. The ambiguous looks on their faces as they sat quietly at the foot of the bed emboldened her.

"Becuz I feel… Uhhh… I empathize wit'chu, girl," Devon proclaimed, rubbing Shella's back, "I'ma help ya. I'ma make sho' y'all make it outta here safely an' y'all gotta safe place ta go to."

Shella didn't respond. She just wept harder. She was traumatized, and had been lied to so much lately that she didn't know what or who to believe.

"I know exactly how you feel, but, girl, you gotta knock all that cryin' off right now," Devon said loud and clear. "You gotta tighten up so you can help me come up wit a exit plan. Time is run—"

"Ayo, Dee!" Bizzy interrupted, walking into the bedroom so quick it seemed rude. "I gotta—" He hit the brakes. "What da fuck goin' on in here?" he wanted to know after stumbling into the passion-charged atmosphere.

Devon scrambled off the bed and bellied up to Bizzy. "Ain't nuttin'. I was… I was…" She glanced over her shoulder at Shella before facing her confounded brother. "She knows da deadline is rite around da corner, so I'm just consolin' her, tryna keep her calm an' her mind off this bullshit. She terrified that her husband ain't gonna come through an' save them." Devon shrugged nonchalantly, hoping she was believed. "Wassup, tho'? You ran up in here like it's about ta go down."

Bizzy didn't know Devon's ways intimately. Yet, he knew her well enough to know that she was acting strangely. Side-eyeing her, he said somewhat warily, "Lemme holla at'chu real quick." He nodded in the direction of the hallway. Once there, he added, "I got da call."

"Ta let 'em go?" Devon blurted out, sounding more delighted than she'd liked.

Bizzy also picked up on the unusual happiness in her response. "Naw," he retorted. His answer almost threw Devon into a panic.

Devon was ready to go back on her word and object to the next course of action. But she caught sight of the long-slide Glock 34 dangling by Bizzy's side. Seeing that not only caused her to bite her tongue, but it also intimidated her. The detached look in his eyes scared her even more, though. *Fuck, it looks like I done ran out of time,* she thought while playing it as cool as possible. *There must be something I can do to buy me some time to whip up a sketchy yet doable plan.*

"Well... Do ya need me ta do anythang?" Devon asked, feigning to be a team player.

"Yeah. Since it's evident you all buddy-buddy wit that bitch in there, tell her they been spared. Then, get 'em in da SUV in da garage. Continue ta small talk wit da bitch ta keep her unsuspectin' of what's really in play fo' 'em. I'll be there shortly."

"Ai'ight. But if you don't mind me askin', what's really in play fo' 'em?"

"You ain't gotta worry 'bout that. You an' RahRah can go home once I leave here wit 'em."

"Ya sho' ya don't need our help? Ya gon' have ya hands full wit four people," Devon said, trying to worm herself into Bizzy's plan for Shella and the kids.

"I done killed a four-hundred-pound muthafucka recently an' had ta dispose of his fat ass body. So, I think I can handle a woman an' three kids." Bizzy grinned like the Grinch. "Anywayz, after I was done takin' care of them, I was gonna go visit G-Ma befo' I went back overseas. I think it would make her Christmas if she saw both of us. What do—"

At that moment, both Bizzy and Devon heard an all too familiar sound. They might've been miles away from the nearest ghetto but there was no mistaking that sound, even if it was faint.

Sensing danger on the horizon, Bizzy shot down the stairs. Midway, he collided with RahRah.

"I was just on my way up ta tell ya that sumone let off a round nearby," Rah said, his chest heaving slightly from loss of breath.

"I heard it. Now come wit me. Let's check da scene out. Devon, you stay wit them."

Side by side, Bizzy and Rah quickly went to investigate the situation.

Devon gladly did as she was told. She hustled back into the bedroom and locked the door. She then untucked her .380. Until her brothers declared that the coast was clear, she was going to hunker down and defend every life in the room, if necessary.

"Was that a gunshot I heard?" asked Shella, visibly overcome with fear.

Trying not to overreact, but knowing she would fail in the attempt, Devon said as calm as possible, "Er'body get in da closet. Now!"

***

"That vas foolish… Very foolish of you."

"*Nyet,* having only one watchman outside vas very foolish of them."

"*Da.* But you still should have let me shoot him vith silenced gun. Maybe you give them heads-up now. Also, someone maybe call police."

"Then vee need to get moving." The Russian shrugged.

"Hold it down, you two," Arkady told his comrades, Maksim and Ivan, after they had expeditiously placed the big Latino in the trunk of his own car. "Vee don't know if guards inside heard gunshot. Hopefully, they didn't, and vee still have element of surprise."

Saying no more, the stalwart trio marched toward the house across the street. The porch light was on, as well as a few interior lights, but that didn't give them pause. They had specific orders. And they were going to do whatever was necessary to carry them out.

"Remember, not a scratch on the family. Yuri said they could be of use later," Arkady said as they narrowed the gap between them and the house. "Maksim, go to back of house. No one escapes. Yuri vill not tolerate us letting family slip away."

Maksim nodded with a shrouded smile. He hoped that someone – anyone – would attempt to run off because it would give him a reason to shoot to kill. Besides, he knew that Yuri only wanted the family alive because they could be sold to forced labor or sex traffickers.

As the battle-scarred Maksim broke off from the others, the porch light went out and the interior dimmed suddenly.

"Hurry, Maksim. I think vee been spotted."

Maksim scurried around a corner to the rear of the house.

Arkady and Ivan dashed to the front door. Ivan, compact and powerful like a bull terrier, immediately smashed his heavy-duty combat boot into the hardwood door. Having done this many times before, one kick was all it took to bash in the robust door. Crouching low, the specialized duo slipped into the house. The home wasn't completely devoid of light. It wouldn't have mattered to them if it was pitch-black because they were professional killers, trained to target the slightest of movements, the faintest of sounds, and the scantiest of scents. It also didn't matter if they were outnumbered because their elite skills gave them the upper hand. To date, they'd never been outmatched.

With their senses heightened, they advanced together in silence. They used hand signals to communicate. In under two minutes, they cleared the first floor. They then went to the back door and let Maksim in. Disregarding the glaring expression of displeasure on Maksim's mug, Arkady made more gestures with his hand. Once Maksim and Ivan acknowledged his wordless commands with nods, Arkady proceeded up the stairs alone. Maksim and Ivan stood pat; their handguns aimed at different points out ahead of Arkady's path.

Nearing the top, Arkady simultaneously detected a slight shift in the shadows and a faint noise.

All at once, the muzzles of multiple guns flashed.

Arkady pulled back. His comrades returned controlled fire as he did so. Once he made it back down the stairs in one piece, they ceased firing to preserve ammo. He took cover alongside Ivan behind a wall. A few seconds later, the enemy ceased firing. Arkady presumed the opposition was reloading. He snapped his finger to get his comrades' attention. He held up two fingers before pointing upstairs, indicating that there were two shooters.

It was three against two. The odds were heavily in their favor. It was truly impossible, and quite laughable, to think that their reckless foes, proven by their erratic shooting, would prevail in this game of death.

Presumably dealing with amateurs, Arkady deduced that the opposition couldn't exchange ammo clips smoothly, so he gave the signal for them to strike. They sprinted upstairs. And like Arkady had theorized, they caught the two... niggas...? scrambling in their attempt to reload. Mercilessly, Arkady opened fire, prompting Maksim and Ivan to follow suit. After a total of seventeen bullets had been shot, Arkady waved for them to stop.

Firearms still aimed, they stared at the fallen men for a few seconds. When there was no movement or sound, they lowered their weapons slightly. Arkady looked at his watch. There wasn't much time to spare, so he ordered Maksim to inspect the room down the hallway. He directed Ivan to check out another room. He stood guard by the stairs until they finished. When they reconvened, he pointed at the last door. In step with one another, they proceeded toward what had to be the master bedroom. As they got closer, their sharp hearing picked up faint noises beyond the door. They put their backs to the wall and moved along it until they reached the door.

A baby crying could be heard.

Then, they heard someone say, "Please, you gotta shut her up or she's gonna get us all killed."

One, maybe two, left to eliminate, Arkady thought as he signaled his comrades, getting them into position to blitz the room. *We must hurry because the police will be here soon.*

Arkady then held up three fingers. He was telling the others that in three seconds they were going.

Two fingers.

One.

Once more, Ivan put his durable leg and foot to work. His effort sent the flimsy door flying off its hinges.

The universe there upon moved in slow-mo.

Boc Boc Boc Boc Boc Boc

Chapter 20

December 25, 2011/ 7:18am/ Orlando, FL
CHRISTMAS. It came but once a year.

For most Americans, the commemoration of the birth of Christ was, by far, the most awaited holiday of the year. It was a day of merriment and feasting and gift-giving with family and friends. For many people, their best and most lasting memories occurred on that day.

Surely, this Christmas would be an unforgettable one for JuneBug and his family. Despite all that had transpired the last few days, Bug was still confident, albeit marginally, that he'd be able to salvage this year's Christmas story. But first, he had to act fast.

Travelling from Buffalo to Orlando in twenty-four hours without identification or cash, and with a frightened puppy in tow, was a challenging task for anybody. Nevertheless, given the position he was in, Bug made the impossible possible. The lengths he went to reach Orlando was enough to impress the Impossible Mission Force.

To begin with, Bug's intrepid *vato* lifesavers whisked him and Fry off to a nearby dope house. There, his benefactors provided everything they could to help him, such as a change of clothes, about a thousand dollars in cash, and a disposable phone.

Bug immediately cast aside the idea of calling the cellphone number he retained for Adrian on the chance that Adrian hadn't heard what went down in Buffalo yet. He had half a mind to call Agent Murray for help, but decided against it because he couldn't be sure if Agent Lane would credit him with the debacle in Buffalo or not. Besides, he relied on the agents too much already and look where that had got him.

JuneBug went on social media instead. He scrolled through it until he found Lipps, an old acquaintance from his brief stay in Nashville that owed him a favor from their past dealings

Lipps was resourceful and well-connected with a reputation in the streets for making things happen. So, once he understood the gravity of Bug's situation, he pulled quite a few strings and arranged for Bug and Fry to be discreetly transported to Orlando. And although his assistance would've caused Bug to be indebted to him indefinitely, he chose to do it all on the house, for he sympathized with Bug's predicament.

Instead of traditional means of travel, Lipps tapped into his elaborate network of underground contacts. He lined Bug up to be smuggled aboard a private cargo turbojet making a legitimate flight from Buffalo to Tampa Bay. He arranged to hide Bug and a sedated Fry from prying eyes among the crates and goods.

As the time ticked away on the long flight, Bug's stomach persistently aggravated him, and his heart thudded with anticipation. He knew that time wasn't on his side, and every passing second without knowing what condition his family was in was more painful than the aching in his gut. He had to navigate through the pain because, for all he knew, Shella and his kids were suffering more.

Upon reaching the home of the NFL's Buccaneers, the weight of the situation pressed down on Bug's shoulders with great force. Because his circle of trusted people had become smaller than a flyspeck, he took heed of what Lipps had said about having minimal contact with loved ones and allies. Since he required ground transportation, he had no choice but to contact his brother, Andric, to pick him up from a Denny's near the airport. On the way to Orlando, Andric peppered him with questions. He needed Andric more than ever, so he divulged everything. After his full disclosure, he begged his fallible brother, his only full-blooded sibling, to do everything he asked without questioning him and dragging his feet. He also begged Andric to not tell their mother, who was an extreme worrier and the only other person he could trust, no matter what.

Now that JuneBug was back safe in O-Town, his order of business began with Andric taking him to his townhouse in MetroWest. He needed to go there to hurriedly get some scratch, a few hand cannons and clips, his backup phone with important contacts, and his inconspicuous Honda Accord. Having those things would provide some comfort and security as he went about looking for his family.

When Bug's home-sweet-home came into view, it became clear that his buzzard luck hadn't run out. Parked in front were two cars. One of the vehicles was an OPD squad car. The other was a sedan, and it belonged to none other than Mr. Vickers.

JuneBug wasn't sure if Agent Murray had contacted Vickers, as agreed, on his behalf. Because of that uncertainty, Bug instructed Andric to cruise the city while he considered what to do next. After twenty minutes of driving around like joyriders in a stolen whip, he hadn't come up with anything. Andric was of no help, either. With hardly any wax left on the candle that was burning from both ends, he threw in the towel and Googled the Department of Homeland Security. He called the listed number and prayed.

Bug needed Agent Murray like a fish needed water. He was hoping that Murray had made some headway and was in the process of securing his family's safety.

***

December 25, 2011/ 10:37am/ Kauai, HI

When it came to double-dealing, Yuri was a cut above the rest. Before he was recognized as a prodigy for his mastery at chess, Yuri had a particular vision: To independently achieve great economic success. To most, mainly his family, his vision was nothing but a mirage. After he graduated from Moscow University, though, instead of taking over the family's successful fertilizer company, he saw his tyrannical vision realized through cronyism and shady boardroom deals, which included a lot of backbiting and backstabbing. He didn't give a damn about adhering to a standard code of values. And he certainly could care less about dishonoring his prestigious family's name while securing the future he pictured.

Driven by his ambition and desire for unequaled power, he began to dabble in the world of organized crime. Whenever Yuri saw an opening, especially a tight one, he went for it. Fortune favored his venturesome boldness because the tight openings always panned out in his favor, which moved him and his handpicked, arcane group of schemers up the ranks quicker. As he shot ahead, his deceitfulness increased. He ultimately became the embodiment of a saw-scaled viper, the deadliest of terrestrial snakes.

Yuri's dirty tricks provided the most cost-effective, time-saving methods for him to reach the top. He had no adversarial competition that he knew of, thanks to his slickness. However, his alliances were plentiful. Little did he know, though, that his snaky tactics had run their course. His bread-and-butter was finally about to bring his world crashing down on his head, all at once.

"Aloha. Welcome to a place that doesn't exist. I've dubbed it 'The Lair.'"

Following their customary handshake, Yuri turned around and took a few seconds to take in the enchanting landscape.

The view in every direction from the *lanai* was Edenic. The sun shone like a halogen lamp and resembled a succulent citrus fruit. The fluffy clouds looked like clusters of cotton balls. Beyond the tropical greenery and sparkling white sand was brilliantly clear blue water as far as the eyes could see. Besides the jaw-dropping natural sights, the absence of all man-made sounds was surreal. The crashing five-foot waves less than thirty yards away; the nonstop refreshing breeze; the assortment of stirring tropical creatures; all of it gave one an extraordinary peace of mind.

"Havaii is... This... This is magnificent," Yuri said, his head swimming. "It's paradise." He then turned back around and blurted out, "Name the price. I vant this place."

Chuckling. "I can't sell it because this is technically the property of the United States government. But *mi casa* is *su casa.* Just give me a heads up and I'll let you use the place anytime you'd like. Don't get attached, though, because I won't mind forcing you off the premises." *More chuckling.* "Now, c'mon. You must see the layout inside."

They entered the stilted one-storied, low-pitched cottage. After a quick tour of the open and opulent interior, they settled down on the backyard deck. There, their eyes feasted on the best of what nature had to offer and they began to converse.

It had been six years since the last time they had met with each other. To minimize the risk of exposure, there had been hardly any communication between them in that time. But, when absolutely necessary, they had spoke briefly over the phone. Now, they were meeting face-to-face because Sergei disapproved of how Yuri's calling had become more frequent.

"I thought I'd never say this, but it's good to see your recreant face," Yuri said jokingly. "I see that living the hypocrite dream has been good to you."

"Yes, it has. Owning a social security number in a land where hypocrisy is normal has been a dream come true.

You'd love living in America. You'd fit in perfectly, just like I have."

A far cry from you, though, I'd hate conforming to stinking American customs, Yuri thought while grimacing involuntarily. *It's apparent that living amongst the greatest tricksters these past thirteen years has brainwashed you, whether you know it or not.*

"So, I anticipated this sudden meeting you ordered, Yuri. I don't have to be a rocket scientist to know you'd want to get to the bottom of the recent crises and setbacks."

Because he was always on the clock, fully committed to his endeavor, Yuri needed to know exactly why things failed to go silky smooth as intended. Moreover, he needed to know exactly who to kill to prevent any future problems from arising.

Although they were parleying while dining alfresco, the gravity of the moment weighed heavily on Yuri. His gaze drilled into Sergei's soul before he spoke. *"Da,* let's discuss vhat took place. But first, need I remind you that trust is a rare and fragile commodity, especially in this business we're involved in. That's vhy alliances like ours are integral, even if they're imperfect. Netting unimaginable profit, vhile punishing the U. S. of A. is the ultimate goal. Do vee still share that same sentiment… uncle?"

With a face now completely devoid of expression, Sergei looked intently at his brother's son. Then, in impeccable English that he'd honed over the years, he said, "I knew beforehand that being a sleeper agent with no support or lifelines would be a challenge. I knew it would require a lot of ingenuity to be accepted by wary Americans. I met that challenge because I'm a master of deception, in case you've forgotten, my finest pupil. You didn't mislead your associates, and I didn't infiltrate the federal government to put in place all the roadblocks and complications over the years just to back out now. We're trapped in this, just to be frank with you. Now, let's skip the rhetorical questions and avoid quibbling for the sake of quibbling. Air your grievances so we can brainstorm, make the necessary adjustments, and get back on schedule. By no means will we not finish what we started."

"How did this container become compromised?" Yuri forthrightly asked.

"That's a great leadoff question," Sergei professed in hushed undertones before breaking eye contact with Yuri. He looked blankly off in the distance. "To date, we've shared a great deal of info with each other, Yuri. The real-time inside info I've provided you not only kept you ahead of all law enforcement agencies in the world, making you effectively invisible, but it also made you an inerrant mastermind in the eyes of your men. And what you have provided me is helping to fulfill my obligation with the Americans to topple the secret criminal society in Russia. Thanks to each other, we're almost invincible... key word, *almost.* Although we take extreme measures when passing along info, it's within the realm of possibility that someone has intercepted one of our calls and deciphered our coded messages."

Sergei eyed Yuri again, then continued. "Now, to answer your question. Aside from the info I quickly, yet carefully, dug up and relayed to you that helped you find that family and relocate the container, the dragnet I have out there still hasn't turned up a clue. The second after I determine who orchestrated the theft, though, you'll be informed." His eyes became steely. "So, after this meeting has concluded, don't reach out to me if I don't contact you first, okay? You've called me too much recently. I have to set up another untraceable channel of communication for us."

Yuri understood.

But the thing he didn't understand was the icy look. *Is he holding me at fault for the breach in our communication?* he wondered. *I only call when I'm in a crunch, and it was crunch time when I called.*

After several unsettling seconds, Yuri went on. "Vhat came to be of our container?"

"Homeland Security is holding it on the Fort Drum military base at the moment."

"Can it be reclaimed?"

Sergei frowned. "After HLS found and identified the components with the krokodil, they looked for the individual, or individuals, that booked the shipment. When their search didn't produce an immediate result, they surmised that a dark cell of Russians in America was close to finishing a tactical weapon. That's when they consulted with me, wanting to know why I hadn't obtained any info about it. Therefore, unfortunate for us, getting our hands on that cargo will be impossible. It's a lost cause. So, we need to figure out how to get more components and how to make sure the Iranians, Iraqis, or North Koreans will be blamed for our handiwork."

Yuri's face showed signs of defeat.

Sergei's frown deepened. He was not yet defeated. "When all else fails, we don't. This is just another obstacle we'll get around. You know that Americans are shortsighted. And you also know that war is a series of catastrophes that are overcome and result in victory for the diligent."

"Bravo. But victory loves preparation," Yuri replied in Russian.

"True. But... relax. Tough luck doesn't last forever. However, tough people do, and there are none tougher than Russians. We're true soldiers. And true soldiers fight not because they hate what's in front of them – America, in our case. They fight because they love what's behind them – our Mother Russia. Our enemies will be traumatized for a long time. Their mettle will be broken beyond repair. Our time to loom over the world is nigh, for the great don't stay great, nor do the small stay small."

"Is the nuclear physicist safe still?" Yuri resumed.

"Yes. After I successfully integrated him with the other one-point-six-million expatriated Russians living in New York state, I relocated him to Memphis. He's still on standby, awaiting further orders. For now, he'll continue to pose as a struggling baker. I'm confident he isn't in danger as long as he remains under the government's radar. He's a nobody, and he'll stay a nobody if I can help it."

Yuri's expression revealed uncertainty.

"Your resemblance to my noble brother, Sasha, is incredible," Sergei said with a faint smile.

It had been nearly thirty years since Sergei last saw his brother's face, or any of his other siblings for that matter. He'd been alienated from his family when he was a teenager once it became clear to his parents that he was dead set on doing what he wanted without regard to others... just like Yuri. When he eventually learned that Yuri had also become a black sheep in the family, he immediately reached out to his nephew. There was no need to brainwash Yuri with his "death to America" propaganda, since Yuri already harbored negative feelings for America. Once in alliance, they concocted their nefarious plan and commenced to implement it.

"Yuri," Sergei added, "our plan to flood Florida's streets with our poison is squashed for the moment. But rest assured, we will crush that monkey, Obama, any day now. It will be us – your dirty money and my dirty doings – that pays sanctimonious America back for humiliating our forefathers. Our vengeful deeds will also sour relations between America and Russia and undo that preposterous treaty the spineless Dmitry Medvedev foolishly signed with the hypocrites."

A mental image of the White House being blown to smithereens tickled Yuri's ugly insides pink, causing him to grin hideously.

"It's great to see my words have put you back in a good mood," Sergei declared. "Now that I've fielded your most important questions, we need to figure out two things. You need to procure more parts for the weapon, and I need to find another way to get them into America undetected. We have a tight schedule, so we need to get busy." He paused for a second. "You have the money to take care of all of this, correct? I don't know about you, but I'm going to have to grease many palms to make this happen again."

Yuri's war chest was running on fumes. He didn't have the money to take care of everything. As of now, he only had rainy day funds. He would've had plenty of money at his disposal if the last load of krokodil hadn't been seized. He had banked on replenishing his coffer once the proceeds from selling the krokodil was divided with his secret collaborator, who facilitated the distribution of the drug within the U.S.

"Da, I'll finance everything," Yuri said just to keep Sergei from worrying.

The pair then discussed the few loose ends they needed to tie up once the weapon was operational; they never left anything to chance when so much was on the line. One of those troublesome loose ends tied itself when their expendable operatives, Arkady and the men with him, were killed in Orlando and Buffalo. Their most concerning wild card, however, was the nuclear physicist. As soon as the innovative weapon was in place and armed, they were going to kill him, too. After that, they would kick back and enjoy life somewhere tropical and watch as America collapsed.

Well, Yuri couldn't kick back until after the traitorous Oleg was dealt with. *I haven't uncovered anything that suggests Oleg is onto me,* he deduced. *But just to be on the safe side, he must be eliminated. He's replaceable.*

"Do you hear that?" Sergei said abruptly, tilting his head toward the sky.

"Hear vhat exactly?" a bewildered Yuri asked, looking skyward, too.

Sergei stood up fast. Squint-eyed, he examined the skyline closely. The low whirring sound he heard became louder. Before long he knew exactly what the distinctive sound was. It was a bird, not native but mechanical.

"Did you follow my instructions to get here?" Sergei was quick to ask.

"Carefully," Yuri countered, confused.

Then Yuri recognized what was heading toward them.

"I don't believe you. They wouldn't be here otherwise. You've betrayed us!" Sergei darted into the cottage.

I made no mistakes following his directions, so they aren't here because of me, Yuri thought as the whirring sound quickened. He got to his feet. It was at that moment he sighted the five helicopters.

"Oleg!" Yuri impulsively blurted out loud. He then scampered into the cottage because there was nowhere else to run.

Crossing the threshold, he wasn't two steps inside of the place when he came upon something that startled him. "Sergei?" he uttered, his tone filled with dread.

"We're fucked because of you," Sergei shouted, with a gun pointed at his nephew. "I had everything carefully arranged for this meeting, but you... Your carelessness will now cause us to rot in a decrepit U.S. federal penitentiary." The mere thought of imprisonment enraged him. The gun trembled in his hand as the barrel repositioned. His twitching finger applied pressure to the hair trigger. "You'll rot there. Not me!"

BLAM

The non-durable door to the cottage burst inward.

"Hands up!"

"Don't move!"

The commands were conflicting, so Yuri just remained still. He was in shock and frozen in place, anyway. His focus was on the smoking, bleeding hole in his uncle's temple when the agents seized him.

"Yuri Komarov," the agent said, getting all up in his face once he was cuffed. "You're under federal arrest for money laundering, human trafficking, murder, and conspiring to commit a terrorist act on United States soil." The agent subsequently read him his rights. "Now, get his hideous Russian ass out of here. And get a body bag for that two-faced son-of-a-bitch, shall we?"

Because Yuri was still transfixed, he had to be hauled away. He couldn't believe what was happening. With Sergei's help, he was supposed to be five steps ahead of the law. He wasn't destined for this outcome. He was destined for worldwide recognition, or so he thought. *This can't be how it ends,* he said to himself as he was loaded onto a chopper. *It WON'T end like this, I swear. Death and destruction will befall America! And Oleg will pay for all of this.*

Meanwhile, the arresting agent walked down to the beach to smoke a cigarette. As soon as they were sure they were alone, they pulled out a secured satellite phone. They placed a call while constantly surveilling their surroundings. Once the person on the other end picked up, they said, "Yuri is in custody... He's dead... It seems he shot himself just before we nailed him... INTERPOL should be picking up Yuri's conspirators as we speak. I wanted to be here personally to take down the two-headed hydra... Their assets have been seized... Agreed, we do make a great team. I'm looking forward to the next adventure you have for me... No problem. You tag 'em and I'll bag 'em." *Laughter.* "...Gracias, jefe. *Hasta luego.*"

Agent Lane ended the call. She then pocketed the satellite phone, tossed the cigarette butt, and returned to the cottage to bark orders with a beaming smile on her face.

***

Simultaneously, at a quiet location five time zones away...

"...Good. And Sergei Glinka...? Terrific. But, out of curiosity, how did he perish? In a ton of pain, I hope... He chose a coward's death, I see. So, what about the other Russians...? And their assets...? *Bien hecho.* Well done. You did great. Actually, *we* did great once again. We make a great team... Well, I should have intel on the Italian Mafia in Calabria shortly. You're going to have a very busy schedule ahead..." *Laughter.* "Anyhow, your money will be delivered to you at once. Again, great job. Now, adios..."

With a crooked smile on his suntanned face, Cesar said, "Another unsuspecting ally eliminated."

"At this rate, you'll be the largest producer of narcotics, the sole king of the drug world, sooner than expected," Adrian added.

"I must thank my old partners for my success. I wouldn't be where I am today if they lived by these words... TRUST. NOBODY. EVER! Don't you ever forget that if you wish to keep making it in this walk of life. You can't expect loyalty from anyone that commits crimes for money, *mi hijo.* Every boss *should* know that alliances in this world are short, subject to shifting loyalties and treacherous betrayals. Yuri knew this, but the prospect of collaborating with me to move his krokodil beyond Europe and Asia exposed him. Our collaboration was structured in such a way that neither of us would know the full extent of each other's operations. But he erred badly when he thought I'd slow down my dealings just to go all in on spreading that poison internationally. I took advantage of his mistake because an intelligent man can play a fool, but a fool can't play an intelligent man." Cesar winked.

Cesar couldn't help being who he was: a devious cutthroat. His father an insolent, self-centered pig and a woman beater, so his upbringing bore witness to many incidents of wanton violence.

"I understand, *padre,*" Adrian replied. "But I still think you gave that *puta* too much money this time. You should've stuck with her usual million dollars."

"She deserved what I gave her because I had to fall back on her once it became obvious my plan to poison Yuri's own people was going awry. If not for her, The Russians would've got that container back and fulfilled their mission. That would've been the cause of ruin to my most thriving enterprise. Besides, *mi hijo,* it's okay to throw your dog a big, juicy bone on occasion. It keeps them loyal."

"Again, I understand. But why give her ten million dollars?" Adrian asked, puzzled.

"I didn't give her a dime."

"Huh? You just said her money will—"

"That was some of Yuri's money... before it was seized." Cesar smiled before happily explaining. "Vicente used his great hacking skills to breach Yuri's high-level security systems. After a little game of cat-and-mouse in the virtual world, Vicente infiltrated Yuri's heavily fortified servers that guarded his wealth in multiple offshore accounts. The moment Vicente confirmed that the breach was successful, I watched the digits on the screen that represented Yuri's wealth be rerouted and diverted to my offshore accounts."

Before Adrian offered his praise for the feat, he asked, "Can't that money be traced?"

"Your brother leaves no digital trace. He's a ghost in the digital realm," Cesar bragged about his other son, a computer geek.

"Don't you think it's time to dismiss Lane? I know she's a valuable asset, but you've been using her far too long now. I think her elimination would be to your benefit."

Cesar took a few seconds to consider what his most prudent child proposed. "You're right. Once Lane delivers that rat bastard JuneBug to me, I'll send her after... Oh, let's see... I'll send her after EL Chapo next. I'll forewarn him, though, so it'll be a suicide mission for her. Her spiteful co-workers will finally get what they have wished for."

That decision settled, the father and son, whose relationship for the last two decades was primarily based on business, talked about… business, of course. One of the several matters they discussed was strengthening Cesar's paramilitary force. Cesar wanted to add to his fifty thousand guerillas, for he knew revenge was a double-edged sword. With the additional weapons he'd secretly swiped from Yuri, Cesar's forces would be heavily armed and ready for the day when karma decided to come knocking on his door.

Chapter 21

January 2, 2012/ 10:51am/ Mobile, AL

With its bayous and moss-draped oaks, Mobile was a town steeped in history... albeit a lot of it was horrendous. Even so, the down-home yet ratchet city could become a sanctuary for a few of its newest arrivals. It just might be the place where their fractured spirits were patched up. It could also be the place for them to begin anew and get on with their lives without worrying about the shadows of their past, and the demons in their closets. That was all wishful thinking, for sure.

Despite the birthplace of the original Mardi Gras festival welcoming them with open arms some days ago, Devon, Miracle and Shella still felt as if death was right around the corner from the two-story house bestowed to Devon. They knew that their most recent decisions and mistakes would leave lasting scars on their souls. Karma, that intangible force that demanded balance, had woven its threads through their lives and forever changed them... for the better? Or the worse?

Mentally, Shella was beyond just being "traumatized." She felt abandoned and soulless.

Devon and Miracle, on the other hand, weren't nearly as afflicted and disoriented as Shella. Because they'd experienced more suffering and bad breaks to date than the average person experienced in their lifetime, they were able to attempt to comfort the shell-shocked Shella. They couldn't let Shella fall to pieces, anyway, for not only were their lives on the line, but also the lives of all their kids. They needed to be on point, a strong unit, to stay alive long enough to bounce back before possibly bouncing out. Until the decision to stay in Mobile or resettle elsewhere was made, they'd be a makeshift family, one that was formed by the cruel twists of fate.

Devon just hoped that Old Lady Luck had determined to be sympathetic towards them from this point on. *Damn, big bro, you're supposed to be here with us,* she ruefully said to herself, fighting back tears. *I should've let you go home to be with your jits on Christmas.*

"What's the matter, Dee?" Kamani asked once he had entered the living room and saw Devon long-faced.

Devon had a vicious migraine. None of the over-the-counter pills she took alleviated the pain, so she really didn't want to be bothered. But she inhaled deeply and exhaled before saying, "I'm just lyin' here becuz my head hurts, bad."

Kamani wasn't dumb. He knew his second mom well enough to know when something was really weighing on her. Instead of saying anything, he approached the davenport she was lying on and hugged her tightly for a while. After the tender embrace, he let her be.

Shortly after Kamani walked out of the living room, in walked his mother, Miracle, from the kitchen. "Devon, I need to put somethin' on my stomach so I can take my med—" She broke off her statement upon seeing Devon's red, watery eyes. "You still thinkin' about RahRah, aren't ya?" she inquired, walking toward the couch. She then sat down next to her lover and gently wiped the tears from Devon's eyes before they fell.

"It's my fault... all my fault he's dead." Devon snuffled. Then she asked, "How Shella an' da kids?"

"Surprisingly, the boys and baby are good. Kamani has been a huge help with them. But Shella..." Miracle sighed.

"Reality hasn't sunk in for her yet. She left everything and everybody she knew back in Orlando. Once she realizes that goin' back home will endanger her and her kids' lives, she'll break all the way down. We can relate to her because we been down that road many times together. Our love for each other was what kept us together. We eventually recovered enough to move on. But Shella is feelin' like she's on her own, even though we're all in the same boat. We're basically strangers to her, so we're goin' to have to show her through our actions that we got her back. She'll come around little by little the more we show her and her kids we're trustworthy."

Stomach growling

"I'm hungry as a bear, Dee," Miracle said immediately after her stomach quieted. "As I was sayin' when I first came in, I need to eat before I take my painkillers. I think it'll be okay for us to finally leave the house. It's beautiful outside. We been cooped up in here since we arrived. If Biz—"

"Don't say his name," Devon rudely cut Miracle off. Then, "Fo'give me," she said in a calmer tone, "but, please, don't *ever* mention his name around me *ever* again. He's dead to me."

"First, I accept your apology. Then I want to apologize for… for bein' inconsiderate." Miracle leaned forward and kissed Devon. "Now get up, take a shower with ya funky booty self, and let's go out to eat. Even though the boys are fine with it, I'm tired of delivered food, aren't you?"

Devon didn't move a muscle. Her head hurt too bad.

Miracle stood up. She grabbed Devon by the wrist and pulled. "Get uuup! Let's go." She pulled again. "We're blessed and lucky to be alive. We can't change our destiny, anyway, so why live in fear?" She sucked her teeth, then answered her own question. "I'm not. And neither are you." She pulled some more.

"Okay okay okay. Stop befo' you hurt yaself. I'm gettin'up." Devon sat up. "Go 'head an' get er'body ready."

Miracle smiled. "We'll be ready to leave in… fifteen minutes?"

"Gimme a hour. My head killin' me, so I'ma be movin' a lil' slow."

"You sure you don't want a Percocet? I swear it will knock that migraine out."

"Naw, I'm fifty-four. I don't wanna get hooked on 'em."

"I can understand that. Even though I need 'em to manage the aftereffects of my trauma, they make me feel sooo good." Miracle then set off to round up the crew for the outing.

Devon called out to Miracle just before she got out of sight. Once Miracle turned around, Devon said, "When we come back, we're packin' up an' leavin'. I ain't spendin' anotha nite in this fuckin' house becuz I don't feel safe. I feel like da Clean-Up Crew is lookin' fo' me ta find out what happened ta *him.*"

Miracle nodded. "Where are we goin'?"

"We can go whereva. We got three million dollars on hand, on top of whateva we get from da eventual sale of StudioX."

"How about Jamaica? We can live near Mandeville where my father was born. I know that area well because I travelled there a lot. Almost everybody is related around there. I think that would be the last place anybody would look for us."

Ignoring her migraine, Devon thought about Miracle's suggestion for a brief time. "We'll give it a shot," she ultimately concluded. "Unda one condition, howeva."

"Okay."

"Death may be inevitable, and destiny may be unavoidable, but I'ma go all out ta duck those muthafuckas. So, da second I sense danger, we're outta there. No ands, ifs or buts about it. Death ain't gon' take me easy."

"That's fine with me. I just hope Shella won't have a problem with leavin' da country."

"Well, I'm leavin' it up to you ta convince her ta come wit us."

"Why you leavin' it all up to me? You're the best sweet-talker I know, the one with the platinum tongue."

"You're well-spoken, too. But, rite now, my mindset ain't on track an' she needs sumone who's empathetic."

"What if I can't convince her to come with us?"

"Once ya explain to her that she has no one ta turn to fo' help or protection if she leaves us, she should see that comin' wit us is best fo' her an' her family." Devon paused briefly. "Ta be honest, she has no otha options. She's eitha wit us or they gotta go... not the baby girl, tho'." Unfeeling, Devon shrugged. "No mercy. I ain't gamblin' wit our lives."

Miracle understood that damaged people were dangerous, so she knew that Devon was ready and willing to do what was necessary to survive. And sadly, she was, too. She could at least try to convince Devon to let Shella and her boys go to fend for themselves, but she chose to side with whatever Devon wanted to do. She didn't want Devon to kill them, if that's what "they gotta go" truly meant, so she prayed that Shella would make the right decision.

As soon as Miracle disappeared, Devon removed her .380 from between the couch's cushions. She admired it in silence for a moment, then she softly spoke to it endearingly. "Now that Rah is gone, it's me an' you against da world, fo' real." She tenderly stroked the pistol. "Thank you fo' neva failin' me. I know we're destined ta make it ta da end togetha." She kissed the gun's front sight. "You're all I need in this life of sin." At that, Devon stood and tucked away her trusted protector. The next chapter of her life had begun.

***

"Woodson, Byron," the Orange County detention center C.O. said over the PA system. "Get dressed. You have an attorney visit."

"Look who's ten fuckin' days late," Bizzy said out loud as he cast the bullshit urban novel he was reading onto the bottom bunk. "It shouldn't be long now befo' I finally get away from these young wild niggaz." He brushed his grill and groomed his face. Next, he gingerly rubbed his bruised and sore chest. Then, he put on his blue jumpsuit and, lastly, clipped his ID card onto the breast pocket. Once he was done arranging himself, he shook his head disappointedly at the blurred man in the scuffed mirror.

The last ten days had challenged Bizzy's nerves of steel. The longer he sat in lockup, the more worried he became. He wasn't worried about the painful contusion covering his torso; he knew that they would heal completely soon. He also wasn't too concerned about the backlog of lucrative "contracts" that were awaiting him in Peru. And the unfinished business he had with JuneBug, no problem, since he'd find him in the blink of an eye with Cesar's help.

Bizzy *was* worried about Devon's whereabouts, though. He just wanted to know if she was safe… and that she hadn't set him up again.

Bizzy, for good reason, worried the most about being implicated for something that he'd done before he fled to Peru. He was amazed when he was booked without any outstanding warrants. But still, he didn't need his booked name notifying an awaiting agency. He wasn't a praying man, yet he prayed every day that his father's lawyer would get him released before it was too late.

"Woodson, report to the front for your attorney visit."

Bizzy strolled out of the cell with his head held high.

"Yo', Tally, they called ya fo' visit."

No shit, Sherlock, Bizzy said to himself, ignoring his young, wild and stupid cellie. All eyes in the common area were on Bizzy until he exited the pod. He was then escorted by a C.O. to see his attorney.

"What took you so long ta come see me?" Bizzy snarled once the C.O. went away. "I woulda called you ASAP, but I ain't memorize ya number. I know ya been contacted by sumone, tho', an' they told you I was locked up."

"Sorry for not arriving sooner, Mr. Woodson," a seated Matthew O'Hare said with a slight Irish accent. "Today's the earliest I've been in a long time." He laughed in an attempt to lighten the mood. Bizzy's face let him know that he failed terribly, so he got serious. "I was in my native Ireland on vacation when I received the call about your arrest. I cut the trip short and came as soon as I could. Now, please take a seat. We don't have any more time to waste."

Bizzy sat. He was all ears for good news.

Matthew O'Hare was well-known all over the Sunshine State. His profound knowledge of both Florida state and federal law, his volubility, and his "no bullshit" attitude had gotten Bizzy and Demetrius out of trouble many times over the years. The last time he served as Bizzy's lawyer was in 2008 when Bizzy unknowingly got entangled in his father's RockBottom Family conspiracy. Because Demetrius and his RBF crew, and all those linked to them, were labeled high profile criminals, he had to really work hard to get the government to reduce Bizzy's original charge of drug distribution. In the end, he worked out a deal that resulted in Bizzy doing ten months in Club Fed for illegal use of a cellphone. Overall, neither Bizzy nor Demetrius had done hard time, all thanks to Matthew O'Hare.

O'Hare opened the briefcase on the table. He pulled out a packet of papers and skimmed through a few pages. "This should be a walk in the park," he confidently said. "But I'm interested in knowing why you were caught shoplifting at Walmart?"

"They can't hear us, rite?" Bizzy asked out of caution, although he already knew the answer.

"I'll castrate the DA, the US attorney, *and* the Attorney General with relish if there's a camera or microphone in this room."

"Well, I needed supplies an', becuz I was literally on da run, I ain't have time ta pay."

"Why were you running?"

Bizzy didn't hold back. He told O'Hare everything, play by play.

Once Bizzy had run through his story, O'Hare calmly pulled a notepad and pen out of the briefcase. Subsequently, he asked, "Where did you discard the Kevlar vest and handgun again?"

"Befo' I went inside that Walmart, I tossed that shit in a dumpsta nearby."

"Where's this Walmart located, Mr. Woodson? Be specific. It's imperative."

"Uhh... I ain't too familiar wit that area, but I believe I was on Conroy Road... Or is it Conroy Windermere Road...? It's one or da otha. They da same road, tho'. So, it's on that road an'... Apopka Vineland. Yeah, that's it. I'm havin' trouble rememberin' that shit becuz I was tryna put a lotta space between me an' da sirens. Once it sounded like they were catchin' up ta me, I got rid of that shit in a hurry."

O'Hare jotted down what had said. He was going to pass the information to Adrian without delay. Although ten days had passed by, he needed Adrian to send someone to try to locate the gun and vest before they potentially fell into the wrong hands.

"I'm good then, rite?" Bizzy asked in a hopeful manner.

"If by that you mean you haven't been connected to that slaughterhouse, then, yes, you're good."

Bizzy flashed one of his Grinch-like smiles.

"But," O'Hare began again, bursting Bizzy's bubble, "from what I saw on the local news this morning, the police are still actively looking for several individuals the neighbors witnessed fleeing the scene. So, for now, you're good. You'd be even better, though, when the Kevlar vest and handgun are safely in our associates' hands."

Bizzy's eyes were glued to the TV every time the live local news aired, so he was up on the "Massacre in Isleworth" case. He knew that the police weren't going to make much headway after it was reported there was a dearth of actionable evidence collected on the scene. He breathed a sigh of relief when the police suspected a botched drug deal resulted in the deaths of the four found in the house. What kept him on edge was the police refusing to close the case until they found and questioned three people of interest: A male seen leaving the scene on foot, and two females with three kids in a late model Kia.

Why'd you take my car and leave me behind, lil' sis? Bizzy wondered for the hundredth time. *I just know you checked on RahRah, but did you check to see if I was alive? Or did you find me unconscious and just chose to leave me for dead?*

Bizzy swore on God that he'd get those answers direct from the source...

"Who?"

Bizzy, who was lost in thought, said, "What?"

"You just said a name," O'Hare responded. "I believe you said 'Devon.'"

"Uhhh... Naw, I-I... Man, fuck all that! Focus on this Larceny charge I got. They ain't gimme a bond at my initial appearance. They said I was a flight risk becuz I told 'em I was from outta state an' visitin' family fo' da holidays. So, can you get me out soon or what? I need ta get outta here an' disappear back ta Peru."

"I'll pull some strings and get you a bond hearing."

"How soon?"

"Tuesday."

"That's... That's tomorrow."

"Correct. See, I have influence in the great state of Florida, Mr. Woodson. *But...*"

"But what?"

"Worst case scenario, I'll have to contact *el jefe*. He has *mucho* influence in all levels of government in the U.S." O'Hare winked. He then began to pack up. He rose from the table. "Now you hang in there for one more day, Mr. Woodson."

They shook hands before O'Hare left.

As Bizzy waited in the chilly room for the C.O. to escort him back to the pod, he dove into the depths of his mind. He daydreamed about his boys, and how he was going to shower them with love and attention soon. He then visualized his future "kill" list. He fumed while adding a couple of names to it. Sometime tomorrow, he hoped to be back in Peru conducting business as usual. He would expeditiously fulfill his contracts with Cesar while progressively making plans for each person that he'd pay a surprise visit to.

"You know I'm still breathin'," Bizzy whispered to himself, thinking about the last name on his list. "We'll bump into each otha again. It's guaranteed. An' I know what da outcome is gonna be. I just hope I don't have ta do it in front of G-Ma."

***

His heart, ordinarily cold, was now heavy. Oftentimes hopeful, he felt dead on the inside. Usually clearheaded, the lonely passage of time had left him unable to think or concentrate.

Where's my family?

The longer that question went unanswered the more Bug deteriorated mentally and physically. He was in complete shambles over the whereabouts of his wife and kids. He didn't know which should be higher on his priority list: a mental institution or surgery.

Karma was making it perfectly clear that he hadn't yet atoned for his greed.

Even though Bug knew he should've bowed out of the game for good after he'd been shot, never in a million years would he have predicted his life getting any worse thereafter. It was a bitter pill to swallow, but he accepted that his get-rich-quick vision was the driving force that led to his current suffering. He wasn't culpable of his cancer, of course, because that was genetics. Other than that, every tragic event that followed his cancer diagnosis was credited to his ledger. Blue's death and his family's abduction happened because of his needless hunger for gouda.

I should've known better than to trust that high-yellow nigga.

While no news was good news in some cases, the void in communication with Agent Murray also had a role in perpetuating Bug's hapless condition.

Bug had talked to a number of personnel at the Department of Homeland Security just to get a hold of Agent Murray. Murray was out in the field when they finally spoke. He readily lit into the agent. He reminded the agent about their written agreement. Murray assured him that he was in Orlando diligently searching for his family. When the agent said that he was too busy to meet, he promised to call Bug daily.

Strangely, the only law enforcement officer that began to blow his phone up was Mr. Vickers. For all he knew, Murray had contacted his probation officer. Bug wasn't one hundred percent sure if Murray had called Vickers on his behalf, so he ignored Vickers' barrage of calls. Besides, keeping in touch with Murray was more important.

When Murray didn't call the next day as promised, Bug's outrage skyrocketed. He tried again and again to reach the dishonest American *federali*. After three days of countless calls to the DHS, he caved and answered Mr. Vickers call.

Bug assumed that Vickers was only calling to say that he'd violated his probation and needed to self-surrender. Instead, Vickers informed him that Murray had spoken up for him and arranged for his probation to be shelved. That was excellent news, but he demanded to know how he could reach Agent Murray. Mr. Vickers summarily ignored him and suggested he go to one of the police stations in Orlando for his safety. Upon hearing that nonsense, he hung up in

Vickers' face because he wasn't going back home to be merked by one of Adrian's hitmen.

JuneBug was on his own now.

The road had been extra rocky for Bug, often looking as if there was no way forward. Still, he was keeping his weary eyes on the route ahead. Nothing would distract him. No roadblock or bottleneck would impede him from his primary mission. He'd risk it all, his money, his health, his reputation, just to get his family back.

"Shella has sacrificed fo' me since I've known her, so I'll neva stop lookin' fo' her an' my kids," Bug said to Fry as he drove aimlessly on a meagerly travelled side road in the panhandle of Florida. "No matter what I have ta go through, I'ma do it fo' them, lil' buddy. They're alive. I can feel it." He petted Fry, who was curled up in the passenger seat and sporadically wagging his stubby tail. "An' once I find you, boo, I swear I'll getta job at Burger King, if that's what it takes, an' we can struggle together," he said with the sincerity of a confessional.

JuneBug's quest for the road to riches was finished forever. He had played the game, and he lost terribly. Furthermore, he was adamant that he wasn't going to be a man lured back into the game due to greed. All the money in the world would not make him relapse.

However, only time would tell if Bug was being truthful...

...because money encouraged evil, and no one knew the meaning of "enough."

Stomach rumbles.

Lock Down Publications and Ca$h Presents
Assisted Publishing Packages

Due to an increase in the price of services we have increased our prices. The prices below reflect the price increase as of 11/1/24.

BASIC PACKAGE	UPGRADED PACKAGE
$699	**$1000**
Editing	Typing
Cover Design	Editing
Formatting	Cover Design
	Formatting
	Upload eBooks to Amazon
	Upload Paperback to Amazon
ADVANCE PACKAGE	**LDP SUPREME PACKAGE**
$1,400	**$1,700**
Typing	Typing
Editing (line editing/content)	Editing (line editing/content)
Cover Design	Cover Design
Formatting	Formatting
Copyright Registration	Copyright Registration
Proofreading	Proofreading
Upload eBooks to Amazon	Set up Amazon Account
Upload Paperback to Amazon	Upload eBooks to Amazon
	Upload Paperback to Amazon
	Advertise on LDP's Amazon and Facebook Page

***Other services available upon request.
Additional charges may apply

Lock Down Publications
P.O. Box 944
Stockbridge, GA 30281-9998
Phone: 470 303-9761
Email: lockdownpublications@gmail.com

Submission Guideline

Submit the first three chapters of your completed manuscript to ldpsubmissions@gmail.com. In the subject line add **Your Book's Title**. The manuscript must be in a Word Doc file and sent as an attachment. Document should be in Times New Roman, double spaced, and in size 12 font. Also, provide your synopsis and full contact information. If sending multiple submissions, they must each be in a separate email.

Have a story but no way to send it electronically? You can still submit to LDP/Ca$h Presents. Send in the first three chapters, written or typed, of your completed manuscript to:

LDP: Submissions Dept
P.O. Box 944
Stockbridge, GA 30281-9998

DO NOT send original manuscript. Must be a duplicate. Provide your synopsis and a cover letter containing your full contact information.

Thanks for considering LDP and Ca$h Presents.

NEW RELEASES

BLOODLINE OF A SAVAGE 1,2&3
THESE VICIOUS STREETS 1,2&3
RELENTLESS GOON
RELENTLESS GOON 2
BY PRINCE A. TAUHID

THE BUTTERFLY MAFIA 1-3
BY FUMIYA PAYNE

A THUG'S STREET PRINCESS 1,2&3
BY MEESHA

CITY OF SMOKE 1& 2
BY MOLOTTI

STEPPERS 1,2&3
THE REAL BADDIES OF CHI-RAQ
BY KING RIO

THE LANE 1&2
BY KEN-KEN SPENCE

THUG OF SPADES 1,2&3
LOVE IN THE TRENCHES 2
CORNER BOY CHRONICLES
BY COREY ROBINSON

TIL DEATH 3
BY ARYANNA

THE BIRTH OF A GANGSTER 4
BY DELMONT PLAYER

PRODUCT OF THE STREETS 1&2
BY DEMOND "MONEY" ANDERSON

NO TIME FOR ERROR
BY KEESE

MONEY HUNGRY DEMONS 1,2&3
BY TRANAY ADAMS

HUNGRY FOR MONEY 1&2
BY SLIMBOS

A THUGGISH PASSION
KILLAZ ON STANDBY 1&2
LAND OF DA HOOLIGANZ 1,2&3
FRESH OFF DA PORCH
BY IRA B.

COUNTDOWN OF A KILLA 1&2
GUNS DOWN, BOTTOMS UP 1&2
SEX, MURDA AND GOD
BY LO-LIFE

THE LEVEL UP 1&2
BY LUXURY KING

FO'EVA ROLLIN' 1&2
BY ASSA RAYMOND BAKER

HUB CITY MENACE 1&2
BY J. WHITE

KILLA CREW
DYING FOR LIKES
BY ARYANNA

A GANGSTA'S KARMA 5 | FLAME

IF YOU CROSS ME ONCE 6
ANGEL 5
By Anthony Fields

IMMA DIE BOUT MINE 5
By Aryanna

A THUGS STREET PRINCESS 3
EMBRACING THE LOVE OF A BOSS
By Meesha

PRODUCT OF THE STREETS 3
By Demond Money Anderson

STANDING ON HER BUSINESS
BY DG SANTANA

GET IT IN SLUGS 1&2
B. STALLS

CORNER BOYS 2
By Corey Robinson

THE MURDER QUEENS 6&7
By Michael Gallon

CITY OF SMOKE 3
By Molotti

CONFESSIONS OF A DOPEBOY
By Nicholas Lock

TENDER
BY KHUFU

THA TAKEOVER
By Keith Chandler

BETRAYAL OF A G 2
By Ray Vinci

CRIME BOSS 4
By Playa Ray

Coming Soon from Lock Down Publications/Ca$h Presents

RAN OFF ON THE PLUG 2 by **PAPER BOI RARI**
STREET REDEMPTION by **TONY DANIELS**
SAVAGE FAMILY EMPIRE by **PRINCE TAUHID**
BAD BITCHES WIT' GUNZ by **DIESEL**
THE SINGLE LADIES by **DIESEL**
COKE BY THE TRUCKLOAD by **DIESEL**
PROBLEM SOLVED by **DIESEL**
TIPPIN' THE SCALES by **DIESEL**
OPPS CRY TOO by **SAYNOMORE**
A GANGSTA'S KARMA by **FLAME**

AVAILABLE NOW

RESTRAINING ORDER 1 & 2
By **CA$H & Coffee**

LOVE KNOWS NO BOUNDARIES 1-3
By **Coffee**

RAISED AS A GOON I, II, III & IV
BRED BY THE SLUMS I, II, III
BLAST FOR ME I & II
ROTTEN TO THE CORE I II III
A BRONX TALE I, II, III
DUFFLE BAG CARTEL I II III IV V VI
HEARTLESS GOON I II III IV V
A SAVAGE DOPEBOY I II
DRUG LORDS I II III
CUTTHROAT MAFIA I II
KING OF THE TRENCHES
By **Ghost**

LAY IT DOWN I & II
LAST OF A DYING BREED I II
BLOOD STAINS OF A SHOTTA I & II III
By **Jamaica**

LOYAL TO THE GAME I II III
LIFE OF SIN I, II III
By **TJ & Jelissa**

IF LOVING HIM IS WRONG…I & II
LOVE ME EVEN WHEN IT HURTS I II III
By **Jelissa**

PUSH IT TO THE LIMIT
By **Bre' Hayes**

BLOODY COMMAS I & II
SKI MASK CARTEL I, II & III
KING OF NEW YORK I II, III IV V
RISE TO POWER I II III
COKE KINGS I II III IV V
BORN HEARTLESS I II III IV
KING OF THE TRAP I II
By **T.J. Edwards**

WHEN THE STREETS CLAP BACK I & II III
THE HEART OF A SAVAGE I II III IV
MONEY MAFIA I II
LOYAL TO THE SOIL I II III
By **Jibril Williams**

A DISTINGUISHED THUG STOLE MY HEART I - III
LOVE SHOULDN'T HURT I II III IV
RENEGADE BOYS 1-4
PAID IN KARMA 1-3
SAVAGE STORMS 1-3
AN UNFORESEEN LOVE 1-3
BABY, I'M WINTERTIME COLD 1-3
A THUG'S STREET PRINCESS 1&2
By **Meesha**

CUM FOR ME 1-8
An LDP Erotica Collaboration

BLOOD OF A BOSS 1-5
SHADOWS OF THE GAME
TRAP BASTARD
By **Askari**

A GANGSTER'S CODE 1-3
A GANGSTER'S SYN 1-3
THE SAVAGE LIFE 1-3
CHAINED TO THE STREETS 1-3
BLOOD ON THE MONEY 1-3
A GANGSTA'S PAIN 1-3
BEAUTIFUL LIES AND UGLY TRUTHS
CHURCH IN THESE STREETS
By **J-Blunt**

THE STREETS BLEED MURDER 1-3
THE HEART OF A GANGSTA 1-3
By **Jerry Jackson**

WHEN A GOOD GIRL GOES BAD
By **Adrienne**

THE COST OF LOYALTY 1-3
By **Kweli**

BRIDE OF A HUSTLA 1-3
THE FETTI GIRLS 1-3
CORRUPTED BY A GANGSTA 1-4
BLINDED BY HIS LOVE
THE PRICE YOU PAY FOR LOVE 1-3
DOPE GIRL MAGIC 1-3
By **Destiny Skai**

A KINGPIN'S AMBITION
A KINGPIN'S AMBITION II
I MURDER FOR THE DOUGH
By **Ambitious**

A DOPEBOY'S PRAYER
By **Eddie "Wolf" Lee**

TRUE SAVAGE 1-7
DOPE BOY MAGIC 1-3
MIDNIGHT CARTEL 1-3
CITY OF KINGZ 1&2
NIGHTMARE ON SILENT AVE
THE PLUG OF LIL MEXICO 1&2
CLASSIC CITY
By **Chris Green**

LOVE & CHASIN' PAPER
By **Qay Crockett**

THE KING CARTEL 1-3
By **Frank Gresham**

THESE NIGGAS AIN'T LOYAL 1-3
By **Nikki Tee**

GANGSTA SHYT 1-3
By **CATO**

THE ULTIMATE BETRAYAL
By **Phoenix**

BOSS'N UP 1-3
By **Royal Nicole**

I LOVE YOU TO DEATH
By **Destiny J**

BROOKLYN HUSTLAZ
By **Boogsy Morina**

GANGSTA CITY
By **Teddy Duke**

TO DIE IN VAIN
SINS OF A HUSTLA
By **ASAD**

I RIDE FOR MY HITTA
I STILL RIDE FOR MY HITTA
By **Misty Holt**

A GANGSTER'S REVENGE 1-4
THE BOSS MAN'S DAUGHTERS 1-5
A SAVAGE LOVE 1&2
BAE BELONGS TO ME 1&2
A HUSTLER'S DECEIT 1-3
WHAT BAD BITCHES DO 1-3
SOUL OF A MONSTER 1-3
KILL ZONE
A DOPE BOY'S QUEEN 1-3
TIL DEATH 1-3
IMMA DIE BOUT MINE 1-5
By **Aryanna**

BROOKLYN ON LOCK 1 & 2
By **Sonovia**

A DRUG KING AND HIS DIAMOND 1-3
A DOPEMAN'S RICHES
HER MAN, MINE'S TOO 1&2
CASH MONEY HO'S
THE WIFEY I USED TO BE 1&2
PRETTY GIRLS DO NASTY THINGS
By **Nicole Goosby**

THE STREETS ARE CALLING
By **Duquie Wilson**

LIPSTICK KILLAH 1-3
CRIME OF PASSION 1-3
FRIEND OR FOE 1-3
By **Mimi**

TRAPHOUSE KING 1-3
KINGPIN KILLAZ 1-3
STREET KINGS 1&2
PAID IN BLOOD 1&2
CARTEL KILLAZ 1-3
DOPE GODS 1&2
By **Hood Rich**

STEADY MOBBN' 1-3
THE STREETS STAINED MY SOUL 1-3
By **Marcellus Allen**

WHO SHOT YA 1-3
SON OF A DOPE FIEND 1-4
HEAVEN GOT A GHETTO 1&2
SKI MASK MONEY 1&2
By **Renta**

GORILLAZ IN THE BAY 1-4
TEARS OF A GANGSTA 1/&2
3X KRAZY 1&2
STRAIGHT BEAST MODE 1&2
By **DE'KARI**

TRIGGADALE 1-3
MURDA WAS THE CASE 1-3
By **Elijah R. Freeman**

MARRIED TO A BOSS 1-3
By **Destiny Skai & Chris Green**

SLAUGHTER GANG 1-3
RUTHLESS HEART 1-3
By **Willie Slaughter**

GOD BLESS THE TRAPPERS 1-3
THESE SCANDALOUS STREETS 1-3
FEAR MY GANGSTA 1-5
THESE STREETS DON'T LOVE NOBODY 1-2
BURY ME A G 1-5
A GANGSTA'S EMPIRE 1-4
THE DOPEMAN'S BODYGAURD 1&2
THE REALEST KILLAZ 1-3
THE LAST OF THE OGS 1-3
By **Tranay Adams**

KINGZ OF THE GAME 1-7
CRIME BOSS 1-4
By **Playa Ray**

FUK SHYT
By **Blakk Diamond**

DON'T F#CK WITH MY HEART 1&2
By **Linnea**

ADDICTED TO THE DRAMA 1-3
IN THE ARM OF HIS BOSS
By **Jamila**

LOYALTY AIN'T PROMISED 1&2
By **Keith Williams**

FOREVER GANGSTA 1&2
GLOCKS ON SATIN SHEETS 1&2
By **Adrian Dulan**

YAYO 1-4
A SHOOTER'S AMBITION 1&2
BRED IN THE GAME
By **S. Allen**

TRAP GOD 1-3
RICH $AVAGE 1-3
MONEY IN THE GRAVE 1-3
CARTEL MONEY
By **Martell Troublesome Bolden**

TOE TAGZ 1-4
LEVELS TO THIS SHYT 1&2
IT'S JUST ME AND YOU
By **Ah'Million**

KINGPIN DREAMS 1-3
RAN OFF ON DA PLUG
By **Paper Boi Rari**

THE STREETS MADE ME 1-3
By **Larry D. Wright**

CONFESSIONS OF A GANGSTA 1-4
CONFESSIONS OF A JACKBOY 1-3
CONFESSIONS OF A HITMAN
By **Nicholas Lock**

I'M NOTHING WITHOUT HIS LOVE
SINS OF A THUG
TO THE THUG I LOVED BEFORE
A GANGSTA SAVED XMAS
IN A HUSTLER I TRUST
By **Monet Dragun**

A GANGSTA'S KARMA 5 | FLAME

QUIET MONEY 1-3
THUG LIFE 1-3
EXTENDED CLIP 1&2
A GANGSTA'S PARADISE
By **Trai'Quan**

CAUGHT UP IN THE LIFE 1-3
THE STREETS NEVER LET GO 1-3
By **Robert Baptiste**

NEW TO THE GAME 1-3
MONEY, MURDER & MEMORIES 1-3
By **Malik D. Rice**

THE LIFE OF A HOOD STAR
By **Ca$h & Rashia Wilson**

THE STREETS WILL NEVER CLOSE 1-4
By **K'ajji**

LIFE OF A SAVAGE 1-4
A GANGSTA'S QUR'AN 1-4
MURDA SEASON 1-3
GANGLAND CARTEL 1-3
CHI'RAQ GANGSTAS 1-4
KILLERS ON ELM STREET 1-3
JACK BOYZ N DA BRONX 1-3
A DOPEBOY'S DREAM 1-3
JACK BOYS VS DOPE BOYS 1-3
COKE GIRLZ
COKE BOYS
SOSA GANG 1&2
BRONX SAVAGES
BODYMORE KINGPINS
BLOOD OF A GOON
By **Romell Tukes**

CREAM 2-3
THE STREETS WILL TALK
By **Yolanda Moore**

CONCRETE KILLA 1-3
VICIOUS LOYALTY 1-3
By **Kingpen**

THE ULTIMATE SACRIFICE 1-6
KHADIFI
IF YOU CROSS ME ONCE 1-5
ANGEL 1-4
IN THE BLINK OF AN EYE
By **Anthony Fields**

NIGHTMARES OF A HUSTLA 1-3
BLOOD AND GAMES 1&2
By **King Dream**

HARD AND RUTHLESS 1&2
MOB TOWN 251
THE BILLIONAIRE BENTLEYS 1-3
REAL G'S MOVE IN SILENCE
By **Von Diesel**

MOB TIES 1-7
SOUL OF A HUSTLER, HEART OF A KILLER 1-3
GORILLAZ IN THE TRENCHES
By **SayNoMore**

BODYMORE MURDERLAND 1-3
THE BIRTH OF A GANGSTER 1-4
By **Delmont Player**

FOR THE LOVE OF A BOSS 1&2
By **C. D. Blue**

KILLA KOUNTY 1-5
By **Khufu**

MOBBED UP 1-4
THE BRICK MAN 1-5
THE COCAINE PRINCESS 1-10
STEPPERS 1-3
SUPER GREMLIN 1-4
By **King Rio**

MONEY GAME 1&2
By **Smoove Dolla**

A GANGSTA'S KARMA 1-4
By **FLAME**

KING OF THE TRENCHES 1-3
By **GHOST & TRANAY ADAMS**

QUEEN OF THE ZOO 1&2
By **Black Migo**

GRIMEY WAYS 1-3
BETRAYAL OF A G
By **Ray Vinci**

XMAS WITH AN ATL SHOOTER
By **Ca$h & Destiny Skai**

KING KILLA 1&2
By **Vincent "Vitto" Holloway**

BETRAYAL OF A THUG 1&2
By **Fre$h**

A GANGSTA'S KARMA 5 | FLAME

THE MURDER QUEENS 1-6
By **Michael Gallon**

FOR THE LOVE OF BLOOD 1-4
By **Jamel Mitchell**

HOOD CONSIGLIERE 1&2
NO TIME FOR ERROR
By **Keese**

PROTÉGÉ OF A LEGEND 1&2
LOVE IN THE TRENCHES 1&2
By **Corey Robinson**

THE PLUG'S RUTHLESS DAUGHTER 1&2
By **Tony Daniels**

BORN IN THE GRAVE 1-3
CRIME PAYS 1&2
By **Self Made Tay**

MOAN IN MY MOUTH
By **XTASY**

TORN BETWEEN A GANGSTER AND A
GENTLEMAN
By **J-BLUNT & Miss Kim**

HERE TODAY GONE TOMORROW 1&2
By **Fly Rock**

PILLOW PRINCESS
By **S. Hawkins**

SANCTIFIED AND HORNY
by **XTASY**

WOMEN LIE MEN LIE 1-4
FIFTY SHADES OF SNOW 1-3
STACK BEFORE YOU SPLURGE
GIRLS FALL LIKE DOMINOES
NAÏVE TO THE STREETS
By **ROY MILLIGAN**

LOYALTY IS EVERYTHING 1-3
CITY OF SMOKE 1&2
By **Molotti**

THE BUTTERFLY MAFIA 1-4
SALUTE MY SAVAGERY 1&2
By **Fumiya Payne**

THE LANE 1&2
By **Ken-Ken Spence**

THE PUSSY TRAP 1-5
By **Nene Capri**

DIRTY DNA
By **Blaque**

BOOKS BY LDP'S CEO, CA$H

TRUST IN NO MAN
TRUST IN NO MAN 2
TRUST IN NO MAN 3
BONDED BY BLOOD
SHORTY GOT A THUG
THUGS CRY
THUGS CRY 2
THUGS CRY 3
TRUST NO BITCH
TRUST NO BITCH 2
TRUST NO BITCH 3
TIL MY CASKET DROPS
RESTRAINING ORDER
RESTRAINING ORDER 2
IN LOVE WITH A CONVICT
LIFE OF A HOOD STAR
XMAS WITH AN ATL SHOOTER

www.ingramcontent.com/pod-product-compliance
Lightning Source LLC
Chambersburg PA
CBHW070449260626
47161CB00004B/1247